TARGET!

"Damn!" Barraka exclaimed in a low angry voice. "They're lost."

"What?"

"They're lost," Barraka repeated, pointing to the log. It was already turning away from the shore. "Keep that gun firing at the Krauts."

The .50 opened up; its tracers stabbed thin lines of light into the fog across the river.

Barraka was on his feet.

"Where the hell are you goin'?" Keller questioned.

"If someone doesn't get them, the Krauts' machine guns will." He jumped clear of the boulders and ran down the bank. "This way," Barraka shouted, wading into the water.

The log turned toward Barraka as a flare burst overhead and machine gun slugs ripped into the water in a line heading straight at him. . . .

NEW ADVENTURES FROM ZEBRA!

THE BLACK EAGLES:
HANOI HELLGROUND (1249, $2.95)
by John Lansing
They're the best jungle fighters the United States has to offer, and no matter where Charlie is hiding, they'll find him. They're the greatest unsung heroes of the dirtiest, most challenging war of all time. They're THE BLACK EAGLES.

THE BLACK EAGLES #2:
MEKONG MASSACRE (1294, $2.50)
by John Lansing
Falconi and his Black Eagle combat team are about to stake a claim on Colonel Nguyen Chi Roi—and give the Commie his due. But American intelligence wants the colonel alive, making this the Black Eagles' toughest assignment ever!

THE BLACK EAGLES #3:
NIGHTMARE IN LAOS (1341, $2.50)
by John Lansing
There's a hot rumor that Russians in Laos are secretly building a nuclear reactor. And the American command isn't overreacting when they order it knocked out—quietly—and fast!

MCLEANE'S RANGER #2:
TARGET RABAUL (1271, $2.50)
by John Darby
Rabaul—it was one of the keys to the control of the Pacific and the Japanese had a lock on it. When nothing else worked, the Allies called on their most formidable weapon—McLeane's Rangers, the jungle fighters who don't know the meaning of the word quit!

SWEET VIETNAM (1423, $3.50)
by Richard Parque
Every American flier hoped to blast "The Dragonman," the ace North Vietnamese pilot, to pieces. Major Vic Benedetti was no different. Sending "The Dragonman" down in a spiral of smoke and flames was what he lived for, worked for, prayed for—and might die for . . .

Available wherever paperbacks are sold, or order direct from the Publisher. Send cover price plus 50¢ per copy for mailing and handling to Zebra Books, 475 Park Avenue South, New York, N.Y. 10016. DO NOT SEND CASH.

Beyond Valor

BY FRANK GERON

ZEBRA BOOKS
KENSINGTON PUBLISHING CORP.

ZEBRA BOOKS

are published by

Kensington Publishing Corp.
475 Park Avenue South
New York, N.Y. 10016

First printing: August, 1984

Printed in the United States of America

This book is respectfully dedicated to the Italian Partisans, whose daring and courage saved the lives of thousands of Italian Jews. . . .

WAR DEPARTMENT SECRET CLASSIFIED
MESSAGE CENTER

Combined Chiefs of Staff
Oct. 5, 1943

Command General
Allied Force Hq
Casserta, Italy

Number: WARX 8371
Topsec book message to Clark for immediate action, from SHAEF, London from Eisenhower.
Mission to Servigliano, Italy is subject
Ref. is made to Mess. 842 to you Hq date Oct., 1943 from Co. Gen. Italy.
Maj. Mitchell Barraka, 0239564, your command, 34th Div., 16th Inf. Bn. is hereby TDY to + his Hq for an indefinite period of time. Ordered to take command of units of 82nd partisan GP operating in the area of Servigliano, Italy. Purpose of command to free prisoner Servigliano and accompany to Swiss border. Return to previous unit after mission is completed. Authorized two other men.

End.

Originator CC/S

Information: Gen. Somervill., Adm. Leahy.,
Gen. Arnold, Gen. Bissell,
Gen. Hilldring, Adm. King,
Mr. McCloy, C of S.

I

Maj. Mitchell Barraka sat next to the driver of the jeep. Grimly silent, he peered through the rain-spattered windshield or glanced at the passing landscape through the open side of the jeep . . . the terrain was hilly. To wrest it from the Germans had taken weeks of hard fighting, and now the two exhausted armies were beginning to dig in for the coming winter months.

Everywhere there were signs of the struggles that had taken place. Burnt-out Tiger tanks and Shermans dotted the sides of the road or stood on the slopes and along the crests of the hills. All of the farmhouses had suffered some damage, and, though many were nothing more than charred ruins, people still lived in them.

The jeep crested a hill, and beyond a long line of Lombardy poplars the small walled town of San Giovonie came into view. A few of the towers with their crenelated openings were still standing. But practically all the gray stone wall facing the road had been leveled by American artillery fire before the town had been taken by direct infantry assault.

"I heard about this place," the young driver said.

Barraka turned to him. The driver's face was badly pockmarked. "What did you hear?" he asked.

"The Krauts fought hard to keep it."

"They fight hard to keep everything," Barraka answered.

The driver shook his head. "I ain't seen no combat yet . . . I just come over from the States ten days ago," he explained. "Right out of Fort Dix and onto a troop ship."

Barraka shrugged but didn't think it necessary to comment. He had been with one division or another since the invasion of Sicily and the subsequent landing in Italy at Salerno with the 34th Division of General Clark's Fifth Army.

"Sir, think we'll be movin' forward again?" the young man asked, unable to keep the quaver out of his voice.

"Not till spring," Barraka told him.

"Maybe it'll be all over by then," the driver said with a wide smile.

Again Barraka didn't think any response was required. The war would be over when the Krauts had no more fight left in them, and from what he had seen in the last few weeks they could still slug it out before pulling back to make another stand. Fighting the Krauts had taught him to respect them.

The church bells began to ring, sending a flock of pigeons into the air, despite the downpour.

When Barraka came out on the square the women were already hurrying to the Romanesque church opposite the ochre-colored town hall. All of them were dressed in black, even the young ones. Among them were several men. But they were very old. There were a few boys, but no teenagers.

The jeep swung around the white marble fountain in the middle of the square and stopped in front of the town hall, now headquarters for the 34th Division of the United States Army.

Barraka lifted himself out of the mud-spattered vehicle. "Don't know how long I'm going to be," he told the driver. "But there's no sense waiting in the jeep. . . . There's a cafe on the other side of the square. I'll meet you there. Go easy on the vino . . . I don't want to wind up in a ditch on the way back."

The driver laughed, gunned the engine, and drove off across the square, raising a curtain of muddy water on either side of the jeep as it rolled over the wet cobblestones.

More from habit than from need, Barraka shifted his web belt and felt the weight of the .45 on his right side and the canteen on his left. He was a tall, lean man with deep blue eyes and corn-silk hair. He turned toward the town hall with its Roman arched doorway and with a long stride he started for the entrance, where two poncho-covered sentries immediately saluted him as he came up to the top step.

Barraka returned their salute and hurried indoors. He had requested this meeting with General Ross Williams shortly after he had received orders to lead an Italian Partisan unit in a rescue operation that in his opinion was absolutely suicidal. His orders had come all the way from the Joint Chiefs of Staff, but he wasn't about to throw his life away and the lives of the men he would take with him just to rescue a few hundred Jews. That wasn't the way the war was being fought, at least not the way he had been fighting it, or wanted to fight it.

General Ross Williams was a chunky man with pepper-and-salt hair and dark gray eyes. He had come up through the ranks and won his two stars by what he did, rather than by who he knew in Washington.

The men in the 34th were proud to serve under him, and he was proud to lead them. They trusted him and he tried to keep that trust, though all too frequently he would have to send them into a fight, knowing they would have to take heavy casualties. But whenever that happened he would always be on the line where the fighting was the heaviest. Many times he was known to have carried the wounded back to the aide station himself.

Barraka had met Williams on two other occasions. Once they had been in the Sistine Chapel at the same time, and just three weeks earlier the general had come down to Battalion to award several Silver Stars to the men. Barraka had received an oak leaf cluster for the silver star he already had.

Dispensing with the usual military formality, Williams greeted Barraka with a vigorous handshake. Gesturing to the chair alongside his ornate Italian desk, he said, "I hope you didn't have any trouble coming here. There are still some Krauts in the woods about five miles down the road . . . once the rain stops I'll send some men in to flush them out." He spoke in a slow Texas drawl.

"No trouble," Barraka answered, noting that the general looked older and very tired.

Williams sat down. Lighting up a dark Cuban cigar, he commented, "I think I know why you're here . . . but why don't you tell me in your own words."

Digging inside the field jacket for his orders, Barraka said, "I request a reassignment. I'm not the man for this job." He placed the orders on the desk and leaned slightly forward.

"Why not? You've worked with the Eyetalian Partisans before. That's your specialty."

"Yes sir," Barraka answered. "But always on missions that had some chance of succeeding."

Williams took a deep drag on the cigar that made its tip flare red. Then he blew three successive smoke rings before he said, "This is a very special mission."

"I know that, sir," Barraka responded.

"You're going to move some three hundred Jews to the Swiss border," Williams said.

Barraka leaned back into the chair. He wanted to shout at Williams, but instead he kept silent.

"I know how you feel," Williams said to him.

"No sir, with all due respect to you, I don't think you do," Barraka answered.

"I don't have much feeling for Jews myself," Williams said. "But I'd also have to say I've known a few good ones."

Barraka didn't say anything. Before going to the University of Minnesota, he had never known a Jew. But at the university there had been one from New York with him in the Civil Engineering Department and another in the English Department. He didn't know the names of either one of them. And there was a young woman on campus who was also supposed to be a Jewess, but he had never seen her.

"I can't reassign you," Williams told him. "If I didn't think you were the man for the job, I wouldn't have sent your name up to the Joint Chiefs of Staff. If we don't get to them, they'll be shipped to Buchenwald, Germany."

"Buchenwald?"

"It's supposed to be a death camp," Williams said, blowing three more smoke rings. "But off the record, I think some of our propaganda boys have been working overtime. I don't think Buchenwald or any of the other ones are anything more than prison camps, similar to our own for POWs. What do you think?"

"About the same as yourself, sir. But there are certainly a lot of rumors around, especially among the Jewish officers."

Williams nodded and blew another smoke ring before he said, "Don't ask me why I didn't send a Jewish officer's name up to the Joint Chiefs. Some of them are damn good. But I wanted someone who wouldn't get emotionally involved and I wanted someone who had a record of dealing with the partisans. I know you won't get emotionally involved and your work with the partisans has been the best in Italy, so you were my logical choice."

"May I be frank, sir?"

"I would be insulted if you were anything else."

"Do you really think the world will miss three hundred Jews?"

"No, I don't. But that's not the point. I know for a fact that a great deal of pressure has been put on our government and the British to free them. You and I know the damn Jews in America have enough money to buy whatever they want. Well, they must have paid a good price for this operation."

"What about the lives of the men who—"

"I'm sorry, major, but you're going," Williams said firmly.

"Then with your permission, sir," Barraka responded, "I'll—"

Williams shook his head. "There isn't any time for you to do anything, except choose the two men you want with you. Three nights from tonight you will rendezvous with leaders of the partisan unit. Vito Volterra is the unit's commander and his second is Agostino Mastrada. They will lead you to Servigliano. By the way, both of them are Jews. I didn't think there were any Jews in Italy before this whole business started; then I found out there are rabbis and Jews who lead partisan units. I tell you, Italy is just full of crazy contradictions like that. At least with the Krauts once you get a line on them, it's always the same line. They don't change. But with Guineas—well, I think you know what I mean."

"May I again speak frankly, sir?"

"Go ahead," Williams said.

"Wouldn't it be easier to make a parachute drop and—"

"Too costly in men and material," Williams answered. "Believe me, you'll have all the support we can give you. Besides, a small group has a better chance of making it to the border."

"Once the Jews are across into Switzerland, what do I do?" Barraka asked. "I still have to make my way back."

"We won't be going anywhere until spring," Williams answered. "Get the Jews across the border and the partisans will bring you back here."

"Sounds like a snap," Barraka replied, purposely snapping his fingers to emphasize the sarcasm of his words. "It's just a fucking throwaway mission!"

Williams's eyes narrowed. "I was asked for the name of the best man for the job," he said sharply. "I gave them your name. You're the best man for the job. You may not like the job and you may not like Jews, but I don't give a flying fuck if you do or don't, because major, you're it. You're going to do the job!"

"Yes, sir!"

Williams's eyes opened again. Drawing contentedly on his cigar, he stood up and said, "If you hadn't requested this meeting Barraka, I would have sent for you. I know your record and I am sure you're the right man."

Barraka clenched his teeth and glared at the general.

"Come see me when you get back," Williams said, extending his hand as the two of them stood up. "I'm not promising anything, but if you pull it off successfully, I think I'll be able to get you a couple of weeks in London or maybe a bond-selling tour back in the States."

"Thank you, sir!" Barraka answered, ending the meeting with a formal salute rather than a handshake.

Barraka was pissed, more pissed than he had ever been in the army or out of it. He hurried along the corridor and out into the rainswept square. The guards at the doorway saluted him and he returned it.

Barraka made straight for the jeep. He was about to hit the horn, when he changed his mind and went into the cafe.

The driver was sitting at a table, saw him, and started to stand.

"It's all right," Barraka told him. "I need a drink." He sat down opposite the young man.

"Not much of a place," the driver commented.

Barraka looked around him. The walls were yellow with age and dirt, but they had been white once. The tables were knocked together out of crate wood. The chairs were wicker backed. Even though it was the last week in October, flies were everywhere. There was sawdust on the stone floor and on one side there was something resembling a bar, where the proprietor stood watching him.

In a quick burst of Italian, Barraka asked the proprietor for Grappa. His command of the language brought an astonished look to the man's face and a broad smile of appreciation to the driver's.

"I am sorry, major," the proprietor said, "I have no Grappa. But the local wine is very good."

"Is he drinking it?" Barraka asked, pointing to the bottle that was already on the table.

"Yes. It is all I have."

"Bring another bottle," Barraka said and turned his attention to the driver. "What's your name?"

"Thomas Higgins . . . but most of the guys I know call me Tim, or Timmy."

"Okay, Tim," Barraka said, "for a little while, let's forget we're in the fucking army. Okay?"

"Sure, major."

"Mitch," Barraka said, extending his hand across

the table. "My name is Mitch."

The proprietor brought another bottle of wine to the table. He dragged his left leg.

"Where did you get hit?" Barraka questioned, pointing to the stiff leg.

"Tobruk," the man answered.

"Isn't that some place in Africa?" Tim asked.

Barraka translated Tim's question.

"*Si, si,*" the proprietor laughed. "It is some place in Africa." He spoke these few words in English, saying them very slowly.

Barraka drank the wine straight from the bottle. Drinking didn't make him any the less pissed. More and more he was beginning to realize how much he hated the war, hated the killing, and was beginning to hate the army, which was something he had never thought he would do. He had enlisted the day after Pearl Harbor, and now, almost three years later, the patriotic fervor was gone, its place having been filled by an enormous feeling of grim determination to survive, despite the mistakes made by the army, even the mistake of sending him to rescue Jews. . . .

When he finally climbed back into the jeep Barraka was still pissed and slightly drunk.

"What I don't get," Tim said, "is how you speak the language."

"My mother taught me," Barraka replied, closing his eyes.

Tim guffawed.

Barraka nodded. "It's true," he said. But he didn't bother to explain that his mother, a French-Canadian by birth, had been a Romance language instructor at the university before her marriage. And as long as he could remember, he had been able to switch without any difficulty from English to French, Italian, or Spanish. When the time had come for him to fulfill his language requirement at the university, he had been able to do it without ever having to attend a class.

Yet Kip, his father, was only able to manage a passable Spanish and a very halting French. The enunciated vowels of Italian completely destroyed him. He never seemed to be able to open his tight-lipped midwestern mouth wide enough to make the sounds come out right. He complained that the Italians had to gesticulate in order to make themselves understood. And, as though it was some breach of courtesy, that was something he could never bring himself to do.

Barraka wondered if his father ever had dealings with Jews. After all, he was president of a bank, albeit a small one. And everyone knew that Jews were always involved with financial matters; even Williams had said so.

Barraka pursed his lips. He felt he'd been given an impossible assignment because some bonehead in Washington or London had decided that it would be as easy for him to move three hundred men, women, and children through mountainous country with a fucking enemy breathing down his neck as to move one man through the same country, dodging the same enemy. Barraka was furious with General Williams for ignoring the fact that three hundred people was not a small group, that they might not have the stamina to walk across mountainous country, even if he could get them out of the prison camp. But generals had the privilege of rank; they could choose to be absolutely deaf, dumb, and blind, whenever it suited their purpose.

The jeep ground to a halt.

"The bridge is out," Tim announced.

Barraka opened his eyes. The windshield was blurred by the rain and then cleared by the wipers. His own vision was blurred. He rubbed his eyes with the back of his hands and focused on the wooden bridge ahead of them. The center portion was down and the portion that remained standing was badly splintered.

"The river must have—"

"River, shit!" Barraka exclaimed, suddenly realizing there was a burnt-out house off the road, not far from the bridge. "Put it in reverse," he said in a calm voice. "Then gun the hell out of it and get us out of here."

The jeep bucked and shot backwards. Tim fought to hold the wheel but it slipped from his grip.

A sudden burst of machine gun fire erupted from the window of the farmhouse.

"Holy Mother of God!" Tim shouted, gaining control of the wheel again just as the rear of the jeep dropped into a narrow ditch alongside the road.

Another burst of fire came from the window. The slugs whamped along the roadway and chewed up several of the smaller trees nearby, causing them to fall on top of the jeep.

"Grab your piece," Barraka ordered. He dropped to the ground, rolled away from the jeep and bellied it to the woods on the other side of the ditch. "Come on, Tim," he shouted. "Come on!"

A short burst smashed into the front of the jeep. A sudden explosion blew away the hood and sent a red plume of flame leaping out of the engine block.

Tim screamed and leaped from the burning vehicle. On fire, he ran toward the bridge.

Barraka watched him, hoping the machine gun would open up and cut him down. But it remained silent. He forced himself to remain motionless, knowing that as soon as he made any move toward the roadway the machine gun would open up on him.

Tim dropped before he reached the splintered end of the bridge and screamed as he continued to burn.

Suddenly Barraka saw five figures in the familiar black uniforms of the Waffen SS leap up and run out from behind the walls.

A moment later a half track cut across the field to the right of the abandoned house.

The crew chief must have seen the Germans because the vehicle swung toward them.

Barraka ran from the edge of the woods to where Tim lay moaning. The air around him smelt of burnt flesh and hair.

From somewhere behind the farmhouse came two short bursts from the quad-mounted machine guns on the half track.

Barraka bent over the still smoking boy.

"Kill me," Tim whispered, trembling from the pain. "For the love of God, Mitch, kill me."

Barraka shook his head. He couldn't speak.

"Kill me, kill me!" Tim pleaded. "Don't let me live, kill me!"

With a silent nod, Barraka put the carbine to the left side of Tim's head and pulled the trigger. There was a sudden explosion. The carbine jumped up and to the right. At the same instant, a thick stream of gray matter, blood, and bits of bone splattered onto the muddy roadway. By the time the half track had rumbled up to him, Barraka had Tim's dog tags in his hand.

The sergeant looked down at the body and said, "Not much more you could've done, major."

"It was what he wanted," Barraka answered, forcing the words out of his constricted throat. "He was so fucking young!"

"Sorry we didn't get here a few minutes earlier," the sergeant told him. "But we were out yonder. As soon as we heard the firing, I came this way."

"Thanks."

"Got a tarp to cover him with," the sergeant offered.

Barraka nodded, took the canvas, and dropped it over Tim. He upended Tim's piece in the mud, placed his helmet on the butt, and then draped one of the dog tags over it.

"Where you headin'?" the sergeant asked.

"The Sixteenth Infantry Battalion."

"Climb aboard, major. You'll arrive in style," the sergeant said, reaching down to help Barraka up into the half track.

II

Barraka pushed aside the wet tent flap and entered the orderly room of Headquarters Company. The company clerk looked up from his typing.

Barraka ignored him. He went straight to Captain Harman, the company CO.

"Next time," Barraka said, tossing the remaining dog tag on the field desk in front of the captain, "when I ask for a driver, don't assign some fucking civilian."

Hartman was a heavy-set man, with brown hair and large hands. He picked up the dog tag and started to read aloud, "Thomas Higgins 6243—"

"Remember what I said about giving a civilian the next time I ask for a driver," Barraka told him again.

"Cooly," Hartman called to the company clerk, "who the hell is—I mean was, Thomas Higgins?"

"One of the new bunch we got about ten days ago . . . straight from the States they was."

"What was his MOS?"

"All of 'em come as infantry riflemen," Cooly answered.

Hartman pushed himself away from the olive-drab field desk and stood up. He was as tall as Barraka and much broader.

"You heard, major," he said. "Higgins was a trained infantryman. His paper said he was."

"Trained your ass!"

"Major," Hartman said, "I don't know what happened out there, but I didn't purposely send Higgins out to get killed."

"If he knew how to handle himself," Barraka said, "he might have come back."

"I use what I'm sent," Hartman answered wearily.

"Just remember what I said."

"Yes, sir."

Barraka frowned. The son-of-a-bitch was giving him the *yes* treatment. He turned, and glaring at Cooly he stomped out of the tent and went straight toward the battalion command post. He was reasonably sure that by now Hartman would be pouring himself a drink to assuage his feelings. He grimaced. There wasn't a damn thing he could do to make himself feel any better. And he was still pissed about the mission.

Barraka stood in front of the large area map. The position of the 16th was marked in green. The battalion held a two-mile front on the south bank of the Sangro River. The remainder of the division was on their left, and elements of the British Eighth Army were on their right. The German 45th Infantry Division was spread out directly in front of them. Anything north of the river was held by the Germans.

"You won't find Servigliano on that map," a

gravelly voice said from behind him.

He recognized the tone and the strong chocolate scent of the tobacco. Like himself, Col. Jonathan Dodd was a pipe smoker.

Barraka turned.

Dodd was a small, thin man with a well-trimmed black moustache and a practically bald head.

"I received the maps you'll need from Division just after you left this morning," Dodd explained. And then he asked, "Any luck with the general?"

"He told me I was the best man for the job," Barraka answered sourly.

"There's no winning in this man's army," Dodd responded in a serious tone. "If you fuck up they get you, and if you do a good job they still get you . . . either way you can't beat them, at least that's what the enlisted men think."

"They don't seem to be too far away from the mark."

"Let's go take a look at the maps," Dodd suggested.

The two men moved over to the far side of the CP. Dodd picked up two flat metal boxes. "One has the maps; the other has aerial photos of the place. But you can't see too much on them." He opened the box containing the photos first and spread the half-dozen pictures out on the desk. "Two of them of Monte San Martino are the same. This one here shows the camp at Servigliano. The other two are of the surrounding terrain, though the idiots in G-2 didn't bother to mark the coordinates on the photos."

Barraka made several swift sweeps of them and picked out details about the nearby town of San Martino and the prison camp itself. The photos were not very good, but he could see where the towers were located, the barracks, and the powerhouse. A road led from the town to the prison. He guessed there were no more than three kilometers between them and not less than two.

"Helpful?" Dodd asked.

"Colonel, that damn camp is on top of a mountain. . . . Just how the hell am I supposed to get in and take those Jews out?"

"That's something you'll have to figure out," Dodd asnwered.

Barraka shook his head but didn't answer.

"Here are the maps," Dodd said. "There are two of them. One covers the area south of Servigliano to the Sangro River, where we are. The other includes the prison camp and the country north of it, to the Swiss border."

"If the Krauts catch us in any one of those gorges, we will have had it," Barraka grumbled.

"Then make sure they don't catch you, major," Dodd responded.

Barraka used a ruler to measure the distance between the Sangro and the prison camp and said, "That's slightly more than a hundred fifty kilometers."

"Two weeks to get there, give or take a day or two," Dodd estimated.

Barraka measured the distance between Servigliano and the Swiss border and came up with seventy kilometers. "And that distance," he explained, "was between the camp and the nearest point on the border."

"No one said it would be easy," Dodd responded.

"It will be damn near impossible," Barraka shot back. "Look at those goddamn mountains that sit between the camp and the border."

"The Germans have the same mountains to face. And you'll have more than a hundred partisans to help you," Dodd told him. "Two of them are due in here by two thousand hours tonight. They'll be crossing the river at Charley Company's position . . . you might want to go down and meet them."

"Is that an order?"

"No . . . but you guys will be spending a lot of time together for the next few weeks. Just remember: If you fuck up, you don't stand much of a chance of getting back to us."

Barraka flushed. "I'll do what I must do," Barraka said. "But I sure as hell don't have to like what I'm doing, or like the people I'm doing it with, or the people I'm doing it for, or do I?"

"No, major, you sure as hell don't have to like anything or anyone," Dodd answered. "But it sure as hell isn't going to help you to hate them, either."

"I don't hate them," Barraka said. "I just don't think the operation has a snowball's chance in hell of succeeding."

"Then you can rest easy, major," Dodd told him. "You didn't make the decision to rescue the Jews. You're only the poor bastard who's going to have to do it. Now tell me who you want to take with you."

"Lieutenant William Koss and Sergeant John Yancy," Barraka answered. "They've been behind the lines with me before. Koss is with Able Company and Yancy is with Dog."

"They'll report to you at oh-eight-hundred hours

tomorrow morning," the colonel said. "You tell me when you're ready to go, and we'll set something up. Now if you'll excuse me . . ."

Barraka took the maps and photos with him when he left the CP. Outside, the sun was beginning to break through the clouds. Long shafts of yellow light came out of ragged blue holes in the overcast sky. Barraka looked at the sky for a long time. The shift in the light was beautiful, stunningly dramatic and out of place with the reality of his mood. He shook his head and walked slowly to this tent. Tim was very much on his mind. Never before had he been forced to kill one of his own men, and, though he had done it as an act of mercy, it made his dark mood ever darker.

Barraka's pup tent was in the woods, several hundred yards from the CP. He shared it with Capt. Joseph Keller, a rangy, taciturn man with cool gray eyes, from Four Corners, Wyoming. Barraka and Keller had bunked together ever since Barraka had been with the 16th. Beside Koss and Yancy, he considered Keller as good a friend as he could have. He particularly liked the man's silences; they complemented his own.

Neither he nor Keller spoke too much about their past lives; they said very little about the future and just enough about the present to maintain some sort of bond between them. Sometimes they chowed together, but not very often.

When Barraka approached the tent, Keller was just crawling out of it.

"I thought I'd be able to sack out for a while,"

Keller explained, as he stood up and saw Barraka. "But there's some trouble with the phones on the left flank. . . . The rain must have seeped through to the wires, or the Krauts did some cutting." He hunkered down and reached in along the side of the tent, withdrawing a carbine, then a helmet and his web belt. When he stood up again, he told Barraka, "There's a couple of letters for you. . . . I picked them up at mail call."

"Thanks."

Keller nodded, put his helmet on, buckled his web belt, and slung the carbine over his right shoulder. He walked toward the CP with a long, slow stride.

Barraka dropped down and pushed the two metal boxes into the tent. Then he crawled after them. The dim inside smelled of sweat and dampness. His two V-mail letters were on the top of his field pack. He took both of them and stuffed them into the breast pocket of his fatigues, then wormed his way back out of the tent. He stood up and went over to a sun-splashed tree stump and sat down.

One letter was from Kip, his father. The other came from Helen Wright, a blue-eyed, honey-colored blonde with full breasts whom he had dated before leaving for the army, and with whom he had come to have an understanding in the last few months. She had decided to stop dating other men and to wait for him to come home.

Almost as if he were weighing them, Barraka held his father's letter in his right hand and Helen's in his left. He decided to read his father's first and put Helen's back into his breast pocket.

The letter was dated ten days before. Ever since Rome had been taken, the mail didn't take as long as it previously had to make its way from the States to the men on the line. Barraka nodded approvingly and began to read:

Hello Mitch—

I'm writing this from my office. It's Friday night. The bank is closed and everything is still. Though it's only the middle of October, there's more than just a chill in the air, which bespeaks a harsh winter. I do not mind the former, especially when the woods begin to turn and I can spend a few hours out of doors painting those vivid colors. But I could do without a harsh winter.

Though you have been away many years now, I still have difficulty with the reality of the situation, especially during these quiet times, when I suddenly find myself wondering if you are well, if you are safe and dry. But whatever my feelings are, your mother's are of a greater magnitude than I could ever hope to imagine. By the way, she and Helen have become fast friends. They are on the phone almost every night. I must admit, I too find Helen charming.

Your twenty-eighth birthday will be rolling around on Thanksgiving Day. I know Mother and Helen are sending a very large package out to you. We all hope it reaches you in time for you to enjoy it.

In your last letter, you mentioned that you would like to specialize in bridge design and construction when you return home, rather than pick up where you left off in homebuilding. I certainly have no objections to your building bridges. In case I have never mentioned it to you, I have always considered bridges one of the few truly great achievements of mankind.

May God protect and keep you!

Your Loving Father, Kip.

P.S. Your sister Carol has gone out on her first date.

P.P.S. Try to write more often. Your mother needs those letters.

A stray breeze riffled the thin letter paper. Barraka had forgotten that his birthday was about a month away. He looked around him and knew he would be somewhere up near the Swiss border by the time his birthday came. Hopefully he would be alive. He frowned and rubbed his chin. It was one of those very rare moments when Barraka allowed himself to think about the future. He had a desperate need to see himself away from the war, away from the killing and the dying. He imagined a broad river and the kind of suspension bridge he would design to span it . . . and then he shook his head. The mission to Servigliano could put a stop to his bridge building before it ever had a chance to start. But there was nothing he could do to get out of it; he had to go.

Folding his father's letter, he exchanged places with it for Helen's in his breast pocket. Hers was dated five days earlier than his father's.

My Darling—

I have just had a lovely conversation with your mother. We are planning to send you a wonderful surprise for your birthday. I hope it reaches you in time, or at least close to it. To have to celebrate a birthday early or late seems to me to be a sad occurrence. It reminds me of Christmas decorations that remain up into January. I find them very sad also.

Do you remember Gloria Harper? She had a reputation for being something of a tease. Well, she is now a married woman. No one in our crowd knows who the groom is. But she met him at a USO dance. Now this is the strange part of it—he's a Jew. That's right. He comes from Boston, where I was told by Gloria's sister that his father owns a very large furniture store. I can't imagine anyone of the crowd, least of all Gloria, married to a Jew. Some of the girls say that Jewish men prefer Christian women. They also say that a Jewish man's private member is cut smaller shortly after birth. I don't think I ever saw a real Jew. Have you?

Barraka paused. He had dated Gloria Harper several times during his senior year at the university and again after he had formed his own construction company. Once he had her pants off and almost got into her. But she had stopped him and had said she was saving it for her husband. She had then proceeded to give him one of the "best blow jobs" he had ever had up until that time. After that he took her out a few more times and she always went down on him. He couldn't remember why he had lost interest in her and once more focused his attention to Helen's letter.

Darling, it is terribly difficult to translate my feelings for you into words. You would think me utterly shameless if I were to tell you what I dream about, even think about. I want you Mitch, in every way a woman can want a man. I wish you were here now so that you could once again hold me in your arms, and I would not wait to let you make love to me. I would willingly, oh so willingly, give myself to you.

All My Love
Helen

Barraka smiled and folded the letter, replacing it in his breast pocket. The sun was pleasantly warm and he removed his field jacket. He closed his eyes, and for a while he sat basking in the sun.

The erotic portion of Helen's letter brought a familiar tightness to his groin. The last time he had had a woman had been in a small town just south of Modena, and that had been five, six weeks ago. The woman had lived in a farmhouse with her two children. Her husband had been taken prisoner by the British, somewhere in Libya, she thought. He had spent two days and nights with her. When he had left he had given her two cans of food and two chocolate bars. She had kissed him gratefully and had said she would pray for his safety.

"I guess every little bit of prayer helps," Barraka said to himself as he opened his eyes and stood up. A few moments later he folded back the two ends of the tent to let the inside dry and release some of the stench.

Off to the east, at twilight, the Germans began to

shell the British positions. And in almost no time at all artillery fire erupted all along the line on both sides of the river that divided the armies from each other.

The rounds that exploded near the bivouac area of Headquarters Company were off to the left where a battery of 155s was located. The Germans were looking for it and obviously hoped they would find it by meticulously laying down a pattern of fire to cover every square foot of ground. Each evening for the past week they had blasted the same area, but they could not pinpoint the 155s. They either fired too short or too long.

The shelling stopped as quickly as it had begun. The silence seemed to wait for another explosion, but none came.

"They better move their ass some time tonight," Keller said, referring to the 155 unit, "or the Krauts will find them with a lucky round." He and Barraka were standing outside of the CP, looking in the direction of the artillery battery.

Barraka agreed with a wordless grunt.

The two men started to walk.

"I'm goin' over the Charley Company," Keller said. "The old man wants me to be there and report to him when the two Eyetalian partisans come in."

"What do you have to do with them?" Barraka asked.

"I'm going to be your communications officer for the mission," Keller said. "Off the record, I heard you're pissed over the whole thing and went all the way up to Division to get out of it."

"Yeah, you heard right."

"Any chance of you being pulled out of it?"

"None."

"Tough . . . I wouldn't want to go on something like that if I didn't have my heart in it," Keller commented.

"Got no choice," Barraka said with a shrug.

"I best be going down to Charley Company," Keller told him. "You want to come along?"

"Like the colonel said," Barraka answered, "I'm going to spend some time with those guys."

"Are you goin', or aren't you?"

"Tell me, did you ever know any Jews before you were in the army?" Barraka asked.

"Sure," Keller answered. "My grandmother was half Jewish, and, according to my grandfather, that was the best part of her."

"Red dog!" Barraka exclaimed, answering the challenge of a sentry with the password for the day that had begun at 0600 hours that morning. He and Keller waited a moment.

The sentry came out from behind a clump of trees with his piece ready to be thrown up to his shoulder and fired if necessary. He moved closer and asked, "That you, Captain Keller?"

"Yes, and Major Barraka," Keller answered.

"Sorry, sir," the man said. "But we got orders to check everybody. Some Krauts got through a couple of nights ago and killed a few guys near Division earlier today."

Barraka was sure the man was talking about the action at the bridge.

"We'll be comin' through here again," Keller

explained. "I'll have two other men with me. Tell the man who relieves you to be on the lookout for us. I don't want any nervous Nelly waking up the whole area by getting off a few rounds."

"Yes, sir," the man answered.

Barraka and Keller made their way down to a place along the river where several huge boulders provided excellent cover for a heavy machine gun. They dropped down into the open space, and Keller asked the young lieutenant if the Germans had been active on the other side.

"No more than usual," the officer answered.

Barraka peered across the river. At that point it was no more than fifty yards wide. A slight mist lay over its black surface. He could hear the Germans very plainly.

"Are they usually that loud?" he asked, turning toward the lieutenant.

"Sometimes louder."

"What happens if you fire a burst?"

"They'll fire one back, sir. They're settling down for the winter. We can see them chopping down trees and building shelters just beyond the embankment . . . I guess we'll be doing the same soon."

"Probably," Keller answered.

"The colonel said the two of them would be coming in at two thousand hours," Barraka commented.

"I wouldn't bet on it," Keller told him. "I spoke to them two nights ago. They said there was a lot of German activity and they might have difficulty coming across."

Barraka sat up and pushed his helmet back. "I don't understand," Barraka said. "What the hell do you mean, you spoke to them?"

"I've been talkin' to them on the radio," Keller said.

"But you don't speak Italian."

"Volterra speaks English," Keller explained. "Don't ask me where he learned to speak it. He does, and that's all that matters. He and his men have been in the vicinity for several days now."

"I thought there was only two of them," Barraka said.

"Two are comin' across. I don't know how many will be waitin' on the other side. We never have a long conversation. If we did, the Krauts would almost certainly get a fix on 'em."

Barraka shifted his position and settled back against one of the boulders. He took out his pipe, lit it, covered the bowl with his palm, and began to smoke. He had no idea Keller had been in touch with the partisans, not that it mattered much.

Keller settled down next to him and said, "I gave Volterra the exact coordinates of this position. But I don't expect 'em on time."

Barraka didn't say anything. After a while he began thinking about what Helen had written and wondered how she'd be in bed. Some women looked like they'd be fantastic lays, while others talked a good fuck. But others who neither looked like they'd be good nor said anything about it often turned out to be the best lay a man could hope for. Helen looked like she'd be good, very good, and now she was even beginning to talk—or rather write about how much she wanted it. That, Barraka took as a good sign. Then, for no apparent reason, he found himself thinking about Gloria

Harper. Though she gave a good blow job, he guessed she'd be a lousy lay. He couldn't imagine why she'd want to marry a Jew from Boston when there were so many guys in Duluth who were hot for her. Guys who had their foreskins. He wasn't sure that Gloria would know a cock was a cock unless it had a foreskin. But he was sure she'd be a quick learner.

"How deep does the river get off here?" Keller asked, looking up at the lieutenant.

"Ten feet, according to the map," the man answered.

Keller was on his feet and moved closer to the river. "I sure hope those guys can swim," he said. And then he added, "The mist has thickened."

"About sunrise or a little bit before it will be a fog."

"I sure hope we don't have to wait until morning for them to come across," Barraka said.

"So do I," Keller responded.

"What if they don't get across tonight?"

"Then they'll try the night after next. It's arranged for them to skip one night and try the following one."

"And if they don't make it at all?"

"They'll make it," Keller answered, peering intently across the river.

Barraka knocked his pipe clean of ashes against the boulder. "Would you mind if I asked you a personal question?" he said, going to where Keller was.

"I can't tell until you ask it," Keller replied.

"About your grandmother—how did a Jew, even a half-Jew, manage to get to Wyoming?"

Keller grinned. "No mystery there," he said. "She was on her way to Seattle with her family. My grandfather saw her, fell in love with her, and didn't care what the hell she was as long as she agreed to be his wife. I guess she must have felt the same way about him, because when he died I remember her saying to me, 'Joseph, your granddaddy was more than my husband: He was my friend and lover.' Then she smiled and said, 'In a little while I'll be close to him again.' And she was. A month later she was dead. . . . Her name was Hanna," Keller said, without taking his eyes from the river.

The two men fell silent. After a few minutes passed, Barraka stood up and went to where the machine gun was. Its long barrel poked through an opening between two boulders, giving the gunner a good field of fire. He returned to where Keller was, sat down again, and soon was dozing, though his senses were alert. Deep sleep was a luxury that combat had taught him to live without. Barraka heard the muffled voices of men around him and listened to their movements.

Suddenly Barraka was completely overwhelmed by a nightmarish dream of what had happened at the bridge that morning. The action was in slow motion, and Tim's cries of agony came from a way off. His own inarticulate moaning woke him, and, rubbing his eyes, he looked at his watch. It was 0215 hours.

"I'm not going to be fit for shit tomorrow," he commented.

Keller didn't answer; he was asleep.

Barraka looked out over the river. It was completely obscured by the fog. But close inshore it was clear. There was enough of a chill in the air to make him shudder and wish he had some hot coffee, or a double shot of the scotch he had stashed away in his barracks bag.

Suddenly there was shouting from the German side.

Barraka looked questioningly at the lieutenant.

"Could be, sir," the officer said.

Keller awakened. He was instantly alert.

The Germans fired a flare. The bright magnesium light illuminated the fog bank with an incandescent whiteness.

"Can you see anything?" Keller asked.

"Nothing."

"I wished to hell I knew what they were yellin' about," Keller commented.

"From what I can make out," the lieutenant said, "one of their men has been knifed."

Another flare went up just as the first began to dim. A few moments passed. Then there was a burst of machine gun fire.

"Give them a burst," the lieutenant told his men.

The .50 barked.

Small arms fire erupted from the German side of the river. Another flare exploded overhead.

Rifle fire came from both sides of the river. More machine guns began to bang away. Several grenades were thrown and their explosions sent spouts of water into the white fog above the river.

The field phone began to ring. The lieutenant answered it. "Captain," he said, "Colonel Dodd is on the line."

Keller took the phone. "Keller here," he shouted into the mouthpiece, while shielding his right ear from the noise with his hand.

"What the hell is happening down there?" Dodd shouted. "Soon the fuckin' arty will begin firing. I thought they were supposed to come across without the Krauts' knowing it."

"The Krauts started to fire," Keller explained.

"Are they across?"

"No, sir."

"Let me know as soon as they make it," Dodd said and rang off.

Keller handed the phone back to the lieutenant and rejoined Barraka.

"The old man is pissed about the firing," he said.

Barraka didn't answer. He couldn't care less if Dodd was pissed or not.

The firing became more sporadic on either flank. But the Krauts were sending up flares at intervals of about three minutes. And the machine gun on the opposite side of the river continued to fire short bursts that now and then thwacked into a floating object.

"There," Keller exclaimed. "There! See it?"

"What the hell—"

"It's a log," Keller said.

"Shit!" Barraka exclaimed in a low, angry voice. "They're lost."

"What?"

"They're lost," Barraka repeated, pointing to the log. It was already turning away from the shore. "Keep that gun firing at the Krauts."

The .50 opened up; its tracers stabbed thin lines of light into the fog.

Barraka was on his feet.

"Where the hell are you goin'?" Keller questioned.

"If someone doesn't get them, the Krauts' machine guns will." He jumped clear of the boulders and ran down the bank. "This way," Barraka shouted in Italian. "This way."

The log turned toward him.

A flare burst over him. Machine gun slugs slapped into the water close to the log. He was totally exposed.

"Keep down," Barraka shouted in Italian. "Keep down!" He ran to the water's edge and splashed into the river.

The log came close to shore.

"This way!" Barraka shouted. "Toward the left."

A flare burst overhead. More machine gun slugs sliced into the water, ricocheted off the rocks with a pinging sound.

Barraka waded deeper into the river. A red ribbon of tracers swerved off to his right and another went over his head.

The log moved closer to him. Two men emerged from the other side. "Up to the rocks," Barraka told them.

In a low crouch the two men zigzagged toward the rocks. Barraka followed. One of the partisans lost his footing and went down. "Keep going," Barraka shouted to the other, as he stopped and pulled the man to his feet. He was the last man through the opening between the boulders.

Two more flares went up and then the Germans' firing ceased. Within moments the .50 was silent.

Breathless, Barraka dropped against one of the boulders.

The two partisans leaped into the open space,

gasping with fatigue and strain.

"Which one is Volterra?" Keller asked, going up to the two of them.

"I am," one of them said, moving his right hand against his chest. "I am Chaim Volterra."

"Captain Keller," Keller said, offering his hand.

III

Volterra was a short, compact man with a black beard, thick, kinky hair, and dark eyes. He looked up at Barraka. Still gasping for breath, he said, in very clear English, "I wish to thank you." And with a thick hand he gestured toward the river. "Neither I nor Agostino could see more than a meter in front of us."

"It was stupid to kill the Kraut," Barraka said, in Italian, "and even more stupid to try and find a place you couldn't possibly see."

Volterra stiffened and glanced toward Agostino Mastrada, a tall, thin man with a pronounced hooked nose. "I am sorry, major," Volterra said, "but we do not fight the war as you do. We kill Germans whenever we can, especially if they happen to be in our way. And as for attempting to reach this place without being able to see it—well, we are here. Any comment about how we managed to get here would be superfluous." He spoke in English, moving his hard black eyes from Barraka to Keller and back to Barraka again.

"You said what you had to say," Barraka answered.

"And now I'm going to say what I have to."

"By all means major," Volterra said, pulling himself to his feet on his rifle.

"I don't want this mission," he told the two partisans. "But I have it, and you have me. You're right about the way I fight . . . I try not to make mistakes that might get me or my men killed. I don't trust to luck, and when I kill I make sure the man I kill is worth killing." For an instant he saw himself place the carbine's muzzle against Tim's head. . . .

"Any German is worth killing," Mastrada shot back.

"Listen," Barraka said sharply. "I'll tell you when to kill and who to kill. While I command, I command, is that clear? Nothing is done without my orders."

The two partisans looked questioningly at each other, and then, with a shrug, Volterra answered, "There are three hundred people whose lives will depend on whether or not we are successful."

Barraka nodded and turned to Keller, saying, "Get on the horn and tell the ol' man they're across."

"He wants you guys in the CP at a thousand hours," Keller called from the phone.

"We'll be there."

Keller rejoined them. "Come on," he said to Volterra and Mastrada. "I'll see if I can scrounge somethin' out of Battalion mess; then you guys can bed down for a few hours. . . . I had a tent put up a few yards away from the major's and mine."

Barraka went to his tent. As soon as he pushed his carbine inside and crawled after it, he removed his helmet and field jacket. With his hands under his head, he lay awake looking at the apex of the triangle above him. He was too angry to sleep.

He made no excuse for the way he had acted toward the partisans. He had treated them badly. There was no doubt in his mind that they were brave men. From his previous missions with partisans, he had learned to respect them. But this was an entirely different situation. These men were Jews and—he stopped himself.

He was against the mission, not against the Jews. But even the general had a negative reaction to horror stories about the concentration camps. And he was in a position to know what was happening. The general thought it was propaganda financed by money from Jews in Wall Street.

Barraka sighed wearily, turned on his side. He was almost asleep when Keller wormed his way into the tent.

"Mitch?" Keller called, gently shaking Barraka.

"Yeah . . . yeah . . . what is it? What's wrong?" He rolled over and started to sit up.

"I want to ask you something," Keller said.

Barraka settled back.

"Off the record," Keller told him. "Man to man?"

"Go ahead and ask."

"Why did you jump all over those guys?"

Barraka pushed himself up on his elbows and said, "Put yourself in my boots and then tell me what you'd have done. I don't want this mission, and though I have a deep respect for the Italian Partisans, these two are Jews."

"They must be good if they command a unit,"

Keller commented.

"I just didn't want them to get the wrong idea. You know how difficult some Jews can be. I wanted them to know from the very beginning what the score is." He knew he was using words he had heard people use, but they fitted the situation to a tee.

"If I were you, Mitch, I'd speak to the colonel again and try to get yourself relieved."

"Won't do a damn bit of good," Barraka said, dropping down on a blanket. "I'm it, the chosen one to lead God's chosen people . . . now there's a crock."

"What?"

"That whole bit about the Jews' being God's chosen people . . . I mean if that's true, what the hell are the rest of us?" He had asked the question in anger.

Keller didn't answer.

Barraka turned on his side and forced himself to think of Helen. After a while he slept, aware of the footfalls around the tent and the sporadic crack of small arms fire that announced the coming of the first light. He awoke with a start, rubbed his eyes, and wormed his way out of the tent.

The air had a chill to it, but the sky was clear and the sun was beginning to show itself over the high hills to the east. The smell of coffee made him look toward the mess tent.

"Major?"

Barraka turned.

Volterra and Mastrada were sitting on the ground in front of their tent. Each of them had draped an army blanket over his shoulders. Their clothing was ragged and their boots badly torn, with newspaper and cardboard patches in the soles. A German machine pistol lay next to Volterra and a Mannlicher rifle rested across Mastrada's lap.

"The smell of fresh coffee awakened us," Mastrada said in Italian.

Barraka moved closer to where they were sitting. He noticed that each of them wore a Star of David around his neck. Many of the Jewish men in the unit wore them.

Volterra stood up and slung the machine pistol over his shoulder. "I don't want to trouble you," he said. "But I must speak honestly."

"Go ahead and speak."

"Neither Agostino or myself thinks you're the man to lead the mission," he said in a soft, but resolute voice.

"Tell that to the colonel," Barraka answered with a shrug.

"I intend to," Volterra said. "You see, major, I have no doubt of your ability. In fact, Captain Keller told us of your success with other partisan units. But this mission is very, very different, and neither of us feels you're the right man for it."

"Fine and dandy," Barraka replied, very much aware of the man's hard black eyes. There was little doubt that Volterra was not afraid of him. "But until I'm relieved, either at your request or my own, I'm still in command. Is that clear?"

"Yes, major."

"You go on up to the mess tent, get something to eat. Then you find the supply sergeant and tell him I want you to be issued clothing and boots." Without waiting for an answer, Barraka turned and went to wash. He was furious with Volterra for having spoken to him that way. He doused his face with ice cold water, ran his hand over his skin, and decided he could do with a shave.

By the time Barraka walked back to the tent to pick up his shaving gear and toothbrush, Keller was up and doing his exercises.

"Listen," Keller said, "I didn't mean to push into your business last night."

"Forget it," Barraka told him.

"Thanks," Keller responded.

"Just so you know what these guys are up to," Barraka explained, "they told me they don't think I'm fit to command their unit and they're going to ask the colonel to relieve me. See what I meant about Jews. Now do you understand?"

"Maybe they can do what you couldn't?"

Barraka shrugged. "I don't give a fuck what they do," he said.

Master Sergeant Jack Yancy had been regular army since 1938. Before that he had been with the CCC building roads in Alabama. He was broad-shouldered, a chunky man with light brown hair, freckles on his arms and neck, and cat-green eyes. He sipped his hot coffee slowly as he listened to Barraka giving him and Lieutenant William Koss the lowdown on the mission.

The three of them sat cross-legged on the ground, not far from the mess tent. Barraka had his back against a pine tree. Yancy and Koss faced the major.

Koss was a thin man with delicate features and a soft voice. He came from the Yorkville section of New

York City. His parents were former German nationals, but when Hitler came to power they had decided that Germany was no longer the place to raise their son. Before Koss was drafted into the army he had taught English literature and German at New York University. He spoke fluent German.

Yancy and Koss worked well together. Yancy had a grudging respect for Koss's education and former position, while Koss realized that Yancy was the man to have at his side especially when the chips were down, and that probably no one in the army knew more about using explosives than he did.

"I think it's a lousy mission," Barraka said. "But this is a lousy war."

"Meanin'," Yancy commented in his southern drawl, "you're bein' extra kind by takin' us away from a lousy war to go on a little old lousy mission?"

With a hint of a smile, Barraka said, "The three of us are good buddies. . . . I'd never want you to think I was in on something good without taking you along."

"All that firin' last night," Yancy asked, "was it because of the Eyeties?"

"They came across," Barraka answered. "Almost got themselves blown out of the water."

"Almost don't count none."

"There's one other thing," Barraka said, "I think you should know. The two partisans are Jews."

"Shit, man," Yancy responded, "that doesn't make one bit of difference as long as they're not chicken when it comes to killin'."

Barraka looked at Bill, who was a Catholic.

"Yance said it," Koss told him.

Yancy scrambled to his feet. "If this meetin' is over,

I'm goin' get me some good powdered eggs and fried spam. You guys want some?"

Both Barraka and Koss shook their heads.

"Mitch," Bill asked after Yancy left them, "what's really bothering you about this mission?"

Barraka was about to disclaim that he was bothered by anything more than the military stupidity of the mission, but instead he said, "I just don't think it's an army mission. Those people will be well cared for once they reach Germany. And, more to the point, our lives are being put on the line. In my opinion, it's not worth it, even for three hundred Jews."

Koss shook his head. "You're wrong. Those camps are not just internment camps."

"You believe that crap—"

"Mitch, they're death camps. I know what I am talking about. If those Jews are sent to Buchenwald, they'll be killed."

Barraka finished his coffee and put the canteen cup down on the ground. "How can you be so sure?" he asked.

"We have family left in Germany. My folks receive letters from them through friends in Sweden. The Germans are systematically killing the Jews."

Barraka shrugged, stood up, and announced he was going for more coffee. "I'll see you in the CP at a thousand," he said and went toward the mess tent. The idea that anyone, even Krauts, would systematically kill a people was too absurd for him to believe.

Volterra and Mastrada were wearing GI issue but, their unkempt beards still made them look scruffy.

They stood next to Colonel Dodd, studying a large situation map that showed the disposition of the battalion's men along the river.

Keller was close to them, while Barraka, Yancy, and Koss were several paces off to one side.

The colonel hadn't wasted any time. As soon as they had all gathered together, he had led them to the map. "The way I see it," he said, "your best place to cross back would be here. Close to the British. The river narrows down to less than ten meters, and it's not more than two meters deep." He tapped the map with a pointer.

"Colonel," Volterra said, "with all due respect to your effort on our behalf, we must settle a particular matter before we continue."

Barraka stiffened. He was once again aware of the man's soft but resolute voice. He hadn't thought Volterra would broach the matter of having him relieved before everyone. He could feel the color rise in his cheeks.

Colonel Dodd lowered the pointer, and with a nod he said, "You have me at an advantage, Signor Commander. I don't know what particular matter must be settled."

"Major Barraka—"

"Major Barraka!" Dodd exclaimed, wheeling around to face him. "Have you any idea what this particular matter is all about?"

"Colonel," Volterra said patiently, "as commander of the partisan unit that will attack the prison camp, I must respectfully ask that Major Barraka be relieved and another officer assigned to take his place."

Dodd faced Volterra. His face was flushed. "On

what grounds, Signor Commander?"

"He has no feeling for the mission, or the people who will place their lives in his hands," Volterra said. "I do not think that the major should—"

Dodd shook his head. "Major Barraka has no choice in the matter," he told him. "He's the man best qualified for the job."

"Technically, I have no doubt of that," Volterra said, still keeping the tone in his voice soft. "But that is only part of the skill he will need to see those people across the border. I do not mean to insult the major, but I think he lacks compassion."

His pride hurt, Barraka stepped forward. He was practically quivering with anger. "Sir," he addressed Dodd, "with your permission, I'd like to speak."

"Permission granted," Dodd answered.

"To set the record straight," Barraka began, "I asked to be relieved. I went to the general and asked. I wouldn't object if I were relieved this minute. But that's not the way it's going to be. I'm going north with you, and it'll be my skill and the skill of my two men that will get those people out of the prison camp and, with luck, to the border. And as for compassion, you're right. I don't have much of it left for anyone but my own men. I've seen enough of them killed because someone made a mistake."

"Is that all, major?" Dodd asked.

"Yes, sir."

Dodd turned toward Volterra and asked, "Shall we continue, Signor Commander?"

Volterra nodded.

Dodd pointed to the place on the map where they would cross the river and said, "Here we'll create a diversion on the opposite end of the battalion, while to the east the rest of the divisional artillery will start firing. We'll make it look as if we intend to cross over in strength on the eastern flank of our position on the river."

Radio communications procedures were discussed. It was agreed that radio transmission from the partisans would not exceed two minutes and that three different frequencies would be used. It was left to Volterra and Keller to work out the sequencing and code expression for special situations.

"Once you get close to the camp you will be in the area of the Sixteenth Infantry Brigade," Dodd said. "It's commanded by Colonel Eric Von Kunstler . . . Signor Commander, what do you know about him?"

"He has served on the Russian front. He is very professional. My men and his have clashed several times. But none of the actions involved more than a dozen men. Kunstler leaves the running of Servigliano to Captain Gissiking. But recently, just before the people were brought to Servigliano, SS Captain Muller was assigned to Kunstler's command. Muller has a platoon of SS men with him. Muller reports directly to Karl Wolfe, the overall commander of the Waffen-SS in Italy. Kunstler and Muller do not see eye to eye on a great many things."

"Any other officer I should know about?"

"Major Radish, Kunstler's executive officer," Volterra answered. "He's not a field man, but he is a very good administrator."

"Major," Dodd said, "as of now, the planning and execution of the mission is in your hands."

"What is your unit's total strength?" Barraka

asked, looking at Volterra.

"Fifty men and women."

"How many are waiting for us on the other side of the river?"

"Six. We intend to link up with them outside of Catanio. That's thirty kilometers behind the German line at the river."

"How many Krauts in the brigade's area?" Barraka asked.

"It varies from month to month," Volterra said. "But never less than ten thousand."

"All under Kunstler's command?"

"Yes. But not all of them are line troops. I'd say about half are combat ready."

"Fifty of us against five thousand Krauts," Barraka said. "It might as well be a thousand to one."

"Has either of you anything else to say?" Dodd asked, looking at Volterra and then Barraka.

"Nothing more," Barraka answered.

"Nothing," Volterra said.

"Tomorrow morning. About oh-one-hundred hours."

"I'll arrange to have your support," Dodd said. "Well, gentlemen, if you need anything by way of supplies, ask Captain Fawer. I've already told him to give you whatever you need. He paused. "I hope the success of the mission will not be jeopardized by personal preferences."

"I want to come back alive, colonel," Barraka answered.

"All of us want to come back alive," Volterra said.

Barraka pursed his lips and remained silent.

A moment later they were dismissed and filed

rapidly out of the CP.

Barraka sat down on a stump and filled his pipe with tobacco. Most of headquarters area was behind him, and, through the trees to his right, he could look across the river to the German-held side.

He found himself wondering if he would be as violently opposed to the mission if the prisoners at Servigliano were—say, Yugoslavians, or even Italian Catholics, rather than Jews. The question made him puff vigorously on his pipe.

Of course! The insanity of the mission was the real reason for his anger. Suddenly he recognized the real possibility that he might be losing his nerve. He had seen it happen to other men. Could it be happening to him?

The question stunned Barraka. If he was losing his nerve, Koss and Yancy would recognize the symptoms long before he would. It wasn't a pleasant thought, and it brought goose bumps to his skin when he realized they would be deep in German-held country before any of the telltale signs would appear. Barraka hoped he would be man enough to turn over his command to Koss if he wasn't fit to lead.

"So there you are!"

Barraka turned and saw the Catholic chaplain, Pierce Brennan, coming toward him.

"I've been looking all over for you," the chaplain told him. He spoke with a definite New York accent. "This was one place I hadn't tried before." He was a tall man, with a square face, bright blue eyes, and a firm handshake.

Barraka stood up. Like himself, the priest was a field soldier. His uniform was mud-spattered, and his chin was darkened by a two-day beard.

They shook hands. "I've got a bottle of scotch and I'll split it with you," Barraka offered.

The priest said, "Let's walk."

Barraka nodded. They walked toward the far side of the company area.

"Tell me what happened to Thomas Higgins," the Padre said.

Barraka shot a quick glance at him.

"I get to see the names of all the casualties. Tim came from my parish in Greenpoint. I know his family and they know mine. We were born and raised in the same neighborhood."

Barraka reached down, plucked a blade of grass, and began chewing on it.

"I spoke to Captain Hartman," the priest told him. "He just said you threw Tim's dog tag on his desk and cursed him out for sending a 'fucking civilian.'"

"That's what I said," Barraka answered. "They send them over here younger and younger with less and less training." He stopped abruptly and faced the priest. "They're sending schoolkids against seasoned troops. Kids who—ah, what the hell is the use of telling you? You know."

"Yes, I know."

Barraka started to walk again. "You can write to Tim's family and tell them he died fighting for his country. Tell them they can be proud of him."

"Yes, but I would have written that anyway."

Barraka said nothing. He threw away the blade of grass and picked another.

"Now would you tell me what really happened?" the priest asked gently.

Barraka stopped. "We were ambushed," he said. "I rolled free of the jeep. Tim was too frightened to move. The jeep took a burst and went up in flames. Tim caught fire. When I finally could get to him, most of his skin was charred. He pleaded with me to help him." He paused to clear his throat.

"You stayed with him until he died?" the priest questioned.

Barraka shook his head. "There was nothing anyone could do for him, Padre. He was dying. I put an end to his suffering."

"Holy Mother of God!" the priest exclaimed, crossing himself.

"I didn't think you'd like it," Barraka said. "But that's really what happened."

The priest put his hand on Barraka's shoulder and gently squeezed.

"It was the merciful thing to do," Barraka told him.

After a long pause, the priest said, "Then there's nothing else to say about it, is there?"

Barraka shook his head. "I'm tired of this fucking war . . . do you know what I mean, Father?"

"Yes."

"Everything I do I feel in my gut. I even *think* with my gut, if that makes any sense."

"The only hope we have is that peace will soon come," the priest said.

"It won't come soon enough to stop me from going north," Barraka said. "It won't come soon enough for that."

"No, it won't. The colonel told me about your mission."

"Did he tell you I thought it was another throwaway deal . . . only this time Lieutenant Koss, Sergeant Yancy, and I are being thrown away, and there isn't a damn thing I can do about it."

"He told me."

"Well, what do you think?" Barraka asked.

"I think you'll do what must be done to get those people out, just as you did what had to be done when Tim was dying."

Barraka didn't answer.

"I'll pray for you, Mitch."

"Thanks," Barraka said with a smile. "Pray real hard. It's going to be one bitch of a mission."

The priest nodded, shook hands with Barraka, and walked away. Then he stopped, turned, and said, "Tim was going to be my assistant. His orders came through this morning."

Barraka made an open gesture with his hands. "I'm sorry, Father."

"God watch over you and those with you," the priest said.

After a few minutes passed, Barraka knocked the dead ashes from his pipe and left the stump. He decided to write to Helen and his parents. He wouldn't have another opportunity until he returned from the mission . . . if he returned.

Volterra called to Barraka. "Excuse me, major, I'd like to have a word with you."

Barraka slowed his pace.

Volterra fell in alongside of him. "If I'm killed," he said matter-of-factly, "Mastrada will assume my place. But should he, too, be killed before we reach Catanio, you and your men will link up with mine at a farmhouse a few kilometers to the east of the town. I've drawn a map of the surrounding country for you." Reaching into his jacket pocket, he withdrew a piece of paper. "You'll notice that the Germans have several detachments of troops nearby."

Barraka scanned the paper.

"The troops are noncombatant," Volterra explained. "Mainly medical and ambulatory wounded, which is why Catanio was chosen for our meeting place. We won't be near any field units."

"And should something happen to me," Barraka said, "my command will go to Lieutenant Koss."

"That is certainly understood."

They were past the immediate area of Headquarters Company. The contour of the land changed from the gentle slope leading to the river to a steeper one that came to an end at the crest of a hill. A convoy of deuce and halfs were coming toward them, bringing up supplies.

"The Germans also are digging in for the winter," Volterra commented. He looked back toward the river. "The winter will give them time to rest, regroup, and resupply. And in the spring they will fight with new strength."

"Yes," Barraka agreed.

"Shall I ask your medical officer for cyanide capsules? If we have to leave someone, he won't be treated kindly by the Germans."

"I know it."

"Then I'll see that each man has one," Volterra said. He stopped speaking. Because his attempt to draw Barraka into a conversation had been rebuffed, Volterra saw no reason to extend himself any more than the military situation required. He had no doubt the American High Command had chosen the wrong man for the mission. But there was nothing he could do about it. He had to live with Barraka and hope that the man's expertise was sufficiently great to outweigh his obvious hatred of Jews. If it did not, if his anti-Semitism proved detrimental to the object of the mission, Volterra decided he would have to be killed. But that was the kind of decision he would make at a particular time and place. And he would do it at that particular moment. That he might have to kill Barraka some time in the not-too-distant future made him glance at the man and shake his head at the incongruity of their being comrades-in-arms and at the same time enemies in their hearts. But the war was full of such inconsistencies; it was part of its absolute absurdity.

At 2430 the artillery began to fire to the west of where Barraka's team was going to cross the river. A thin, swirling mist lay over the water. The opposite bank appeared and disappeared according to the vagaries of a light breeze.

The Germans were quick to answer the fire. Two minutes after the initial salvo, both sides were engaged in a fierce artillery duel. For moments on end the night was turned into sudden bursts of dazzling whiteness, or the blackness was shredded with short, swiftly darting tongues of flame. The ground shook. Each explosion reverberated between the walls of the low hills on either side of the river.

Keller went down to the point of departure with Barraka and the other men. He was connected directly to Division by a field phone that had been strung earlier that day. Now and then he spoke to Colonel Dodd who was up in Division relaying the information to General Williams.

"Williams and Dodd wish you the best of luck," he said to Barraka, who was lying on his belly and looking intently across the river.

Barraka answered with a swift obscene gesture.

"Major Barraka thanks you," Keller said, shielding the phone's mouthpiece with his hand.

Volterra was close to Barraka, focusing his attention on the opposite bank. He touched Barraka on the shoulder and said in a loud whisper, "Can we have the artillery move over this way? The Germans might get suspicious about why it all seems to be so concentrated to the west."

"Keller," Barraka called, "ask the colonel to move the fire to the east a few miles."

Keller relayed the message, and the pattern of fire shifted slightly to the right.

Barraka checked his watch and said, "We've still got fifteen minutes before we go. He left the bank and squatted down in front of Koss and Yancy. "You guys sure you have everything you need?" he asked.

"As much as we can carry," Koss answered.

Keller moved close and said, "You were just assigned the code name Cross Over. I'll be known as

Will o' the Wisp."

"What?" Barraka asked, squinting up at him.

"The mission will be officially known as Operation Cross Over."

Barraka pursed his lips and shook his head. "Pass the information to Volterra."

"You want a swig?" Yancy asked, offering a bottle to Barraka.

"Wine?"

"Shit no, Mitch," Yancy said. "When I do a man's job, I drink a man's drink. That's real stuff."

"Real stuff what?"

"Some guys I know in the medics—"

A huge explosion erupted from the far side of the river. Flames suddenly leaped up.

Barraka and the others turned their attention to the fire.

"Ammo or fuel dump," Yancy said.

Secondary explosions sent streaks of flames shooting hundreds of feet into the air.

They settled down again to a background of muffled explosions from the German side of the river.

Barraka took the bottle from Yancy and drank. It burned on the way down, and when it reached his stomach he handed the bottle to Koss.

Koss drank and began to cough.

"Volterra," Yancy called, holding the bottle out to him.

Volterra drank and gave it to Mastrada, who nodded approvingly and said, "It is strong enough to throw at the Germans."

"Never," Yancy answered. "I don't believe in throwing good booze at a bad enemy." And handing the bottle to Keller, he said, "Somethin' to remember me by."

Keller was just about to drink when the field phone rang. He answered it. "Two minutes to go," he said.

Barraka looked at his watch and nodded. He motioned his men to move up to the bank. Off to the northwest the sky was red with flames. "Fuel dump," he said, resting the butt of his carbine on his hip. "Make sure that BAR is high and dry," he cautioned Yancy. He was sweating now and his throat was very dry. "Remember if you run into any trouble, try to get out of it with your knife."

The artillery firing stopped.

Small arms opened up. The river was arched with zigzagging tails of tracers.

"Now!" Barraka exclaimed and swiftly plunged into the river. Volterra went in after him. Yancy followed. Koss came next and Mastrada brought up the rear.

They moved rapidly, keeping as low as possible in the water. The river was swift and very cold. It deepened quickly.

"Watch your footing," Barraka warned, as he almost lost his.

The water came up to their chests and then very swiftly they were neck deep.

"It's up to my fuckin' mouth," Yancy said, spitting water.

"Keep moving," Barraka urged. The water was already beginning to drop away from him. He glanced over his shoulder. They were closer to the German side of the river than to the American.

The river bottom started to slope upward. Barraka hurried. The cold water filled his legs with a pins-and-needles feeling. The bank in front of him was lined with trees almost to the water's edge. He quicked his pace. Within moments he was out of the water. "Hurry!" he said in a low voice. He wanted to get his men into the cover of the trees as quickly as possible. They were almost there when suddenly the sound of German froze him.

Barraka listened carefully. Holding up his hand, he indicated with his fingers that there were two of them. He motioned to Volterra to follow him. The others were to stay close to the cover of the trees.

Barraka moved off, working his way toward the Germans. Once again he was sweating.

Volterra was close by.

Incongruously, Barraka found himself thinking about the two letters he had written that afternoon. One had been to his parents and the other to Helen. In neither had he alluded to anything about the mission. It had never been his way to share his role in the war with them. There wasn't any point to giving them anything more to worry about than they already had. He always wrote about the war as if it were a prolonged travelogue, especially conducted for his benefit. . . .

The voices grew louder.

Barraka saw the two Germans. They were drivers. Their vehicle had broken down on a narrow road that curved close to the bank of the river. One was smoking and the other was tinkering with something under the hood.

"Take the one under the hood," Barraka whispered.

Volterra vanished into the woods.

Two minutes passed. Barraka couldn't see him.

Suddenly there was a thud. The man under the hood

gave a startled scream. He tried to pull the knife from his back. He staggered backward and fell.

Barraka ran forward. Even as the other German was unslinging his rifle, he rushed him, driving the trench knife to the hilt under the man's rib cage.

Volterra came out of the trees.

"Get the others," Barraka said.

The rest of the group came up from the bank of the river.

"Let's move," Barraka told them.

Volterra fell in alongside of him.

"The more distance we put between ourselves and the river," Barraka said, "the safer we're going to be."

"How fast do you want to move?"

"At a run."

"Then let's run," Volterra answered.

Barraka set the pace. The others followed. If they were lucky, they'd be five, maybe six kilometers away from the river before dawn. He looked back. The men were keeping up with him. After an hour, he would give them a ten-minute rest.

The link-up with the other partisans took place at Catanio without incident in the early hours of the third day.

The farmhouse where they met was made of stones and roofed with dull red terra-cotta. The large single room had an earthen floor and was sparsely furnished with an old table, two backless chairs, and a sleeping pallet against one wall. A wood-burning hearth occupied half of one wall and was blackened from years of use. Several scrawny chickens wandered in and out of an open doorway.

The house and the land around it belonged to an old man with a bulbous nose whose name was Rufo. He seemed glad to see Volterra and treated him with a great deal of respect. Though he looked curiously at Barraka and the other Americans, he did not ask who they were, where they came from, or where they were going. He provided wine and bread for all of the men and apologized for not being able to give them meat, explaining that the Germans had taken the few pigs he had and his only cow.

Volterra told Barraka that the old man's son had been killed in Greece and that the daughter-in-law had run off to become a whore for the Germans.

"Am I supposed to feel sorry for him?" Barraka asked. Though he did, he wasn't willing to show it for fear that it might be misinterpreted for weakness. He couldn't risk that happening, especially when he was dealing with these particular Jews.

Volterra's eyes became slits. "I don't think you feel a thing, major," he answered, moving away from where Barraka was resting against the wall. He sat down next to Mastrada and reached for the bottle of wine that his friend had alongside of him.

"He is not an easy man," Mastrada commented, looking at Barraka.

Volterra took another pull on the bottle before he said, "None of us are easy men. . . . If we were, we would not be doing this."

"He is ours and we are his," Mastrada responded with a shrug.

"Only to a point," Volterra said, handing the bottle back to him. "Sooner or later he and I will have to settle our differences."

Mastrada nodded but didn't say anything.

Exhausted, the men slept until midafternoon.

Volterra was the first one up and he roused the others one by one.

The old man provided them with bread and apples. When they left, he kissed Volterra and Mastrada on both cheeks and stood in the doorway to watch them disappear into the gathering twilight.

That night Volterra used the radio for the first time. The conversation between him and Keller lasted no longer than it took for him to identify himself and say that they had reached their first goal.

"Do you have anything to say to him?" he asked, looking at Barraka.

"Nothing," Barraka answered.

Volterra relayed a series of numbers that would, when decoded by Keller, give the day and time of his next transmission. Then he signed off.

For the next several days the band moved northward. They traveled by day, keeping away from the roads. The terrain was more and more difficult to move over. The hills became steep, razor-backed mountains. Each night seemed to be colder than the previous one. Now and then they would see a long convoy of German trucks creeping southward along the floor of a valley, or struggling through a mountain pass.

At the end of each day's march, Volterra would take out a map and show Barraka approximately how far they had come that day. Always, the distance was exceedingly small.

One night, after a particularly slow day, Barraka said, "If we keep creeping along the mountains, we'll be another two weeks. I want to get there . . . do the job, and return to my own unit."

"I want to get there too," Volterra answered quietly, "which is exactly why we are creeping, as you so very well put it, over the backs of the mountains."

Realizing he had let his impatience override his judgment, Barraka said, "I guess haste could make waste."

"It's not worth the risk to find out if it could," Volterra replied, knowing he wasn't going to get anything more out of Barraka, that the man had come as close to making an apology as someone with his prejudices could. . . . Progress was slow. But then slow progress was progress. . . . Volterra smiled.

"What's funny?" Barraka asked.

"That we agree, even if the agreement is somewhat oblique."

Barraka stood up and walked away.

Volterra could not contain himself and laughed softly. It was far better to laugh than be angry. Laughter was the one weapon that disarmed even the most rabid anti-Semite. He had learned how to use it years before when he had been a boy growing up in Ascoli and Verona, and even in the streets of New York, when he had been a student at Cooper Union, studying architecture. But sometimes the laughter came hard, very hard indeed.

Volterra stopped laughing, closed his eyes, and hoped sleep would come quickly.

IV

Colonel Eric Von Kunstler stood at the castle window and admired the saffron sunset that sharply etched the dark mountain peaks against the sky. With each minute that passed, the saffron became suffused with more indigo. A soft knock at the door forced him to turn away from the window. "Come in."

Major Irwin Radish entered the room. The major was in charge of the brigade's intelligence section. Before the war he had been the headmaster of an exceedingly fine gymnasium in Düsseldorf. He was a gnomish-looking man with thick glasses and thinning brown hair. In his five years in the army, he had never been in action.

Kunstler went behind his ornate Quattrocento desk. He switched on a lamp. "I was just admiring the sunset," he said. Now and then he ran his hand over the narrow head of his dog, Dimitri, a mix of German shepherd and Doberman he had found as pup some six months before in a bombed-out building while passing through Hamburg on his way to his present command of the XIth Infantry Brigade.

"They are spectacular," Radish agreed with a nod. "I have a report that might interest you."

"On what?"

"Radio messages," Radish said, placing a sheet of paper on the desk in front of Kunstler. "As you can see, each message was sent from a different position over a period of days."

"Using the code name Cross Over?"

"Yes."

Kunstler went to the far wall. One large map showed the area of his command, which was a large area that went south from where they headquartered in Malveno for twenty kilometers, west for sixty, east for ten, and north to the Swiss border. There were many towns and villages that came under his jurisdiction, including the prison camp at Servigliano and the nearby town of Monte San Martino. A second map, as large as the first, depicted all of Italy.

Radish was close by and said, "If you trace the positions of each transmission on the map, you'll see they're getting closer to us."

"What do you make of it?" Kunstler asked. He was a tall, lean man with iron-gray hair and dark blue eyes. Deeply incised wrinkles ran from his nostrils to the corners of his lips.

"Could be an OSS unit," Radish answered. "But most probably it's combination of OSS and partisans coming up from the south to link up with units already here."

Kunstler lit a cigarette. "I want to know why they're coming," he said. Kunstler had seen action in Russia, had been wounded at Stalingrad, and had been returned home to recuperate. He was married and had a ten-year-old son named Martin, after his father, who had risen to the rank of general during the First World War.

During the six months he had served under Kunstler, Radish had learned that whenever Kunstler asked him what he thought about a particular situation the colonel was not necessarily seeking a personal view, but rather an interpretation that either reflected his own, or at the very least did not differ from it too severely. Though Radish respected and admired Kunstler, he never thought of himself as his friend. Kunstler could trace his family back to the Teutonic knights, and his feelings of friendship, whatever they might be, could only really come into play with someone of his own class.

"Do you remember a report some ten, maybe twelve days ago from army intelligence about the heavy shelling along the American Sector on the Sangro River?" Radish asked, knowing that Kunstler had a remarkable memory and read every report that came down from higher echelons.

"A fuel dump was destroyed."

"Yes . . . but no other action occurred . . . no attempt was made to cross the river."

"Not en masse," Radish answered. "But from the movement of those radio transmissions northward, I would guess that artillery fire covered—"

"Weren't the bodies of two soldiers found near their vehicle?" Kunstler asked, returning to the desk from the window.

Radish had forgotten that information had appeared in a footnote in the report, but now that Kunstler mentioned it, he remembered that both men had been knifed, and he said as much.

"But what would bring them up here?" Kunstler persisted.

"At least three possibilities I can think of on the spur of the moment," Radish answered. "To disrupt our transportation and communication facilities in the event that we are forced to further retreat."

Kunstler stiffened. He let the smoke spill out of his nose before he said, "The armies are settling down for the winter. Both sides are exhausted . . . your second possibility, please."

"The Jews at Servigliano," Radish responded.

Kunstler pointed the cigarette at him and asked, "And what do you think they will be able to do with three hundred-odd men, women, children, and old people? If I told you once, Radish, I told you a dozen or more times that my orders are to hold them there until I receive orders to move them to Bolzano and turn them over to the SS. I will follow my orders!"

"Yes, sir," Radish answered. "But to answer your question . . . suppose the partisans and a few OSS plan to free some of the younger Jews and have them join their ranks."

"Jews don't fight."

"Begging the colonel's pardon," Radish said, "but the leader of the partisans and his second-in-command are Jews."

"They are the exception," Kunstler answered. "There are always exceptions when you deal with men." He set his cigarette down on the lip of the ash tray, opened the top drawer of his desk, and removed a file folder. "This is the file on Volterra and Mastrada," he said. "Volterra is an architect. He studied in the United States. He speaks English and holds a doctor's degree in his field. Mastrada is a lawyer. He does not speak any other language but Italian. He studied at the University of Bologna. Do we at least know where these two are now?"

"According to our source of information, they left this area about a month ago, taking ten men with them."

"And no indication of where they went?"

"None."

Kunstler closed the folder. He picked up the remainder of his cigarette. "Do you think there is any connection between the radio messages and Volterra?"

"I would not discount that possibility."

Kunstler nodded and said, "Until we know more, I want more patrols to sweep the area in front of our sector." He moved to the map on the wall. Using the forefinger of his right hand, he drew an arc in front of the southern face of his command. "They must come through this way, or they will have to go over the mountains here and then use the pass at Pressolana. Put extra patrols there too . . . if we can get them before they rejoin the others, we might be able to save ourselves a great deal of trouble."

"I'll have operations issue the necessary orders," Radish said.

Kunstler went back to the desk and stubbed out the cigarette. "Tell me, how many partisans are there in this area?"

"Seventy-five to a hundred."

"And we can do nothing about capturing them?"

"It's always the same," Radish explained. "We must stay to the roads, while they move over these mountains at will. . . . And you know as well as I do, that even when we move over the roads, we move with great difficulty because the roads are narrow and poorly constructed."

Kunstler went to a sideboard and picked up a bottle of wine. He offered some to Radish. "The roads may be bad, but the wine is still very good. . . . I often wonder why the Italians managed to keep one skill and forget the other."

Radish accepted the wine with a polite nod.

"You know," Kunstler said, "before you came in I was admiring the sunset and thinking to myself how nice it would be to visit this place with my wife and son after the war. I never thought that way about Russia . . . there was nothing but land and sky. You could see to the horizon. It is a place where dimensions are meaningless . . . there is just space. But here, even the highest mountain has its summit. To tell you the truth, Radish, I have come to love Italy."

"I, too, have thought of visiting it after the war."

Kunstler filled their glasses again and said, "I expect the orders to move the Jews from the camp to Bolzano almost any day now."

"It seems such a waste of transportation," Radish said.

Kunstler nodded but did not say anything more. When Radish was gone, he took the report from his desk and once again traced the movement of the radio transmissions. Each one was further and further north. He shook his head. Fighting partisans was not his idea of how a war should be fought, at least not how he wanted to fight what was left of the war for Germany, and, though it was hard to admit it, not much of the war was left in Italy. The best the German army could do would be to bleed the American and British so much that they would have to put off the invasion of France. Perhaps by that time Germany could develop new weapons that would enable them to surrender with honor? Perhaps even unite with the Americans and the others and fight as allies against the Russians?

Kunstler poured himself another glass of wine and drank a solitary toast to that day when Germany and the Allies would fight together to destroy Russia. "That," he said aloud, "would be a war worth all the rest."

"By the day after tomorrow," Volterra said, squatting down close to where Barraka was seated, "we'll enter the Eleventh Brigade's zone."

Barraka looked up from the small fire he was nursing. He and Volterra had avoided having much contact with each other. On a day's march, though, Volterra was almost always at his side, the effort needed to negotiate the high ridges leaving little strength for any superfluous conversation. And when it came time to make camp, Barraka chose to remain aloof from the partisans, though Koss and Yancy mingled freely with them. Yancy played a harmonica, and Julio, one of the partisans, joined him on his ocarina. Both Yancy and Koss were rapidly picking up the language, and it always made Barraka smile to hear Yancy speak Italian with a southern drawl.

Volterra took a map from inside his jacket and opened it. "We're here," he said, pointing to a spot on the map. "Over there to the left is Monte Christo, and we are on the north side of Monte Panginella, which puts us on a line more or less with the pass at Pressolana, here."

The fire blazed up; Barraka warmed his hands over it. He still did not speak.

"I suspect," Volterra said, "that the Germans have monitored our radio transmissions and Kunstler will—"

"What are you trying to tell me, Volterra?" Barraka asked.

Volterra took a deep breath. "Simply that we should avoid the pass at Pressolana and move further north, then backtrack and enter the zone here at Impalo. . . . From there we can easily work our way down to our own area of operations. Naturally, we will maintain radio silence."

"Isn't that something like closing the door to the barn after the horse ran out?" Barraka questioned, squinting at him. And before Volterra could answer the jibe, Barraka asked, "How long will the extra march delay us?"

"The moon will be full for the next few days and we should be able to keep moving for at least eighteen hours."

"Okay, how long?"

"Not more than three, possibly four days."

Though Barraka realized the delay wasn't significant, he did not answer immediately and ran his hand over his chin. There was more than stubble there now. Not only did he have a beard, but he was so filthy he could actually smell himself. "What about food?" he asked. So far they had managed very well. Every two or three days they always managed to be near a farmer who'd be willing to give them a few chickens, rabbits, cheese, bread, and wine.

Though Volterra had never said as much, Barraka was quite sure the line of march had been laid out on the basis of where Volterra knew they would be given food. If he had done that, it was excellent planning.

"Rations will be short," Volterra replied.

Barraka held both his hands toward the fire again.

"When you're ready to give me an answer," Volterra said, "I'll be over there with my men." He stood up and walked away.

Barraka called to him.

He stopped, gnashed his teeth, and turned around.

"Come back here," Barraka said. His tone left no doubt that he wasn't asking, he was ordering him to return.

Volterra went back.

"Can any of your other men use the radio?" Barraka asked, standing up.

"Yes."

"Suppose we send them the way you wanted to go and they continue to make radio transmissions each night?"

"If the Germans have monitored us, they will continue to."

"They will think that whoever is transmitting is moving north and they will suspect they can intercept the group at Impalo."

"The radio moves north while the rest of us slip in through the pass at Pressolana," Volterra said.

"Think it will work?"

"It might."

"Will the men you send be able to slip by the Germans?" Barraka asked.

"Yes."

Barraka filled his pipe and bent down, picking up a glowing ember to light it. He puffed twice on his pipe before he said, "I just don't see why we should waste time, if we don't absolutely have to. Do you?" He tossed the ember back on to the fire.

"No, major," Volterra answered. "There is no reason. I'll tell the rest of the men what the plan is."

"Do that," Barraka said, already stamping out the fire with his feet, for fear that it might be seen by the Germans in the gathering darkness.

Kunstler slept poorly. He was more concerned about the partisans' entering his area of command than he dared show Radish. In Russia he had seen the destruction that a well-organized band of partisans could accomplish. Whole truck convoys were destroyed. Sometimes the partisans took the trucks and left the bodies of the drivers and guards as mute evidence of their ability to strike with impunity.

He was afraid that a combination of OSS officers and partisans might create havoc with the movement of supplies to the south. Should that happen, he would be held responsible. The possibility of its happening drove him from his bed and brought him back to his office and the large map of the area under his command.

He smoked several cigarettes and drank two glasses

of wine, all the while pacing the length of the office and looking at the map. He tried to put himself in Volterra's position and think what he would do. Moving in from the south would offer too much of a risk, though it would be the easiest of all routes into the zone.

"Pressolana would be the choice," he said aloud, while he tapped the map with his forefinger. "But their transmissions are already north of there."

Kunstler went to the window and opened it. The town lay white under a full moon. He returned to the map and scanned the northern boundary of his command. Most of it was contiguous with Switzerland, but there was a narrow strip that was not. He climbed on a small stool and looked closely at that portion of the map. It was very high country, almost three thousand meters. If there wasn't snow there already, there probably would be within a week or so. The small village of Impalo was on the Italian side of the border. Kunstler went to his desk and put through a call to headquarters, southwest, and asked to be connected to the ranking intelligence officer. Within moments he was speaking to a Colonel Weiss about the movement of a group of suspected partisans from the south toward his area.

"Strange you should call at this particular time," Weiss said to him. "I have a report in front of me that suggests the voice is different in the last two transmissions from all of the previous ones. . . . But, of course, we are not absolutely certain. The differences could have been caused by atmospheric conditions, or some difficulty with their radio."

"I understand," Kunstler said. And then he asked if

the village of Impalo might provide access to his area.

"Not according to our map," Weiss answered. "But I see there is a notation to look at aerial photographs. Wait a minute, and I'll get them."

Kunstler lit another cigarette and puffed at it nervously.

Weiss came back on the line. "There's a pass there," he said. "Not much of a pass, and by this time of the year it's probably, or will soon be, snowed over."

Kunstler thanked him and said, "If I can ever be of help to you, please don't hesitate to call." He put the phone down and returned to the map. "I have you, Volterra," he said aloud. "I have you!" He drank another glass of wine, and, knowing exactly how he would deploy his men in and around Impalo, he went back to bed. This time he slept soundly.

It was noon when Barraka and his men neared the pass. They had been moving since first light. The sky was covered with dark gray clouds and a cold wind came blustering off the mountains to the north. Barraka had spent a restless night, and now he was more tired than usual. But he pushed himself to continue, knowing the men depended on him to set the pace.

Some time during the night he had dreamed about Helen. The memory of the dream saddened him; they had been denied each other. The real possibility that he might never make it back to her seldom entered his mind. But whenever it did, he would become angry with her for refusing to go to bed with him on his last leave. They had been alone in her parents' house. Their caresses were becoming more and more passionate. He opened her blouse and kissed her breasts.

"I want you," he told her, moving his hand under her skirt.

"No," she said.

He freed one of her breasts and kissed the nipple.

"I might never come home," he said.

"Please," she said, "don't say that."

"I love you," he told her, moving his hand between her thighs.

"And I love you."

"Then let me—"

Someone touched Barraka on the shoulder. He turned his head.

Koss was alongside of him. "We have a problem," he said.

Barraka stopped. He saw Volterra and Mastrada bending over a man who was stretched out on the ground. "What's wrong?" he asked.

"Better go back there, Mitch," Koss answered.

Barraka moved to them. "How bad?"

"It's Julio, the ocarina player. I think it's his appendix," Volterra said, looking up at him.

Volterra stood up and motioned to Barraka to follow. "There's a doctor not far from the pass. We could carry him there in a few hours, and then be on our way."

"He might not make it, even if we get him to a doctor," Barraka said.

"That's right. But at least he'd have a chance."

Barraka looked toward the stricken man. Despite the thickness of his beard, Julio couldn't have been more than twenty.

"This doctor," Barraka asked, "can he be trusted?"

Volterra nodded. "He's helped us before."

"Have a couple of the men fix up a litter," Barraka told him. He called the other men together. "We're going to bring Julio to a doctor," he said. "But we must hurry. I want to be as far away from the pass as possible before nightfall. No stops from now until we reach the doctor's house. Is that understood?"

"Yes."

"Okay, let's get the hell out of here," Barraka told them, taking the lead again. A litter was created by pushing two rifles through the sleeves of a jacket, and Julio was placed on it.

A short while later, they were on the move again.

Volterra came alongside Barraka. "Thanks," he said. "Julio's popular."

"If it meant going one step out of our way," Barraka said, "I'd have left him."

"I understand only too well the kind of leader you are," Volterra said, making no effort to keep the sarcasm out of his voice.

"I doubt it," Barraka replied. "But whether you do or don't, doesn't make a damn bit of difference."

Volterra dropped back to his place in the line of march. He was angry, angry with Barraka and with himself for letting Barraka make him angry. Knowing someone like Barraka was a unique experience, something he would be able to tell his grandchildren about if he was lucky enough to live long enough to marry and raise children of his own.

But the more Volterra thought about Barraka's attitude toward Julio, the more Volterra realized that, despite its cold-bloodedness, it was essentially right. The mission came first, and any detour for any reason could jeopardize it. He fell in alongside Barraka again and said, "For what it's worth, I do understand."

Barraka looked at him for several moments. The glacial coldness in his blue eyes dissolved. "I do what I think must be done. But whatever I do, I'll never jeopardize the mission—that much I can assure you."

"I understand," Volterra replied.

By the time they reached the vicinity of Pressolana it was raining heavily. Rather than risk being trapped in the narrow space of the pass, Barraka ordered the men to make their way over the flanks of nearby Monte Gallina and then pick up the roadway that would take them to the doctor's house.

They were soon in a valley where grass was still very green. Scattered on the slopes of the hills were the huts of the goatherders.

Barraka sent two men forward to act as scouts, and Yancy took the point. The road was narrow and twisting. Two deuce and halfs going in opposite directions would just about be able to pass each other if they slowed down.

One of the scouts came back and said there was a house about four hundred meters in front of them, around a sharp curve in the road.

"The doctor's house," Volterra said.

Barraka ordered them forward at a run. He and Volterra vaulted over the low wall and worked their way through the grape arbor. When they reached the door, Barraka flung it open. With his carbine in firing position, he rushed into the small foyer.

Volterra followed.

The doctor, an old bent man with glasses perched on the bridge of his nose, was at the table in the dining room. He was too startled to speak, but his elderly housekeeper screamed.

"Silence," Barraka barked.

The woman dropped the dish she was holding and sat down.

Volterra stepped out from behind Barraka and said, "Dr. Klaus, one of my men needs help."

"Where is he?" Klaus asked, getting to his feet.

Volterra called to the men carrying Julio.

"Bring him into the room there," Klaus said, gesturing toward a closed door off to the right of the parlor.

Julio was carried into the room, Klaus followed, and when the two litter bearers left he closed the door.

"The name Klaus isn't Italian," Barraka said in a whisper.

"The Austrians held this part of Italy . . . many families up here have German-sounding names," Volterra explained.

Barraka uttered a wordless sound of understanding. He looked toward the table. There was freshly baked bread on it. A large china tureen of minestrone soup, roast chicken, and a bottle of wine. He licked his lips and asked the woman if she had any more bread.

She nodded.

Suddenly he heard the sound of a truck moving

along the road. And then one of the men called out, "Germans!"

Barraka whirled around and started for the door.

"Cover me," Volterra said. "Keep your men here. If we need help, then you make the decision to give it or get out. You'll be able to make your way to Servigliano from here without me."

Barraka stepped aside.

Volterra ran from the door in a low crouch. He signaled his men to follow him.

The truck was moving slowly toward the house from the north.

Barraka put Yancy with his BAR behind the window, while he and Koss took the old woman upstairs and covered the road from a high elevation.

"Can you see Volterra?" Koss asked.

"The rain is too heavy . . . that damn truck is taking a long time to get there."

"What about the doctor?"

"Volterra says he's a friend," Barraka answered. He wiped the sweat from his forehead. A few minutes ago he had been cold and wet, and now he felt as if he was in the clutch of a fever. He glanced back at the woman.

Her eyes were wide with fear. She was on her knees praying.

"The truck!" Koss exclaimed.

Barraka looked down at the road.

The green mud-splattered troop carrier came down the road. The vehicle slowed down.

"It's going to stop," Koss said.

A sergeant swung down from the cab and shouted an order. The men in the rear jumped free. There was a squad of them. Several moved to the side of the road, unbuttoned their flies, and began to urinate.

"Goddamn, just a piss call," Koss said.

The sergeant said something to the driver and started toward the gate, calling as he moved for someone to come to the door. He stopped and again shouted to the men.

"My God," Barraka exclaimed, "they're coming in here."

Suddenly a burst of small arms fire erupted from the other side of the road. Three of the Germans fell.

The sergeant dropped to the ground and called to his men to return the fire. He managed to lob a grenade toward the woods on the other side of the road. It fell short and sent a plume of mud into the air.

The Germans were firing from the prone position.

Barraka could see three of Volterra's men working their way around the left flank.

The Germans spotted them and turned some of their fire on them.

"Are we going to help them?" Koss asked.

Barraka nodded and crashing the window out with the butt of his carbine, he began to fire. Koss opened up and Yancy worked the BAR from right to left.

Three of the remaining Germans threw away their rifles and started to yell, "Don't shoot . . . Don't shoot!"

Volterra and several of his men came running across the road. Those on the right flank joined him.

"Anyone catch it?" Barraka shouted from the window.

The sergeant stood up. He was bleeding from the shoulder. The other three men weren't hit.

Barraka and Koss raced down the steps and out of the house. Yancy came up behind them.

Volterra herded the four men against the truck. "We don't take prisoners," he said, looking at Barraka. Then, without waiting for a response, he squeezed the trigger of his machine pistol.

The four men crumpled into the mud.

"Take what we can use," Barraka told the partisans, and then to Volterra he said. "What about the doctor and his housekeeper?"

"They'll go with us."

"Let's go back and find out about Julio . . . we've got to get the hell out of here as soon as possible."

Volterra agreed and together they went into the house.

Klaus was waiting for them in the parlor. "The boy is dying," he said. "Apparently the appendix must have burst."

"How long will he last?" Volterra asked.

"Too long for you and your men to remain here," Klaus answered.

"I'll take care of it," Volterra said.

Barraka nodded and turned his attention to Klaus. "You and your housekeeper will have to go with us. If the Germans find you here—"

Klaus nodded and called to his housekeeper, telling her to pack a few things. "We're going away for a while. Perhaps a long while."

A single shot came from the rear of the house. A few moments later, Volterra came out of the room. "Have we time to bury him?" he asked softly.

"Do it quickly," Barraka answered, aware of the strained expression on Volterra's face. He understood

Volterra's anguish: It was his own. Tim's death flashed into his mind, and for an instant he thought of saying something to assuage Volterra's pain. But instead, he turned to the doctor. "I'm going to take what food you have and pass it out to my men."

"Give them some wine, too," Klaus told him. "They will need it on a night like this."

Major Radish enjoyed a cup of coffee and scanned the various reports that had come down from army headquarters in the morning's pouch. Radish always had coffee and a piece of pastry. This morning it was peach tart. The morning before it had been an apple turnover, generously covered with cinnamon. Unlike Colonel Kunstler, he had no affinity for the Spartan way of life.

The reports were dull. Both armies had indeed settled down for the winter, and Radish hoped he would be reassigned to Germany before the spring. If it did not happen, there was no doubt in his mind he would be taken prisoner by the Allies. He hoped by the Americans, rather than the British.

Radish finished the last bit of the tart and washed it down with a swallow of coffee. None of the intelligence reports were worth showing to Kunstler. He gathered them into a pile, called an aide to file them, and was about to stand up when the phone rang.

"Major Radish, Eleventh Brigade, Headquarters Company," he said crisply into the mouthpiece.

"This is Lieutenant Gunnar, Company D," the man on the other end said. "This morning one of my patrols found the bodies of ten of our men belonging to—"

"What?" Radish shouted.

"Ten bodies, sir."

"Where?"

"Two kilometers from the Pressolana pass, outside the house of Dr. Klaus."

"Put a guard around the area."

"I've already done that."

"The colonel and I will be there as soon as possible," Radish said. He put down the phone and shook his head. Then, with a sigh, he headed toward Kunstler's office and knocked softly at the door.

Colonel Kunstler and Major Radish sat in the rear of a command car. Two motorcyclists, armed with machine pistols, led the way. A truck carrying a patrol of nine men followed the command car.

"Have you contacted the SS?" Kunstler asked.

"Captain Muller will be there."

Kunstler snorted and looked out the open side. Rain was falling. The sky was leaden and the rich green of summer had an ominous dark hue.

"Just a few days ago," Kunstler said, "I was sure I had Volterra. I was certain he'd try to get through from the north."

"A logical assumption!"

"I don't want the SS in this," Kunstler said.

Radish agreed. "This might have been the work of partisans already in the area, or another group moving in from the south."

Kunstler shook his head. Neither possibility sat well with him. "We'll have to take more forceful counter measures," he said. "That will incite the partisans to make bolder strikes. It'll continue like that until we have a more hostile population here than we already have."

They were stopped by the men in the cordon that Lieutenant Gunnar had set up around the area.

One of the motorcyclists gestured back toward the command car and the guard waved the convoy forward. Within a matter of minutes, Kunstler could see the slaughter. The vehicle came to a halt. He swung himself out and pulled up the collar of his leather trench coat to keep the rain off his neck. He walked slowly toward the lieutenant, saluting him. "Was anyone alive when you arrived?"

"No, sir," Gunnar answered.

Kunstler looked at him for a long moment. The lieutenant was very young.

Another command car came up the road and pulled up behind Kunstler's. Captain Muller emerged, followed by two lieutenants.

Muller offered separate salutes to Kunstler and Radish. Ignoring Lieutenant Gunnar, he turned his attention to the bodies that lay in the road. With his hands behind his back, he rocked back and forth on the balls of his feet. "These men don't have any weapons," he said to Kunstler.

"They probably surrendered and then were shot," Gunnar said.

Muller did not respond.

"For the time being," Kunstler said, answering Muller, "I'd prefer to handle it myself. The SS need not trouble itself over something like this." He had no use for the SS and even less for someone like Muller, whose small, thin frame and ascetic-looking face with its sad brown eyes completely belied his cruelty and lust for power.

"Something like this," Muller replied, with a wave of his hand, "is exactly what the SS should trouble itself about."

Kunstler was not aware that Muller's subordinates had gone off to search the house and grounds until they returned with empty casings from American-made weapons.

"These are from a carbine," Kunstler said, when one of the sergeants showed him the brass casings. "And these are from a BAR."

"American weapons this far north?" Muller questioned.

"No doubt supplied by a parachute drop," Major Radish said.

"Sir," Lieutenant Gunnar said, addressing Kunstler, "there's a freshly dug grave in the woods, just off the roadway."

"At least one of them was killed," Muller said. "I'd have hated to have something like this happen and not have anyone pay for it. Tell me, colonel, do you think that Jew, Volterra, could be responsible for this?"

"He might be," Kunstler answered. He did not want the SS to get Volterra. Volterra and Mastrada belonged to him.

"Yes, I think so too. He must be taken or killed, or we will have much more of this kind of thing."

"I agree."

"Then, have your men do it, colonel," Muller said,

"or I will be forced to take some harsh punitive measures with the locals, and that will only make your command more difficult."

Kunstler went white with anger.

Muller saluted, clicked his heels, and walked back to his command car with the two lieutenants in tow.

V

For most of the night, Barraka and his men climbed over the ridges toward Servigliano. It was hard going. The wet rocks were slippery. More than once Barraka slipped and slid some distance down a slope before he could manage to grab on to a rock and break his fall. All of them had trouble keeping their balance. Volterra and Mastrada fared better than most of the men because they were used to the terrain.

Barraka called a halt at 0400 hours and sought protection from the wind and the rain in an abandoned goatherd's hut on the north side of one of the ridges. He was dog tired. His hands were badly bruised by the rocks he had grabbed on to. Before he dropped down against the wall of the hut, he told Volterra to assign a man to guard duty.

Koss and Yancy settled near him, and Koss said, "The woman won't be able to keep the pace."

With his eyes closed, Barraka nodded. "Will the doctor be able to?" he asked.

"Yes," Koss answered. "He says Tina—that's the

housekeeper's name—has relatives in a hamlet three kilometers beyond Malveno. . . . He asked if she could be sent there, and as for himself, he said, he would like to remain with us."

Barraka looked at his blood-streaked hands and said, "I guess it's the only thing we can do with the woman. Ask Volterra or Mastrada to arrange it. . . . It would have been better if we had left her at the farmhouse on the way and she had gone to her relatives from there."

"What about the doctor?"

"Probably we'll have need of him before this mission is over."

"I'll go talk to Volterra about Tina," Koss told him, standing up.

Barraka settled back and once more closed his eyes. He tried to ignore the pain in his hands, but he couldn't.

"You know," Yancy said, "Volterra and his boys were doin' damn good out there . . . I think they'd have taken those Krauts even without our help."

Barraka looked at him. "What are you trying to tell me, Yance?" he asked.

"Man to man?"

"Man to man," Barraka repeated.

"Okay, here goes, Mitch," Yancy said. "You're giving Volterra and Mastrada a hard time because you got what you think is a shit mission. Bill thinks so, too."

Barraka reached down into his pocket and fished out his pipe, filled it, and when he was smoking it, he told Yancy, "I don't think they'd have taken the Krauts."

"Now we'll never know, will we?" Yancy responded. "But even if you're right, they put up a good scrap. We've both been in enough of them to know that."

Barraka was about to answer, but thought better of it. He wanted to hear more from Yancy.

"Mitch, you're walkin' around as if you got a broom stuck up your ass. I mean Koss and me don't love Jews any more than you do. But Volterra and Mastrada and some of the others, well they're more like us than they are like . . . like Jews. I think you should give them a—"

"A pat on the back?"

"Yes, damn it. Shit man, we're all up to our eyeballs in Krauts. It's the least any of us could do for the others. There's nothin' else when all is said and done, but what the guys alongside of you think of you. These guys are good, Mitch."

Barraka let the pipe go out and rolled the hot bowl between his hands: The heat soothed them.

"That's what I had to say," Yancy told him.

Koss returned with some bread and a bottle of wine. He divided the bread into three pieces and handed the bottle to Barraka, saying, "Rank before youth and beauty."

"Up yours," Barraka responded before he drank and passed the wine to Yancy. "Yance has just been talking to me," he said.

Koss glanced at Yancy.

"I told him what we talked about," Yancy explained.

"We thought it would be best to tell you before it became a problem," Koss said, reaching for the bottle.

Barraka didn't answer.

Koss settled against the wall and finished the bread, then quickly fell asleep.

"Any more wine left?" Yancy asked in a low voice.

"Some," Barraka said, handing the bottle to him.

"Good wine," Yancy commented, draining the bottle. "Now what we could use is women and song."

"Thanks," Barraka said.

"Yeah," Yancy answered with a wave of the empty bottle. "Don't thank me, thank my ol' lady and ol' man for makin' me possible."

"Someday I just might do that," Barraka laughed.

"Listen, if I couldn't find them, how the hell do you expect to?"

Barraka raised his eyebrows.

"I never knew them," Yancy explained laughingly. "I was raised by my aunt and uncle . . . I think my ol' man must have fucked my mother and run; then she had me, took one look at what she had borned, and she ran away too."

Barraka smiled, shook his head, and closed his eyes. . . . He could depend on Yancy and Koss no matter how difficult the situation might become. And he was certain that before the mission was over, all of them would be tested. Perhaps even judged? Barraka hoped none of them, including himself, would be found wanting. His thoughts dwindled to nothing; he slept.

As soon as Kunstler returned to the castle at Malveno, he called a meeting of his company commanders in his office at 1500 hours. But before the meeting began, he said to Radish, "I not only have

Volterra to be concerned about, I also have Captain Muller . . . I tell you, Radish, part of what has happened to us, to Germany, is the result of what the SS has done." He got up and stood by the window.

It was still raining and the tops of the distant mountains were obscured by a heavy cloud cover. Several mud-spattered vehicles were already in the plaza, and he watched one move slowly out of the narrow roadway across the plaza.

"If there are any partisans here," he said, "they will know that something important is going on."

"They always do," Radish answered with a shrug.

"All right, let's begin the meeting," Kunstler told him, turning from the window.

Radish went to the door and opened it, welcoming the company commanders. He bade them enter Kunstler's office, where chairs had already been set up for them in front of the two large maps.

Kunstler wasted no time and got down to the reason for the meeting. "Ten of our men have been killed by partisans," he explained, "and we must find and destroy them before we take more casualties."

The commanders murmured their approval.

Kunstler tapped the map of the area with a pointer as he said, "We must make a systematic search of our command sectors. They must be found and shot, with the exception of Volterra and Mastrada, their leaders. I want those two men alive."

"And so does the SS," Captain Muller said, standing in the half-open doorway. "We want them very much."

Kunstler had not realized that Muller was there. He had not been asked to attend the meeting. Muller moved forward. Every head was turned toward him.

"I am sorry, captain," Kunstler said, "but this meeting is—"

"The SS is deeply concerned about the growing number of partisans in this area," Muller said. "We have reason to believe that—"

"Captain," Kunstler suddenly roared, "leave this room at once and wait in the out area. That, captain, is an order."

Muller stopped. His cheeks and ears were scarlet. He nodded, turned, and left the office.

Kunstler returned his attention to the map, and he said, "I want patrols out at random hours. Each area should be swept at least once a day. And Captain Gissiking, just to be extra cautious, I want you to double-check your field of fire from the towers around the camp at Servigliano."

"Yes, sir," Gissiking answered. He was a corpulent man with a bristly blond moustache and blond hair. He had recently taken a young Italian mistress in the town of San Martino. Though he had a wife in Kiel, he had little hope of ever seeing her again.

"I don't think anything will happen at the camp," Kunstler said. "I think the partisans are here to disrupt our communications and sabotage our supply lines."

The officers nodded their agreement.

"Destroying the partisans in this area is now our primary mission," Kunstler said. "Are there any questions?"

There were none and the men filed out of the office.

"Have Captain Muller come in," Kunstler told Radish.

As soon as the SS officer was in the room, Kunstler asked Radish to close the door, and then he said, "I want you to witness this."

Muller started to speak.

"Silence!" Kunstler barked. "You will not speak until I give permission." He went to his desk and sat down. Leaning forward, he said, "I told you earlier in the day that I would take care of this matter. I did not tell you that to hear myself talk. I do not want you involved unless I summon you. Did I summon you?"

"No."

"Then you came here without being asked?"

"Yes."

"Captain," Kunstler said, "I do not want to see you anywhere near my headquarters again unless I ask you to come. Is that clear?"

"Yes, colonel."

"I hope it is," Kunstler said. "I would not enjoy reporting you to your commanding officer, or to General Kesselring. But I will not hesitate to do either, if you involve yourself in what I have explicitly told you is an army affair. Do you understand?"

Muller managed a choked, "Yes, colonel."

"You may go."

Muller saluted, clicked his heels, and went to the door.

Kunstler did not return the salute.

But just as the captain reached the door, he called to him.

Muller stopped.

"You may report this entire conversation to your superior," Kunstler told him.

"Be assured colonel," Muller answered, "that I

will." He opened the door, stepped out of the office, and closed the door after him.

Kunstler looked at Radish.

"I thought you wanted to remain in the army," Radish said.

"Not with vermin like that," Kunstler answered. "They're not soldiers; they're killers." He reached for a cigarette, lit it, and, looking at the burning tip, said aloud, "I'm beginning to think I smoke too much."

"Perhaps," Radish replied. "Perhaps."

Kunstler stood up and went to the maps. "I wish to God," he murmured, "I knew where they were, Radish. I wish I knew."

Pietro Garjulio's house stood at the north end of the row of eight buildings that made up the hamlet of Ventretti. He was a tall, gaunt man with a sallow complexion and gray eyes that betrayed nothing of his inner self to the outside world. His two sons had been killed on the Russian front and his daughter, Maria, now twenty-three, was his reason for living. He had long since given up caring about his wife. While they lived under the same roof and shared the same bed, he never spoke to her unless it was to give a command. Among the small number of people who lived in the hamlet and the farmers for some distance beyond it, he was known as a hard man.

But Garjulio did not care what people said about him behind his back as long as they showed respect when he came face to face with them. And because he knew how to deal with the Germans, he had managed not only to hold on to what he had, but also to prosper.

He had, in recent months, acquired many of the fields around Ventretti. He was reflecting on his marked fortunes when, without knocking, two armed men entered his house. His oldest brother's daughter was visible just behind them.

Garjulio, Maria, and his wife were at the dinner table. He didn't stop eating and motioned to his daughter and wife not to stop either.

"We've brought your niece," one of the men said, moving aside to let the woman pass. But she did not move.

"I can see that," Garjulio answered.

He recognized them: The taller one was Biaggio Montina, the other Hugo Dorsi. Both had disappeared from the neighborhood about a year ago. Biaggio was a strapping man of about thirty. Hugo was smaller and chunky.

Both men looked greedily at the food on the table.

"Partisans?" Garjulio asked, though it was evident they were.

"Soldiers of freedom," Hugo replied.

Garjulio spit a mouthful of food on the wooden floor.

The two men looked at each other. "Will you take her?" Biaggio asked.

"To honor the memory of my dead brother, Carlo, may he rest in peace, I will not turn her away."

"Then we have nothing more to do here," Biaggio said, looking at his companion.

"Could you perhaps spare some food?" Hugo asked.

"If you take," Garjulio said, "you take without my willingness to give." He stood up and looked defiantly at them. "I give nothing for the likes of you."

The men backed out of the house and closed the door.

"Scum!" Garjulio shouted after them. "Filthy Communist scum . . . may you die tonight and burn in the fires of hell for all eternity." He looked at his niece. "So the old bastard finally threw you out. After years of fucking you, he threw you out."

Tina began to sob. "He didn't . . . I couldn't go with them. I couldn't travel with them."

"Who?"

"The partisans and the Americans."

He gave her a questioning look, then gestured to an empty chair at the table. "Eat; then we'll talk."

Tina wiped her eyes and began to fill her plate with food.

Garjulio even poured her a glass of wine. "Now tell me about the partisans and the Americans."

She told him what had happened at the doctor's house.

"Where did the three Americans come from?" he asked.

"The south," she answered. "From somewhere in the south. Their leader was named Barraka. The other two were called Koss and Yancy."

He asked the same questions in several different ways.

Her answers did not vary.

When he was sure she was telling the truth, Garjulio smiled and told her he was happy to have her in his house.

* * *

From the moment Garjulio heard about the presence of Americans in the vicinity, he knew that Germans would be willing to pay for the information. Twice he went downstairs to drink Grappa and pace. By first light, he was at the kitchen stove warming himself, while he waited for the water to boil for his morning egg. He was already dressed, shaved, and wearing his dark blue Sunday suit and a white shirt.

Garjulio left the house, pausing momentarily outside the door to pull up the collar of his jacket against the chill in the air. With the characteristic stride of a man of determination, he walked toward Malveno.

Garjulio crossed the plaza and met Colonel Kunstler coming out of the castle. They greeted each other courteously, though Garjulio knew he was smiling more than he should have.

"Here to see the major?" Kunstler asked, knowing the man had been helpful in the past.

"No, colonel," Garjulio answered politely. "Today my business is with Captain Muller."

Kunstler nodded and wished him luck. "If I can be of any assistance," he offered, "please feel free to call upon me."

"That's very kind of you," Garjulio said.

"Heil Hitler!" Kunstler exclaimed, raising his arm.

Garjulio returned the salute. He continued across the plaza, while the colonel went a short distance beyond the fountain before he turned to watch him walk up the three steps to the door of the castle, where he was immediately challenged by the two sentries.

With his black hat in his hand, Garjulio stood in front of Muller's desk waiting for the captain to look up from the papers on his desk.

The room was small. There was a window overlooking the street that ran between the castle and church. A large swastika hung on one wall. Behind the captain was an autographed picture of Heinrich Himmler, which, Muller had told him during a previous visit, had been given to him personally by the Reichsführer.

The odor of eau de cologne made Garjulio want to sneeze, but he forced himself to control the need. He could not understand why certain men wanted to smell like a woman.

"I will give you my full attention shortly," Muller said suddenly, breaking the silence in the room.

"Thank you," Garjulio replied respectfully.

Muller did not answer. He moved several papers to one side and made clicking sounds with his tongue. Then he replaced the papers he had previously moved. His actions and sounds were part of a game that enabled him to gain even more of an advantage over a visitor than his position already gave him.

"Well," he finally said, "I can give you my undivided attention." He looked up and smiled.

Garjulio smiled too. He understood the captain's game and had played it before with him.

"What brings you here?" Muller asked.

Garjulio eyed the chair next to the captain's desk and asked permission to sit down.

Muller nodded. He did not like having to deal with

Italians. He thought them an inferior people, good only for farming and certain kinds of hard labor.

"In the past," Garjulio said, "you have dealt fairly with me, and I respect a man who deals fairly with me."

"I am sure," Muller told him, "that you would have received exactly the same treatment from any other German officer."

"Dealing fairly is a matter of honor with me," Garjulio said. "My word and my hand are all I need to seal a business arrangement."

Muller nodded. He wished the man would get to his reason for coming to him.

"I want you to understand," Garjulio said, "that in this matter I have to have your word that I will be well paid."

Muller squinted. "How can I give you my word," he said, "when I don't know what you're talking about?"

Garjulio began to sweat profusely. His throat became very dry. "I must be able to protect myself and my family," he said.

"As long as we are here—"

"Excuse me, captain," Garjulio interrupted, "but may I speak frankly?"

"By all means."

"For now," Garjulio said, "the lines to the south are set for the coming winter. But in the spring the Americans and British will push north again."

Muller flushed. He was furious that a mere peasant presumed to tell him what the military situation would be in the future. "No one knows that for a certainty," he replied tightly. "We are moving more men and materials to the front every day."

"I do not doubt that," Garjulio said. "But if the Americans and British do—"

"What is it you want, Garjulio?" Muller almost shouted.

"Five thousand American dollars."

"What?" Muller bellowed, leaping to his feet. "How dare you ask for—"

Garjulio wiped his brow. But he stubbornly repeated his request.

"The insolence," Muller said, "is what I dislike most about you. Insolence under the guise of having a happy and easygoing nature." He shook his head. "All of you are thieves and liars."

Garjulio shrugged. "These are hard times. We do what we must in order to survive."

Muller gave a snort of disdain.

"I am sorry if I angered you," Garjulio said. "Perhaps, it would be better if I go." He started to get up.

"Sit!" Muller commanded.

Muller picked up his ceremonial dagger, and slapped the blade across the palm of his left hand. "You know," he said, "I don't have to pay you at all for the information."

"Captain," Garjulio answered, "I came here as a friend, not an enemy. But even in friendship there must be a certain amount of realism. I am known by my neighbors to favor the Germans. I must be able to protect myself if your army is forced to move further north. The only way I'll be able to do that is if I have enough money to—"

"I understand," Muller told him.

Garjulio smiled.

"I will pay you what you asked," Muller said. "But only if I judge the information to be worth that much."

"I wouldn't expect it to be any other way."

"Now, tell me what you think is worth so much money."

"There is a band of partisans close by," Garjulio said. "They are led by two Jews: Volterra and Mastrada."

Muller put his dagger down and asked, "Do you know where the partisans are?"

Garjulio shook his head. "But the two who were at my house are from this vicinity." He told him their names.

Muller picked up the phone and ordered the immediate arrest of the families of both men. "We'll see if we can't smoke Biaggio and Dorsi out."

"I do not think they will come back," Garjulio commented. "They are Communists and have no sense of honor, dignity, or duty."

Muller set his elbows on the desk. "So far what you have told me is not worth the sum you asked for."

"If that was all I had to tell you," Garjulio answered, "I would have been a fool to ask for so much money."

"I'm listening."

Garjulio took a deep breath. "There are three Americans traveling with them."

Muller started to stand and changed his mind. "You have proof?"

"Their names are Barraka, Koss, and Yancy."

Muller leaned back into his chair. The presence of Americans would most certainly account for the ammunition casings found around the truck and in the doctor's house.

"Have you told anyone else about the Americans?" Muller asked.

Garjulio shook his head.

"You must not mention it, not even to Colonel Kunstler. And make sure no one in your family does either, or I will have to—I don't have to tell you what I will do, do I?"

"Rest assured that neither I, nor anyone else in my family, will speak of the matter."

Muller nodded. He was already beginning to develop a plan to use the presence of Americans in the Eleventh Brigade's sector to undermine Kunstler's position with army headquarters. . . . A good commander would never have let the partisans slip into the area, much less annihilate an entire patrol. The longer Kunstler remained ignorant of the Americans, the more time Muller would have to develop his plan and the more chance it had of succeeding.

"Is the information worth the price?" Garjulio asked.

"A thousand perhaps? But no more than that."

Garjulio made a pretense of being greatly upset.

VI

At dawn, Barraka and Volterra made their way up to the top of a ridge. The valley below was still dark.

"It's there," Volterra said, gesturing to the right. "The Germans leveled the top of the mountain to build the camp."

Barraka scanned the area with his field glasses.

"You'll get a better look at it as soon as the mist burns away," Volterra said.

Barraka could already see the camp was well guarded. There were towers at each of the four corners, and at least three strands of barbed wire topped the chain metal fence that enclosed the compound.

"Monte San Matino," Volterra explained, "is on the side of the mountain just to the right of the camp at Servigliano. We have a friend there, a man named Giorgio."

Barraka moved his glasses on to the village that clung to the side of the mountain. Here and there wisps of smoke floated out of a chimney.

"How many people in the village?" Barraka asked.

"Seventy, give or take a few."

"How many Krauts at the camp?"

"Eighty, perhaps ninety, including thirty Italian soldiers."

Barraka turned and whistled for Koss and Yancy to join him. "That's the camp at Servigliano," he said, handing Yancy the field glasses. "Monte San Martino is off to the right. Volterra says there are about eighty soldiers."

"It sure as hell don't take that many to guard it," Yancy said. "Those machine guns in the towers have a clear field of fire in every direction."

Barraka turned the glasses on the camp again. He could see the figures of people moving.

"They should be having a head count," Volterra told them.

"That's what they seem to be doing," Barraka said. "They're forming up into groups." A few minutes later, Barraka and Volterra moved down to the other men.

"By tonight," Volterra said, "we'll meet the rest of my men."

"How close will we be to the camp?" Barraka asked.

"On the side of the mountain above Monte San Martino."

"Let's move out," Barraka called, slipping his knapsack on and picking up his carbine.

Though he had only seen it from a distance, the sight of the camp worried him. The Germans had all the advantages, not the least of which was its physical location. The reality was far more frightening than the reconnaissance photographs had shown. He and his men would be cut down before they got halfway up the slope. The mission, as far as he was concerned, was still suicidal.

Volterra moved slightly to the right. "Once we're in the valley," he said, "we'll stay off the roads. There's a place where the road to Monte San Martino cuts through the woods. But by the time we reach it, it should be near twilight."

"What difference does that make?"

"The Germans are afraid to move after dark," Volterra said. "Then we control the roads."

Toward noon, they were on the northern slope of the mountain. They went swiftly down toward the wooded portion of the valley. Monte San Martino glistened white in the afternoon sunlight. They moved in deep shadows that here and there were slashed with sunlight.

Barraka remembered the time he and his father had gone camping for a few days in the northern part of the state, near the Canadian border. It was late fall and the weather was cool and crisp. The second night out they had been sitting at the campfire at twilight when a huge bull moose came down to the edge of the lake to drink. The animal was silhouetted against an orange-yellow sky. They had watched him in absolute silence. Several times the moose looked their way but did not bolt.

After he was gone, Kip had said, "I don't think I'll ever forget that."

"I don't think I will either," Mitch answered. . . .

He hadn't forgotten it. He wondered if Kip had.

"You look like you're deep in thought," Volterra said.

Barraka plucked a blade of grass and chewed on it. "I was remembering."

"Good memories, I hope?"

Barraka nodded.

"Wait!" Volterra exclaimed, holding up his hand.

Barraka signaled a halt. "What's wrong?" he asked.

Volterra motioned to him to be silent. "Scatter!" he whispered.

"Take cover," Barraka ordered.

Koss and Yancy came forward.

"Germans," Volterra said, pointing to the right.

"Yancy, over there," Barraka said, pointing to a stump that Yancy could use to rest the BAR on.

Volterra motioned them to keep low.

Barraka slipped the safety off his carbine.

The men bellied down on the forest floor.

Barraka caught a glimpse of black uniforms. "SS," he said. "Koss, can you make out what they're saying?"

Koss lifted his head. "They're looking for partisans," he said. "Yesterday there was a fire fight between them. They're coming our way."

"How many?" Volterra asked.

"Three."

Barraka lowered his carbine and unsheathed his trench knife. Koss did the same. Mastrada motioned he would go with them.

"Make some noise," Barraka told Volterra. "But not until you hear me whistle."

"Good luck," Volterra whispered.

The three men crawled along the floor of the forest and started to circle behind the SS.

"There are two more," Barraka said, pointing off

to the left. "They must have stumbled into a full patrol. Let's get the hell out of here!" He led them at crawl back to where Volterra and the others were waiting.

The Germans began firing to the left of them.

Volterra and Mastrada were on their feet.

"Get down!" Barraka ordered. "Get the hell down!"

"We can help."

"We can get ourselves killed!"

The Germans shouted to each other. A grenade went off, sending a shower of pine needles and earth upwards. A man screamed. A burst from a machine pistol chewed into a tree. More rifle fire. Then silence.

Germans were shouting again.

"They're telling their friends they killed four partisans," Koss translated.

"We could still get them," Mastrada said.

"Just stay where you are," Barraka warned, pointing his carbine at him, "or I'll put a bullet in you myself."

Volterra reached out and put his hand on Mastrada's arm. "Wait," he said gently. "Wait." He moved his eyes to Barraka but remained silent.

He had no doubt that Barraka would kill Mastrada, if it meant saving the others to continue their mission.

Barraka lowered his carbine. "Okay," he said, "let's take a look."

The bodies of the four partisans were sprawled behind a clump of wild berry bushes.

"They didn't have any cover," Barraka said disgustedly. "If they had been professionals, they would have known better."

Volterra and Mastrada moved from body to body

without speaking.

"Take their weapons," Barraka told them, "and let's get the fuck out of here. I don't want to run into more SS."

"Can we bury them?" Mastrada asked.

"Sure. Then we'll take time to hold services."

Mastrada flushed. "Listen, you son of a whore," he said in a low growl, "these men were my friends." Without warning he threw himself at Barraka and sent him crashing against a nearby tree. He jumped on him and grabbed hold of his head, trying to pound it against the ground.

Barraka drove his fist into Mastrada's face. Blood spurted from his nose and poured over him.

Mastrada let go of his head and began to strangle him.

Barraka pushed the palm of his hand against the underside of Mastrada's jaw with such force he broke Mastrada's hold. In an instant, Barraka rolled free and was on his feet. His trench knife came out from its sheath. "C'mon, you Jew bastard," he growled. "C'mon, and let's settle this once and for all!" The words were out before he could stop them. He had held them in too damn long. Now all he wanted was to get these damn Jews out of his life. They didn't belong there. He wanted to be free of them.

Mastrada drew his knife.

Barraka began to circle him.

Then suddenly Yancy said, "We don't have time for this shit, Mitch!"

Barraka looked at him, took a deep breath, and lowered the knife. He had let his anger get the best of him. It was wrong.

"If you don't kill him," Mastrada told Volterra, "I will."

"If I were you, I wouldn't try it," Barraka said, "at least until I get your people to the border."

They began to move through the forest again, Barraka in the lead and Volterra at his side. For several hours, neither one spoke. As the afternoon wore on, the weather began to change. Heavy clouds came rolling down from the northeast.

"There's the smell of rain," Volterra finally said.

Barraka made a sound that was neither a signal of agreement or disagreement. The right side of his chest hurt. He guessed that Mastrada had bruised a couple of his ribs.

The forest became dark and when the rain did come, it was cold and windblown. The men pushed doggedly on.

Suddenly Barraka called a halt. His face was white, and his heart was pounding.

"I have to rest for a few minutes," he told Volterra. He touched the right side of his chest. "Mastrada has a hard head."

"Have Klaus look at it."

Barraka shook his head. "Later. When we link up with the rest of your men."

"We should be doing that in an hour or two."

"I'm okay now," Barraka told him. "Let's push on."

"Are you sure?"

Barraka nodded and ordered the men forward.

Volterra walked close to Barraka. "Mastrada was wrong," he said. "He knows how you feel about the mission and about Jews. He pushed you too hard."

Barraka wiped the rain from his eyes and looked at him. He wanted to deny that he was an anti-Semite. But he couldn't, not honestly. Not after what he had said.

"In your place, I too would have stopped him from burying the dead men," Volterra said. "But one of them was his first cousin."

Barraka clenched his teeth; turned away. There was no way he could have known that!

"I know you didn't want this mission," Volterra said. "Moses didn't want to lead the Israelites out of Egypt either. But God commanded him to do what he didn't want to do."

"I know the story."

"I don't like you, major," Volterra said, "but I know you'll do everything you can to carry out the mission, and I respect you for that."

For several minutes, Barraka continued to walk without speaking. "I think we'll get along," he eventually said. "Not smoothly, but enough for what has to be done." He turned and offered Volterra his hand.

Volterra shook it.

Suddenly Barraka staggered.

Volterra caught him and called for the doctor.

Barraka found himself stretched out on the wet forest floor. Blurred faces were looking at him. He closed his eyes.

Dr. Klaus taped Barraka's bruised ribs, but Barraka refused a sedative. He allowed Yancy to carry his pack, and to make it easier for him to walk, he asked Volterra to cut a bough from a nearby oak tree for him to use as a staff. Then he ordered the march to continue toward Monte San Martino.

The rain stopped some time before midnight. Within an hour the clouds vanished and the sky was filled with stars.

Barraka was in pain. Each breath he took made him wince. He was forced to pause every few minutes.

Soon the woods began to thin out and the land developed an increasingly steep slope. They were coming to Monte San Martino.

Volterra and Mastrada had changed places in the line. Now it was Mastrada who walked beside Barraka. "We could use the road once we're above the village," he told the American.

Barraka glanced at him. "What about the Krauts?"

Mastrada shrugged. "Only the camp commandant and his driver are usually there. Going up the road would be easier than climbing the slope."

"The SS might still be around."

"Right." He bowed his head.

Mastrada agreed. "I apologize for what happened back—"

"I understand how you felt. Volterra told me your cousin was killed."

"So was his brother, not three months ago," Mastrada answered. "They were my uncle's two sons."

"If you had gone to help them," Barraka said, "you'd have been killed, and maybe the rest of us, too."

"Would you really have shot me?"

"I'd have stopped you," Barraka answered. "And if

it meant having to shoot you to do it, I'd have shot you."

Mastrada nodded. "Will you accept my apology?" he asked.

"Yes."

Mastrada smiled broadly and dropped back to his own position in the line of march. Volterra moved up once more to the head of the column.

The woods were sparse. Above them rose the dark mass of Monte San Martino. Off to their left searchlights played across the prison camp at Servigliano. The beams of light looked like long, accusing fingers.

"They'll have to be taken out, if we hit the camp at night," Barraka said.

"Not if we strike just before they switch them on," Volterra answered.

Despite the pain, Barraka smiled. It was obvious Volterra had developed some sort of a plan.

Suddenly Volterra touched Barraka's arm and pointed off to the right.

Barraka saw two figures. He dropped his staff and unslung his carbine, threw himself to the ground. The jolt was agony.

"Wait," Volterra told him and started to move forward.

"What the hell—"

"They're not Germans," Volterra exclaimed. He moved toward the men and whistled softly.

One of them whistled back.

"This way . . . here we are."

The two men ran toward them. They looked questioningly at Barraka.

"Tell us what happened," Volterra said. "The

introductions can wait. He's a friend. Now it's important I know what's been going on."

"Yesterday Garjulio paid a visit to German headquarters in Malveno. Shortly afterwards our spotters picked up the SS. They were coming this way. The men scattered in groups of threes and fours. But there was a fight between our groups and one of their platoons. Four men are unaccounted for. Mastrada's cousin was with them."

"They're all dead," Barraka told him, grimacing with pain.

The two men were visibly shaken. But neither said anything.

Barraka turned to Volterra. "Isn't Garjulio Tina's uncle?"

"He is."

Barraka ran his hand over his bearded face. "I want this Garjulio killed and his farm burned," he said.

"Are the SS still around?" Volterra asked.

"They're in San Martino and on the roads."

"Above the village?" Barraka asked.

"They probably will be by morning."

"Is there a place from where we can watch the road into the village?"

"Yes," Volterra answered. "It's not too far from here."

"We'll go there," Barraka said. "And see what the Krauts intend doing. In the meantime, have the men regroup here. I'll want to link up with them by tomorrow night at the very latest."

Kunstler was at the desk, Dimitri close beside him. A

bright morning sun filled the window. Now and then he sipped from a mug of hot coffee laced with brandy.

A knock at the door brought his head up. "Come in," he called, leaning against the back of his chair. He had been anticipating this visitor since dawn.

Captain Muller entered. "Heil Hitler!"

"Sit down, captain," Kunstler said.

Muller settled into the chair next to the desk. "May I smoke?"

"Denied," Kunstler snapped. "This is not a social visit. I've just completed a letter to Field Marshal Kesselring in which I ask that you be reassigned."

"Colonel," Muller said, "I respectfully remind you that—"

"By what authority did you order a mission against the partisans?" Kunstler forced himself to keep his voice even.

"The SS has within its rights a freedom of action when it comes to attacking enemies of the Fatherland."

"You sound like a pompous ass," Kunstler said. "You have the right to know what I have written to support my request for your transfer."

Muller shook his head.

"Suit yourself. But until my request is either granted or denied, you will restrict your activities only to administrative work. You will withdraw your men from the area around Monte San Martino and wherever else they are, and until further order from me, they are to remain here in Malveno . . . is that understood?"

"It is, Colonel Kunstler," Muller said. "But it is my

duty as a German officer to inform you that I intend to—"

"I don't give a shit what you intend to do! But I warn you, if you ever conduct a mission without my approval while still in my command, I'll have you tried for disobeying a direct order. Is that clear?"

"Yes, sir."

"Now get the hell out of my office," Kunstler shouted, "and don't bother saluting me."

Muller rushed from the room.

"Well, Dmitri," Kunstler said, reaching down to rub the top of the dog's head, "let's hope that holds him for a while."

The animal licked Kunstler's hand.

VII

Barraka awoke to the smell of coffee, a bright blue sky, and mountains drenched in sunlight. His breath steamed in the cold air. He moved his eyes around him: There were at least fifty men spread out in the sparse woods along the road and behind a stone barrier that he did not remember having seen the previous night. Stiff from sleeping in one position, he moved his hand gently over his chest. The pain was still there, but it was not as intense as it had been. He began to stand when he realized someone had thrown a rough blanket over him. He nodded appreciatively and reached for his staff, pulling himself up on it. A moment later he slung his carbine.

"Over here," Volterra called.

Barraka turned.

"Fresh eggs, bread, and coffee," Volterra shouted from the bottom of a small gully.

Barraka waved acknowledgment and started down toward him. The scent of coffee and frying eggs made his stomach growl. He could not remember when he had eaten last. Probably twenty-four hours had passed since he had had any food.

"Join us," Volterra said, gesturing to the people close by. "I have some good Grappa for the coffee."

Barraka looked for Mastrada but couldn't find him. There were three new faces; one of them obviously belonged to a woman. Though she was dressed in man's clothing and her hair was hidden under a cap, Barraka was too close to be deceived by her attempt to camouflage her sex. He turned his attention back to Volterra, "Where are the Krauts?"

"Gone," Volterra answered. "Pulled out about nine."

"Zero-nine-thirty, to be more precise," one of the new men said with an English accent.

Barraka looked at him.

"Major Thomas Conway, RAF," he said with a broad smile. "And more recently a resident of the camp at Servigliano."

"Major Barraka—"

"No need to, old chap," Conway said, gesturing toward Volterra. "Chaim has already told us who you are."

Barraka looked at the second man.

"Leftenant Stephan Rawlins, British Eighth Army, Tenth Division," he said, "and like the major, a former resident of Servigliano."

Barraka turned toward the woman.

"Rinata Muzio," she said in tight, almost angry-sounding words. "Partisan."

"Your eggs will get cold," Volterra warned, as he handed a canteen cup of coffee to Barraka. "Tell me when," he told him, holding a bottle of Grappa over the steaming coffee. He started to pour.

Barraka took a good belt before he said, "Enough!" He stood up and found a place for himself near Koss.

Volterra came after him with his staff and a large piece of coarsely baked dark bread.

"I don't like surprises," Barraka commented, forking up some of the egg. "I don't even like surprise parties."

Volterra bent down close to him and said, "Neither do I. But under the circumstances," Volterra said, pointing to Barraka's chest, "it was easier to have the men come here than for you to meet them somewhere else."

"I mean our three newcomers."

"Conway and Rawlins asked that you not be told about them until you were here."

"I don't understand."

"They prefer to fight with the partisans than be returned to their own units," Volterra explained.

"Why?"

With a shrug, Volterra answered, "There are certain questions I don't ask when a man tells me he wants to fight with my unit."

"Did they escape from Servigliano?"

"With some help from my men."

"And what about Rinata?" Barraka questioned, looking at her. She was a tall, dark-complexioned woman with sensuous lips and wide eyes whose color he was too far away to determine.

"As she said, a partisan."

Barraka squinted at Volterra but did not press for a more explicit answer about Rinata. "Anything else I should know?"

"Nothing."

"I hope not," Barraka said, sipping the coffee. "I sure as hell hope not."

"But there is something I want to discuss with you."

"Okay."

"It's about your order to kill Garjulio and burn his farm," Volterra responded.

"What about it?"

Volterra dug into his pocket for a pack of cigarettes and offered one to Barraka. "I didn't carry out your orders," Volterra said calmly.

Barraka felt a sudden surge of anger. He nodded but said nothing.

"Aren't you going to ask me why?"

"I expect you to tell me without my having to ask."

Volterra took a deep breath. "To kill him and burn his farm would make those dependent on him destitute . . . the farm provides for all of them."

"Kill him," Barraka exclaimed savagely, "and burn the fucking farm!"

Volterra shook his head. "There's another reason why I won't do it," he said.

Barraka threw the rest of his coffee on the ground and stood up. He knew he was about to be told the real reason why his order wasn't carried out. The other explanation was a blind, a polite Italian way of avoiding facing an unpleasant reality. Because of his experience with partisans he had been exposed to this particular maneuver. It was a way of saving face after having committed some blunder. He wondered what it was this time.

"If we kill him and burn the farm, the Germans will

know it was our work . . . Captain Muller will know . . . Kunstler will know, and they will hunt us down, or at least try to. And if we are hunted, we will not be able to accomplish our mission."

Barraka glared at him.

"So now you understand why I didn't follow your orders," Volterra said.

"Yeah," Barraka answered, "I understand."

"And do you agree I was right?"

"You were right," Barraka grudgingly told him.

"Then we have nothing more to discuss," Volterra said with a smile, "at least not for a while."

"Are these all your men?" Barraka asked.

"A dozen more have gone into San Martino to find out what the Germans were doing there."

"They were looking for us."

"Yes," Volterra admitted, "they were. But why were they pulled out?"

"And you think your men will find out why?"

"They'll try," Volterra answered.

Barraka shrugged and walked away. He resented Volterra now almost as much as he had when he had first met him. But he had to admit that killing Garjulio and burning the farm would have been a bad tactical error . . . perhaps even a fatal one?

Barraka went back to the boulder where he had spent the night, sat down and munched on the piece of bread, regretting having thrown away his coffee. He thought about going down to the gully for more but was too proud to do it.

"Mitch," he told himself, "you're never going to understand Volterra, or any of his people. If you want to come out of it alive, you just have to make the best of a lousy situation. That's the only thing you can do."

Barraka, Koss, and Yancy changed from their uniforms to the inconspicuous clothing worn by the local farmers. The change allowed them to move freely in and out of San Martino and around the outskirts of the village as they checked the accuracy of the maps they had been given. They found them woefully inadequate. In some instances, they were completely wrong, showing such things as bridges where none existed, or omitting a road, where one should have been shown.

By late afternoon, Barraka left Koss and Yancy to continue their work, while he and Volterra went to reconnoiter the prison camp at Servigliano. Though Volterra had brought a detailed layout of the facility, Barraka insisted on making his own sketches.

"The machine guns on the towers have intersecting fields of fire," Volterra explained. "And each of them can fire to the center of the facility where the prisoners are housed in three buildings. One for the women and children and two for the men."

Barraka made a wordless sound and continued to draw a three-dimensional view of the camp.

"There's only one gate to the camp," Volterra said. "It serves as an entrance and an exit. There're always four guards on duty. They have telephone communications to the towers and to the office of the camp commandant."

"Where's the powerhouse?"

"That small building off to the left," Volterra answered. "It's in a separate barbed wire enclosure and is guarded by two men at all times."

"Water supply?"

"From artesian wells."

"Pumped or natural?"

"Natural."

"The guardroom and the barracks must be that long building on the far right?" Barraka said.

"It is," Volterra answered.

Barraka stopped sketching and suggested they move around to the north side of the mountain. "How long did it take the Krauts to level the top of it?" he asked.

"A few weeks," Volterra answered. "But most of that time was spent clearing off the debris. They actually blew the top of it off. You'll see what I mean when we're on the other side."

They worked their way cautiously around the slope. The north face was littered with debris from the top. Huge chunks of rock, some weighing many tons, were scattered all the way down to the base, where there was a small, but swiftly flowing stream.

"If we move those people out this way," Barraka said, "we'd wind up with too many casualties from broken ankles and legs, especially among the old and the children. But those rocks would provide good cover."

They went around to the east face of the mountain. There were a few trees growing on it, but they were down toward the base. The rest of the slope was exposed and would give the machine gunners in at least two of the towers a field day. The same condition existed on the southern slope.

"All we have to do," Barraka said sarcastically, "is

line them up in a column of twos and march them out."

"If it were that easy," Volterra responded softly, "I would not have asked for help . . . we would have done it ourselves."

"It's going to be a bitch to get them out," Barraka said, "and a much bigger bitch to move them to the border."

"Right now," Volterra told him, "I'll settle for getting them out. Then I'll worry about taking them into Switzerland . . . But we must act soon, or the weather will stop us, even if the Germans can't."

Barraka made a face but didn't say anything . . . Volterra was right about the weather. Each day that it remained good was a day wasted. As far as the weather went, they were on borrowed time. But there was another side of the coin, even when it came to the weather. Bad weather would not only hinder them, it would also hinder the Germans.

"We are scheduled to make radio contact tonight," Volterra told him. "Do you have anything you want me to relate to Captain Keller?"

"Tell him to get hold of a bottle of bourbon for me," Barraka answered.

They crossed the bottom of the valley and began their ascent up the road leading to Monte San Martino. The sun was already below the mountains, and though the valley was steeped in quickly darkening twilight the western sky was still a brilliant blue.

Barraka turned up his collar and gathered the old woolen scarf, given to him earlier in the day by Volterra, more tightly around his neck. He walked quickly, using his staff to help him. His breath steamed in the air and his hands felt the bite of the cold.

"Given good weather," Barraka asked, "how many days between here and the border?"

"Six, with luck."

"Six, with luck," Barraka repeated, and after a moment he added, "To elude the Krauts for six days won't be a matter of luck, it will be a fucking miracle . . . believe me, it will be one fucking miracle."

"Call it whatever you please," Volterra answered, "as long as it happens."

Venus and Saturn showed in the eastern sky. Some of the brighter stars came out. The moon rose. Just as the last glimmer of light vanished from the sky, the searchlights at Servigliano came on.

Barraka stopped and watched them. Each one swept over a particular quadrant of the prison at intervals of three minutes.

When Barraka commented about it, Volterra explained, "It's done by a timing mechanism . . . but the men in the towers can assume mechanical control just by pressing a button."

"Kraut efficiency," Barraka responded. "They'll do it every time."

"So you do admire them," Volterra said with a slight chuckle. "I have been wondering about it and now I know."

"I'm an engineer," Barraka answered, "or I was until the war. But I admire anything that's well designed and well built, even if it's made by the enemy."

"I admire them too," Volterra revealed. "But having said that, I would have to add that I hate them . . . I don't think you hate them, at least not on the same level, or with the same intensity that I, and my people, do."

For a while, Barraka thought about what Volterra had said. He admitted his feelings toward the Germans were more impersonal. He killed them because if he didn't, they would kill him. He seldom thought about the reason why he was fighting them. But he did know it was a life-and-death struggle between the Axis Powers and the Allies. And if there was a God, He had to favor the Allies, who were fighting not only to keep their own freedom, but also for the freedom of the people already conquered by the Germans and the Japanese.

"Perhaps in a different place and at some future time," Volterra offered, "we will sit down and talk about it."

Barraka realized he was being given the opportunity to back off and he took it. "Yeah, some day we'll sit down over a bottle of vino and talk about the war and why we were in it."

"I tell you now," Volterra laughed, "if there was any other place for me to be, I would be there. But I'm a Jew, and there is no other place for me but here."

"And I'm not a Jew," Barraka said, "And I'm here because the army says here is where I'm supposed to be. It may not be as all powerful as your reason for being here, but for me, it is."

The two of them laughed until tears filled their eyes.

"It's good to laugh now and then," Volterra said,

"even if we have nothing to laugh at but the joke that was played on us. Mine by my birth and yours by the American army."

They started to laugh all over again.

Muller spent most of the day brooding over the way Kunstler had treated him. Immediately after Kunstler had excluded him from the meeting of company commanders, he had written a full report about it to General Karl Wolfe, the senior area SS officer. In particular, he had noted that Kunstler exhibited characteristics that were, in his opinion, at variance with certain doctrines of National Socialism, and he had suggested that in the interests of the Fatherland, Kunstler should be thoroughly investigated by the SS for possible subversive tendencies. Marked Top Secret, he had sent the letter in the official SS mail pouch. But now, for him to send another letter explaining the latest episode was unthinkable.

Not wanting to sit at the same table with Kunstler, Muller absented himself from lunch and had a tray of food brought to him by his orderly. Though he drank the coffee, he had little appetite for the blood sausage and boiled potatoes that lay steaming on the plate.

Several times, he thought about telephoning General Wolfe to ask for an audience. Once he even picked up the phone, only to put it down again, realizing that Kunstler had powerful connections in the army who would not hesitate to destroy him should he openly attempt to bring the colonel down without sufficient cause.

"Sufficient cause," Muller said aloud. Those two

words were the key to what he had to discover in order to completely discredit Kunstler.

He suddenly had the feeling the walls of the office were pressing in on him. Calling his aide, Muller told him, "I'm going out for a while." He looked at his watch. It was already 1500 hours. "I do not expect to return this afternoon," he said, very precisely. "If I am needed for an emergency, I will either be in my quarters or in the cafe across the plaza. Should I decide to go somewhere else, I will leave word with the duty officer."

A few minutes later Muller crossed the plaza.

The sun was already on the western mountain peaks and the long shadows of late afternoon were beginning to creep across the cobblestones.

He stopped outside the cafe and looked toward Monte San Martino. Though his men had only killed four partisans, he was absolutely certain that they would have gotten many more had he not been forced to withdraw them by Kunstler.

"And for what reason?" Muller muttered. "Probably because he did not initiate the action." With a shake of his head, he entered the cafe and sat down at a table in front of the window overlooking the plaza, a position that afforded him the opportunity to see everyone who entered and left headquarters.

"Ah, captain," Calvino exclaimed, "it is a pleasure to see you." He came out from behind the bar and went toward the table. He was always more obsequious toward Muller than toward the other officers, sensing the man accepted his servility as something due him by right of conquest. "This lovely weather after yesterday's rain is a welcome relief. But soon it will turn cold, and the snows will come."

Muller looked askance at him. He could not understand the minds of the Italians. That Calvino could talk about the coming of snow with such light-heartedness completely mystified him. He dreaded the dark days of winter here in Italy as much as he had when he had been home. Perhaps more so, in this alien country.

"A glass of white wine, captain?" Calvino offered. "I have recently received several bottles of Soave."

"Yes," Muller answered succinctly.

Calvino opened the bottle at the table and poured some wine for Muller to taste. When he received a nod of approval, he filled the glass, saying "This should really be served in a beautiful goblet."

"What difference would that make?" Muller asked idly.

Calvino clicked his tongue and then explained, "Beauty always enhances beauty . . . by serving the wine in a beautiful glass, the drinker is not only pleased by what he tastes but also by what he holds and sees . . . it is much the same when a man possesses a beautiful woman. His pleasure with her is increased many times by her physical beauty. It is a rare man who finds pleasure with an ugly woman."

With a wave of his hand, Muller said, "Spare me your observations."

"Of course," Calvino responded with a smile and withdrew behind the small bar.

Muller sipped the wine. He needed something he might use against Kunstler, something that would force his superiors to take action against the colonel.

"What do you think of the wine?" Calvino called out.

"It would be much better," Muller answered testily, "if you permitted me to drink in silence."

"I am sorry I disturbed you, captain. I was only concerned about—"

"Silence," Muller shouted. "Silence!"

Calvino retreated into the rear room.

Outside the shadows lengthened. Now and then an officer from one of the line units in the brigade entered or left headquarters. A motorcycle dispatch rider came roaring into the plaza and stopped in front of the building.

Muller was an abstemious drinker, and after a glass and a half he moved the bottle off to one side.

The dispatch rider came out of headquarters, donned his helmet, lowered his goggles, and, straddling his motorcycle, he began to jump up and down on the starter to get the engine going. As soon as it sputtered to life, he gunned it and moments later was on his way.

Muller looked at his watch. It was 1615 hours. Within fifteen minutes the cafe would be crowded with officers, among them Major Radish, whom he did not want to see. There would be no way to avoid him, if he remained.

He paid for the wine with German scrip and left the cafe with intentions of going to his quarters, where he would sleep for a while. He was very tired. His feud with Kunstler was taking a toll on his energy and robbing him of sleep.

Muller occupied a small room in the castle. As he

started across the plaza, he suddenly changed his mind and decided to go for a walk, with the hope that the exercise and fresh air might relax him more than a nap would.

He crossed the stone bridge at the north end of the town and went up to the top of a small hill, where he stopped to once again look toward Monte San Martino.

Everything was shrouded in a rapidly deepening twilight, with the exception of the western sky above the peaks on the right, which was ablaze with an orange sunset.

He was just about to turn and walk back to the castle when the searchlights at Servigliano went on, turning the dusk there to a silvery brightness. The transition from deep shadow to brilliant light was so instantaneous that it took him by surprise. And, almost as rapidly, he understood why there were Americans with the partisans.

"The Jews!" he exclaimed aloud. "The Jews are the reason! And Kunstler knows it! Kunstler has been purposely telling everyone the partisans are here to disrupt communications and traffic . . . but he knows what their reason is . . . he knows and is probably helping them."

Muller slapped the side of his boot with his crop. For the first time in days, he felt truly satisfied, truly at peace with himself. Now he had something to work on, something he could sink his teeth into.

Kunstler had overlooked the fact that Volterra and Mastrada were Jews, he told himself. The colonel had either overlooked it, or purposely ignored it. If he could prove one or the other, Muller knew, it would be enough to make Kunstler's position as brigade commander questionable, if not altogether untenable.

By the time he returned to Malveno, Muller had developed an appetite. He had no reason, now, to avoid sitting down with Kunstler. He was pleased to think of himself as the instrument of the colonel's eventual downfall.

"Tell me about the woman," Barraka said, as he and Volterra moved through the darkness toward Monte San Martino. "Is she the only one with your unit?"

"To answer the second question first, she's not the only woman. Several more will arrive by tomorrow. But do not have any doubt about their ability to fight. They kill with the same ferocity as any man and a few, like some men I have known, enjoy it."

Barraka shuddered. Women who killed were completely out of his range of experience. None of the other partisan groups with whom he had previously operated had had any women in their ranks. He had a sudden vision of Helen dressed in men's clothing and pointing a rifle at some man. It was so disturbing, he willed it out of his mind.

"As for Rinata," Volterra said, "I know only that she came from Verona, and that she was a prostitute."

"She told you that?"

"Yes," Volterra answered. "Openly, without shame."

"Does she—"

With a shrug, Volterra said, "She does not sell her body, but this life we lead does not lend itself to the morality of what you or I, or for that matter most of the others in the unit, lived by before the war. Those of us who survive will never be the same."

Barraka only partially understood what Volterra had said. His own values of right and wrong had been drastically changed by the war. But he was sure when he returned home that they would revert to what they had been before he had left.

As they neared the place below San Martino from where they had started earlier that day, Barraka realized the partisans were no longer encamped by the side of the road. "Where are the men?" he asked.

"Some are on the other side of the mountain," Volterra explained. "Others are back in the woods. We never stay more than a night in force in any one place. Even the camp above the village was never manned by more than ten men."

"And where are Koss and Yancy?"

"In San Martino," Volterra said, "waiting for us to join them for dinner. A real dinner of hot food."

"In the town?"

"Yes," Volterra said with a smile. "We have friends who have a house there."

"Listen," Barraka told him, "for a hot dinner, I'd even sit down with the Krauts."

The house was beyond San Martino, but it was close enough to be considered a part of the village. It was a two-story structure, with a huge kitchen downstairs and several bedrooms on the upper level.

Koss, Yancy, and Mastrada were at the table. And Barraka was surprised to find Rinata there, too.

The man and woman who owned the house were old. Volterra treated them with great respect. He introduced Barraka to the elderly couple and when he spoke to them in Italian they smiled broadly. The man's name was Giorgio Pippi. His wife answered to Terisa.

"How would you like a bath?" Volterra asked.

"Almost as much as I'd like a hot meal," Barraka answered.

Volterra smiled. "There's a metal tub in the barn, some strong laundry soap, and several large pots of boiling water."

In the barn Barraka found clean underwear and two heavy sweaters, one a turtleneck. The bath was a delightful luxury. For a few minutes he sat in the steaming hot water and relaxed.

He returned to the house.

"Come on, Mitch," Yancy said, "we're waitin' on you and we're hungry as hell."

Barraka sat down. "I really think you love this life, Yancy."

"Shit man," Yancy answered, "what's not to love . . . good friends, good food, and lots to do and see. Sure it gets a little hairy now and then. But it sure beats the hell out of punchin' a time clock or waitin' on a bread line. I know; I've done both."

Volterra translated what was said in English for Mastrada and Rinata. But Yancy and Koss had enough of a command of Italian to say most of what they wanted to in that language.

The conversation between Yancy and Rinata was very lively. And Yancy's southern drawl, when transferred to Italian, made her laugh.

Giorgio brought out two bottles of red wine. After filling every glass on the table, he offered a toast to all of the men, everywhere, who fought for freedom.

Terisa carried a huge pot of spinach soup to the

table. When that was finished she and Giorgio set down two large platters filled with spaghetti and mushrooms, followed by roast chicken and rabbit.

Yancy and Rinata became involved in a conversation about Rome. They were soon oblivious to the rest of the people at the table.

Barraka wondered if he should say anything to Yancy about Rinata's past. Then, with what amounted to a mental shrug, he decided not to interfere. His obligation to Yancy did not include becoming involved in the man's private life. Yancy was not exactly an innocent man. Barraka was sure that he could take care of himself.

The two bottles of wine were finished and two more were brought.

Just as the third bottle was emptied by Mastrada, Rinata said in a loud voice, "Yes, John Yancy, I will sleep with you."

"Well, I'll be damned!" Yancy exclaimed, and then, looking at Barraka, he said, "Mitch, I didn't even ask her yet."

"But I could tell you were thinking of asking," Rinata said, "so I decided to save you the trouble."

Volterra and Mastrada started to clap. Barraka and Koss joined them. So did Giorgio and Terisa.

Then Giorgio said, "There is nothing in the world so good for a man who fights as a good fuck . . . at least," he added, "that is the way I remember it when I was young."

Everyone laughed.

Taking Rinata by the hand, Yancy asked Giorgio which of the bedrooms he could use.

"The one in the rear," the old man said. "It is quiet there."

When they were gone, Volterra lifted his glass toward the steps and said, "May they bring each other delight this night."

"I'll drink to that," Barraka said, raising his glass.

"So will I," Koss added. "Yance is a damn good man."

"We're all damn good men," Mastrada commented. "If we weren't, none of us would be here."

Each of them drank another glass of wine in silence.

Barraka found himself thinking about Helen. He was angrier now with her than he had ever been for not going to bed with him before he had gone overseas. He pursed his lips and tried to ignore the slow burn in his groin.

"It's almost time to make radio contact," Volterra said. "Tonight we will send from the top of the mountain." He stood up, put on his jacket, and picked up his rifle. He started for the door.

"I'll go with you," Barraka told him. "I need some fresh air."

The two of them left the house and walked silently toward the top of San Martino. The sky was filled with stars. It was cold enough for their breath to steam on the night air.

Barraka asked Volterra about Giorgio.

"An old Communist," Volterra said. "He spent a good many years of his life in prison under Mussolini."

"Communist?" Barraka questioned, surprised.

"Don't worry about it," Volterra responded. "So

am I . . . so are most of the partisans."

"You're joking!"

"We'll talk about it another time," Volterra told him. And gesturing to where the top of the mountain was, he said, "Vincenzo is there with the radio." He whistled. A moment later the signal was answered. "Come," he said, "we want to do this very quickly."

They scrambled to the top of San Martino. Volterra immediately bent down to the radio set.

"The frequencies are adjusted," Vincenzo said, as he turned the generator crank.

Volterra began to call, "This is Cross Over, do you read me?"

"Loud and clear," the voice at the other transmitter answered.

Volterra glanced up at Barraka. He said into the mike, "Say again, do you read me?"

"Loud and clear," came the response.

"That's not Captain Keller," Volterra said to Barraka.

Barraka took the mike and said, "This is Major Barraka . . . where is Keller?"

No response came from the other end.

Barraka repeated what he had just said.

"Captain Keller is dead," the man said. "This is Captain Fennly."

"What happened to Keller?" Barraka asked.

"Killed two days ago by a sniper," Fennly answered.

"The goddamn fucking war!" Barraka swore, in a choked voice. He handed the mike to Volterra. "The goddamn fucking war!" He stood up and walked a short distance away from the radio while Volterra completed the transmission. Barraka's vision was blurred with tears. He wiped his eyes and took several deep breaths.

Volterra came up to him and put a hand on his shoulder. "Let's go back to the house," he said quietly.

"Yeah," Barraka answered, "Let's go back to the house." Then, in a much lower voice, he said, "Keller was a good man, a good soldier."

"Yes," Volterra answered, "I know."

"Did you know his grandmother was part Jewish?"

"Yes. He told me."

Barraka drank another bottle of wine before he stumbled up the steps to the bedroom he was to share with Volterra. When he finally drifted off to sleep, Barraka was once again sitting by a campfire with Kip, watching a bull moose come down to the edge of the lake to drink.

Yancy reached across to the small table next to the bed and took a cigarette from the open pack. He moved gingerly to avoid disturbing Rinata, who was sleeping next to him. The cigarette tasted good. He settled against the back of the bed, using the two goose-feather pillows to prop himself up.

A deep, predawn gray filled the room, and it was cold enough for his breath to steam in the air. He looked toward the window. Outside the gray was several shades lighter. A bare-limbed tree was distorted into a crazy shape by the cheap windowpane glass.

Sleeping in a bed was an unexpected luxury for him, and having a woman was an even more unexpected pleasure. He looked down at Rinata. She was on her back with her thighs slightly splayed. Half of her right breast was uncovered. He put his hand over it, enjoying its warmth and soft resiliency. He touched the nipple and felt it harden.

Rinata opened her eyes and reached up, taking the cigarette out of his mouth to take a long drag on it. "How long have you been awake?" she asked, circling his waist with one arm.

"Not long," he answered. "A bed takes some getting used to again."

"And a woman?"

"Not as much as a bed," Yancy told her, squeezing her breast.

She stuck her tongue out and said, "If I didn't know you better, I would be insulted."

"We fit pretty damn well together," he responded, slipping his hand down to her vagina.

"Yes, it was good."

Yancy laughed and said, "When ol' Yance does it, it's always good."

Rinata reached for his cigarette again and took another deep drag on it.

"Do you know why we're here . . . I mean Mitch, Bill, and myself?" he asked.

She nodded.

"You a Jew?"

"No," she answered. "I'm Catholic."

Yancy stubbed out the cigarette. "Mitch doesn't think the mission has a chance," he said. "What do you think?"

With a shrug that made her naked breasts roll, she answered, "It must be tried . . . if it fails, it'll not have been for want of trying . . . but if we do not try, it'll not have the chance to succeed or fail, and the Germans will ship the Jews to the death camps."

"I guess we can't let the Krauts do that," Yancy said. "I guess it's one of those damn things that just has to be done." Then sliding down closer to her, he added, "Like the thing that must be done now." His fingers played on the lips of her vagina, while he bent over and kissed her mouth. . . .

VIII

Barraka couldn't sleep. He looked at his watch. It was three o'clock in the morning. He left the bed, took the map case, and went downstairs to the kitchen, where he spread the maps out on the table. The one of the local area no longer interested him. He had drawn a more accurate one from his own reconnaissance. But the map of the country between Servigliano and the border worried him. Colonel Dodd had said it wasn't accurate.

Volterra came down the steps. "I couldn't sleep either," he said. He moved to the table and looked down at the map.

"There are just too many unknowns," Barraka said, tapping the map with a piece of wood. "It shows the high places and that's about all."

"There's very little up there," Volterra told him. "Some isolated farmers, but nothing more. I doubt if the Italian army has an accurate map of it."

"We've got to have one. Once we take those people out, we've got to be able to go where the Krauts can't, at least in any numbers." Barraka filled his pipe and went to the stove to light it. "How many days will it take for us—the two of us—to lay out our own route?"

"If we move fast, two days, maybe three."

"I don't want to lose the time. But it'll give us an edge over the Krauts. We'll know exactly which way we're going, but they'll have to guess."

"When do you want to go?"

"Now," Barraka answered, "before dawn."

They crossed the mist-filled valley below the village, swung north around Servigliano, and worked their way into the narrow gorge.

"We've got to make it impossible for any mobile units to follow us," Barraka said.

"There's a series of ridges to the north," Volterra told him. "They're not shown on the map."

"If they're there, we'll use them."

The sun came up, burning off the mist.

"There won't be too many more days like this," Volterra said. Hand over hand they climbed a rock wall that led them to an open expanse between two large hills.

Exhausted, Barraka paused and looked around. The lack of cover made him frown. "It might be better to cross this at night," he said. "We could stay in the north end of the gorge until dusk, make the climb during twilight and be up here by night. Do you think any of them are in good physical shape? It's going to take one helluva push."

"I don't know."

Still breathing hard, Barraka started to walk. "We'll split your men," he said, "into five groups. Each one will move north toward the pass, but by a different route. Then we'll rendezvous at—"

"There's a bridge over the Itillina River we'll have to either bypass or take before we reach the border," Volterra told him.

"Okay, we'll rendezvous close to it."

They moved swiftly, alternating between a jog and a fast walk. They climbed several rock faces and made their way across boulder-strewn ridges.

"I've got to rest for a while," Volterra said.

"Over there," Barraka answered, pointing to a cluster of boulders.

The two men dropped down and leaned against a large rock. Volterra drank from his canteen and passed it to Barraka. "The war seems far away," he said.

Barraka agreed and then drank. He put an empty pipe in his mouth. Every part of his body ached. His hands were cut and bruised from the rocks. But the war did seem to be far away. The sky was very blue and the sun felt warm against his face. If he were a different kind of a man, he might ask himself what he was doing there. But he wasn't given to that kind of thinking and even if he were, he knew it wouldn't change anything: He'd still be there.

"What are you going to do when it's over?" Volterra asked.

Barraka was surprised by the question. "Build bridges," he answered.

"I'll design them and you'll build them," Volterra said with a smile. "That's right, I'm an architect."

Barraka looked at him. He hadn't known what

Volterra had done before the war. Though they had already spent eleven days together, this was the first time they had been alone for an extended period of time.

"Which of our names should be first?" Volterra asked.

Barraka smiled. "The one who can run the longest."

"Then your name is first."

Barraka stood up, gave Volterra his hand and pulled him to his feet.

They didn't stop again until they made camp for the night. They ate bread and cheese and drank wine from a bottle Volterra carried in his knapsack.

Barraka relit his pipe.

"Do you believe in God?" Volterra asked.

"Sure. . . . There must be something, or someone that—" He stopped himself. He had believed in God and the mercy of Christ. But the war had changed his beliefs. He wasn't so sure that everything that happened was in God's hands; he wasn't so sure that man possessed an immortal soul.

"Should I tell you what I believe?" Volterra asked. "I believe that without man there would be no God, and once created, God, through man, orders the world."

"That's too deep for me," Barraka answered. He knocked the ashes from his pipe, and said, "Get some sleep. I'll take the first guard." He pulled the blanket over his shoulders and refilled his pipe. Since he had seen Servigliano, he couldn't think of a way to breach its defenses without mounting a full-scale assault. He had gone over every detail of its layout dozens of times and was unable to find a way to get in and out with a minimum of risk. No matter how he approached the problem, to enter the camp would entail killing the guards, and to do that would expose his men to machine gun fire from at least two of the towers.

He decided to wait until they returned to San Martino before discussing the problem with Volterra, Koss, and the others.

Volterra stirred and moaned in his sleep.

Barraka looked at him. He had tried not to like him, to fault him every way possible. But the truth was that Volterra was a good man. He could trust him, if necessary, with his life. Jew or not, Barraka realized they had forged a bond of friendship as strong as any he had with Koss or Yancy. In the years to come, if he remembered anything about the war, he'd remember Volterra.

Late the following morning they saw the Alps in the distance, and in the early afternoon they reached the bridge. It was made of stone and was so narrow that only one truck at a time could pass over it. There were two soldiers on either end and a small building on the north side of the river. Telephone wires went north and south.

"We'll have to cut those wires," Barraka said. He peered through the glasses again. "I wouldn't be a bit surprised if the Romans put down those bottom stones," he said, "but we're going to have to blow it."

Three kilometers north of the bridge, they came to a German motor pool.

"We're going to have to stop the Germans from going down to the bridge, once the wires are cut," Volterra said.

"It's just a small detachment," Barraka answered.

"I'd say maybe twenty-five men, including mechanics. I don't see more than ten trucks. It shouldn't be hard to take out."

They passed the motor pool and moved through the woods, parallel to the road. The last sixteen kilometers to the border were the easiest, the road snaked its way directly to the pass. Satisfied with the route, they turned back, and by nightfall they were well south of the bridge.

IX

Kunstler entered his office at 0800 hours. His orderly had already switched on the desk lamp and arranged the various intelligence reports in a neat pile.

Kunstler sat down and reached for a mug of hot coffee. He scanned the day's meteorological report. That the forecasts were almost always right was a source of pride for Kunstler. He enjoyed accuracy, whether it was manifested in a meteorological report or in the solution to a particular mathematical puzzle. The forecast was for the weather to worsen throughout the day, with freezing rain predicted for the lower mountain and valley regions and snow at elevations above three thousand meters.

The next report came from the radio monitoring section. Ever since they had picked up and tracked the movement of the partisan radio from the south to the area of Brigade's command, Kunstler read each morning's report with great interest.

He put his mug of coffee down. Pressing his fingers together, he began to see the pieces of a puzzle. Some of the pieces even fit together.

He stood up, put the report inside his tunic, and left the office. "I will be with Captain Muller for a while," he told his aide.

Kunstler went down the hall and entered Muller's office.

"Tell me," he said, "exactly what you know about the partisans operating in this area?" He spoke to him as he would an errant schoolboy.

Muller flushed under the sudden attack. "What are you talking about?"

"Have you read this morning's report from the radio monitoring section?"

Muller shook his head.

"Read it." Kunstler put it in front of Muller.

"Major Barraka," Muller said, scanning it.

"That's right," Kunstler responded. "And it's a good guess that Koss and Yancy are also members of the American army."

"Major Barraka," Muller repeated.

"Now tell me, Captain," Kunstler pressed, "what do you think they are up to?"

Muller blinked.

"The Americans and the partisans. . . . Surely a man with your net of informants must have some thoughts about why a group of partisans would pick up a team of American soldiers and bring them all the way back here . . . and don't tell me they're here to disrupt transportation and communications."

"That's your viewpoint."

"I am interested in yours, Captain Muller. I already know mine."

Muller put the palms of his hands against the edge of

the desk. Kunstler was much more adroit than he had thought him to be and much more savage than he had suspected.

"Let's understand each other," Kunstler said. "I'm not here to badger you. I asked you for your opinion and that's what I want."

"Obviously, the partisans will attempt to strike at the camp at Servigliano."

"And how did you arrive at that conclusion?"

"Volterra and Mastrada are Jews."

"Not good enough."

"They know that the Jews in Servigliano are slated to be shipped to—"

"For what purpose?" Kunstler interrupted. "What the hell would the partisans do with three hundred men, women, and children?"

Muller turned crimson. He was not used to being shouted at, and he suspected that his orderly could hear the colonel.

"Listen," Kunstler said, "I also read today's meteorological report and the forecast for the next two days. The weather will deteriorate, by next week it'll be even worse. That means snow, blizzard conditions; if it moderates, it means freezing rain and wind. Now you sit there and tell me that the partisans are going to attempt to free the prisoners, but you can't tell me what they intend to do with them once they're free."

"I'm a German," Muller said. "I can't think like an Italian and most definitely not like a Jew."

"And I'm only a colonel in the army, but it's an answer I can't accept. Think like an Italian . . . think like a Jew."

"I can't," Muller answered.

"Pity," Kunstler said. "And I thought we were having a meaningful conversation."

Muller raised his eyebrows.

"I happen to agree with you," Kunstler told him. "The partisans will attack the camp at Servigliano. But I don't understand why."

"Perhaps because they hope to bring more men into their ranks?"

"That's a possibility. But it doesn't answer the question of why the Americans are involved."

Muller sat very still. He half expected another verbal assault from Kunstler and was surprised when the major did nothing more than reach across the desk for the monitoring report.

"Sooner or later we'll know," Kunstler said, standing. "Isn't that right, captain?"

"Most certainly."

"I'm pleased you've decided to help us win the war."

Muller flushed for the third time since Kunstler had come into the office.

"Two more points to cover before I leave," Kunstler told him, imitating his manner of speaking. "The first has to do with how I discovered you knew more about the partisans than you're willing to tell me. I happened to pass Garjulio on the day he visited you. It was a few hours before you mounted your attack against the partisans. And this morning when I saw Major Barraka's name in the radio report, I guessed you must have known about his presence, or you wouldn't have had your men attack the partisans. After all, the partisans have been around here for as long as you have, and that was the first time you ordered an attack in strength. Oh yes, I should add that from the time the two soldiers were found knifed on our side of the Sangro River, I've been following the movement of the partisans northward."

Muller said nothing.

"As for the second point," Kunstler continued, "certain friends of mine in army headquarters have intimated that you've become quite a letter writer. My suggestion is that if you must write, write poetry. It's a more personal form of expression and much less apt to lead you into difficulty."

When Barraka and Volterra returned to Pippi's house in San Martino, a freezing rain was falling. Barraka sat down at the table and told Yancy and Koss what he and Volterra had found between the camp and the border.

"But our first problem is to get the people organized. They must be ready to move when we are," he said. "That's what we have to talk about."

Giorgio brought a bottle of Grappa to the table and hot soup for Barraka and Volterra.

Each man looked questioningly at his neighbor but none of them spoke.

Barraka studied the three-dimensional drawing of the camp he had made. "I'm going in through the fence," he said, still looking at the drawing. "There's a place adjacent to the powerhouse that none of the searchlights touches. It's in darkness all of the time."

"Are you sure?" Volterra asked.

"I marked it," Barraka answered. "I'd guess it's wide enough for a man to stand in and long enough for three men. I'll cut the fence, belly my way in, and go out the same way."

"That's trusting a lot to luck," Koss said.

"That's also counting on Jerry not finding the hole," Major Conway said.

Barraka nodded. "If there's another way, I don't see it."

"You might be better off using the powerhouse to get out," Volterra said. "There's only two guards."

"I'd rather not leave any bodies," Barraka said. "I want to go in quietly and leave quietly. The only unavoidable noise will be the wire cutter and that can't be helped. Any questions?" He waited a moment. "Okay, then, that's the way I'm going in."

"It's too dangerous," Volterra said. "Suppose something goes wrong and you're caught?"

"I told you before," Barraka answered, "if something happens to me, you can rely on Koss and Yancy."

"I think several of us should go with you, Mitch, just in case you get into trouble," Koss said.

"I wouldn't try for more than five," Volterra said.

"Are there any local men in your group?" Barraka asked, realizing Koss was right.

"Salvatore Fantana and Carlo Crucci."

"I'll take the two of them and Major Conway. Who else?"

"I'll go," Mastrada said.

"That makes five. We'll go in tomorrow night."

Volterra nodded. He had another radio message to send. "I'll be back in a couple of hours. This time the radio is several kilometers to the north of San Martino."

After dinner Barraka went up to his room and dropped down on the bed. He smoked his pipe until it tasted bitter. Then he spent time looking over his sketches of Servigliano and the set of aerial photographs he had. By midnight, he went downstairs to see if Volterra had returned.

"It's a bad night," Giorgio said.

"Where are the others?"

"Asleep in their rooms, or in the barn."

Barraka went to the door and opened it. A gust of wind drove the rain against him. He pushed the door shut and wiped his face. "It's a goddamn mean night."

"Don't worry about Chaim," Giorgio told him. "He can take care of himself."

"I'm not in the least bit worried about him," Barraka answered.

Giorgio made an open gesture with his hands. "It is not a sign of weakness to be concerned about a comrade."

Barraka went to the door, opened it again, and peered into the rain-filled night. "If he doesn't come soon, I'll wake the others and—" He saw the dark figure of a man moving toward the house. "Chaim?" he called, using Volterra's given name for the first time.

"Yes."

"What the hell is wrong with—" Barraka stopped. There were two men out there, one held by the other.

"Ran into a patrol," Volterra said. "One of the men has a leg wound. Rouse the others. We can't stay here any longer. . . . There are patrols all over the area. I'll tell the others in the barn. Get the others out of the house."

Minutes later every one of the partisans was dressed and armed. They left Pippi's house and slipped into the rain-filled night.

Volterra led them down the north side of the mountain, to a place where there were some trees, but not any real protection from the storm. "I think the Germans are on to us," he said.

Kunstler finished reading the report of the skirmish with the partisans that had taken place the previous night several kilometers to the north of San Martino. He reached down to scratch Dmitri's head and looked at the large map on the wall across the room. Though he could not read the small print, he was able to see the topographical features of the area where the action had taken place.

"What do you suppose they were doing there?" Kunstler asked, shifting his eyes from the map to Radish, who was standing by the window.

"A guess only?"

"Yes, if that's all you can give me."

"They were going to make another radio transmission," Radish said, going to the map. "It's a good place to transmit from."

Kunstler agreed. "Have you read the latest report from our radio monitoring group?"

"I sent it to you first."

Kunstler tapped the right side of his head. "I have it on my desk," he said. "The transmission was started by Volterra and then another man began to speak. He identified himself as Major Barraka."

"Barraka?"

"Yes. Muller found out from one of his informants that Major Barraka is one of three Americans with Volterra's partisan unit. The other two are Lieutenant Koss and Sergeant Yancy. Captain Muller intended to bring this information to your attention after he had ascertained what their mission is."

"Muller said that?" Radish asked.

"Yes, in a manner of speaking," Kunstler said with a smile, "but now, give me your evaluation of the situation."

"I'd prefer to have more facts."

Kunstler stood up and walked to the wall map. He studied it intently for several minutes. Almost as if he were asking himself a question, he said aloud, "But where the devil would they take them?"

Radish allowed a hint of a smile to move across his lips. "Who are you talking about?"

"The Jews at Servigliano," Kunstler said, facing him.

Radish maintained silence.

"Even on the assumption that they would be able to get them out," Kunstler went on, "what would they do with them . . . three hundred men, women, and children. Do they think they could do something with them? Even more preposterous is the idea they'd be able to take them out of the camp."

"I agree," Radish said. "Yet it seems the only plausible explanation for what's been happening."

"As far as the partisans are concerned, yes," Kunstler said, "since, as I remember, Volterra and Mastrada are Jews and perhaps fanatical enough to attempt an attack on the camp. But the presence of the Americans baffles me. Do you think army intelligence in Berlin might have information on the three of them?"

"Most probably on the officers," Radish answered, "and possibly on the sergeant. I'll request their dossiers immediately."

Kunstler sat down at his desk again. Dmitri stretched out close to him.

"We have someone with the partisans, don't we?" Kunstler asked.

"Carlo Crucci," Radish answered. "From the village of San Pietro."

"Can you contact him?"

"Yes, through Garjulio."

"Whatever we pay him for information, double it," Kunstler said. "I want to know every move they make before they make it."

"May I suggest you have Captain Muller arrest anyone in the area suspected of having anything to do with the partisans? They're fed by local people; let's make life difficult for them."

Kunstler glanced to the rain-spattered window. "The sooner the weather turns, the better our chances to put an end to their operations. No, I think it would be a foolish move to arrest anyone now. We don't want to let them know how much we already know."

Radish smiled.

"You may tell Captain Muller," Kunstler added, "that his information was invaluable."

"He'll be most pleased to hear that."

The two men laughed.

Carlo Crucci crossed the bare, rainswept south field

and headed for Garjulio's house. He was related by marriage to Garjulio; his mother's first cousin was Garjulio's wife.

Crucci vaulted over some rocks, crossed a stream, and made his way to the yard, where he saw Garjulio helping one of the hired men unload hay from a wagon. He waved to Garjulio and called out that he only had a few minutes because he was on his way to Malveno.

Garjulio said something to the hired man. Putting the pitchfork aside, he jumped down from the wagon.

Crucci was a short man of about thirty-five, with waxed moustaches, black hair, and small black eyes. He took a few steps toward Garjulio. "We'll go in the house and talk," Garjulio said.

Crucci nodded. He hoped that he would be offered food and wine. Garjulio had some of the best vineyards in the area and the wine he made from the grapes was usually sold to the restaurants in Balzano and Trentino.

They entered the house.

The air was so filled with the strong smell of roast pork that Crucci's mouth watered.

Garjulio gestured to a place at the table, while he went to the sideboard for a bottle and two glasses. "Grappa," he said, filling each of their glasses. He drank his swiftly and filled the glass again. He looked at Crucci with such intensity that Garjulio could not help squinting.

"I came as soon as I could," Crucci said.

"Our friends told me to tell you they want to know what your friends intend doing before they do it," Garjulio told him. "You will find a way to visit me as often as necessary."

Crucci nodded. "Do our friends realize the danger?" he asked.

"Whatever they pay you, they'll double it."

"The danger is very great."

"I was told what to tell you, and I'm telling it to you," Garjulio said.

"Yes, I understand."

"Have you anything to tell our friends now?"

"Something is going to happen at Servigliano," Crucci said.

"When?"

"I don't know," Crucci answered.

"Have you any idea what's going to happen?"

Crucci shook his head.

"Then how do you know something will happen there?" Garjulio asked. He neither trusted nor liked Crucci.

"I heard some talk."

Garjulio did not comment. "Any new men in the unit?" he asked.

"Three Americans . . . a Major Barraka, a Lieutenant Koss, and a Sergeant Yancy. Barraka's in command of the unit now."

Garjulio belched.

There was nothing more for them to say to one another.

Crucci stood up. Garjulio saw him to the door and stood watching him until he was out of sight around the bend of the road below the house. "A fuckin' dandy!" he muttered, closing the door with a bang.

X

The night was black and a freezing rain was falling. Volterra walked alongside Barraka. "I still don't like the idea of your going in," Volterra said.

"And I still don't like the idea of being here altogether," Barraka responded with a smile, stopping in a clearing where Mastrada and the other men were waiting. "Saddle up!" he ordered.

Each of the partisans picked up a bandolier and three grenades. Barraka took two extra clips of ammo for his carbine and the same number of grenades as the others.

They moved out of the woods and made their way across the bottom of the valley toward Servigliano.

None of the men spoke.

At Servigliano the beams of the searchlights were blunted by the heavy rain and the light around the camp was diffused, making it seem as if the top of the mountain was crowned with gold.

Once they started to move up the slope, they made slow progress. Now and then they were drenched by water cascading off the rocks above them. In various places they were forced to climb hand over hand.

Barraka was fearful they were making too much noise, but he knew it couldn't be helped and hoped the rain would muffle their sounds.

It took almost an hour for them to climb up the rock-strewn slope. When they reached the chain metal fence, Barraka and Fontana worked the wire cutter. Each time the blade bit through a strand of metal, it made a loud snapping noise. Barraka swore under his breath and wiped the sweat and rain from his eyes.

Fontana gestured toward the powerhouse.

"I hear them," Barraka whispered, referring to the German soldiers inside. "Let's hope they can't hear us."

Link by link, Barraka and Fontana cut a semicircle out of the fence, large enough for a man to wiggle through; then they moved back to the narrow black rectangle where the other men were waiting.

"Fontana goes first," Barraka said. "Crucci next; then Conway, Mastrada, and myself. Once we're inside, Crucci takes a position between the barracks and the guardhouse . . . Conway stays along the inside wall of the powerhouse, facing the open area between the guardhouse and the barracks. Fontana covers the door to the barracks. Mastrada will go with me. If we run into any trouble, I want each of us to cover the other. Is that clear?"

The men nodded.

Barraka looked at the searchlight and timed its movements.

"Fontana," he said, concentrating on his watch, "get ready . . . go." Crucci followed. Conway went next; then Mastrada; Barraka wiggled through the opening last.

They lay face down in the mud, waiting for the next sweep of the searchlight.

"Did you see that?" Mastrada asked.

"What?" Barraka responded.

"There's a gallows in the center of the yard."

Barraka raised his head. A hanged man pendulated with the wind.

The beam of the searchlight passed close to them. The instant it was gone, they leaped to their feet and ran to their assigned positions.

Barraka, breathless and sweating, made it to the door of the barracks. He looked to where each of the other men was. He could see Fontana was close enough for him to wave to. Crucci and Conway were back in the shadows of the supply building.

Barraka flung open the door. A woman screamed. A fetid smell rushed at him, making his stomach jump. He almost backed away. A single lantern was on the floor at the far end of the room. The dark shapes of men huddled against the walls. Barraka couldn't tell what they looked like, but he could hear the sound of their ragged breathing.

The stink was so powerful Barraka was forced to breathe through his mouth. He hesitated; then, pulling his shoulders back, he stepped forward again. The wooden floor creaked under his weight. He could hear the pounding of his own heart and Mastrada's footfalls behind him.

Barraka moved deeper into the gloom. On either side of a narrow central aisle, six bunks were piled one on top of the other. They were pallets of wood without any blankets. A man couldn't sit up in them. The rain poured in through the leaks and ran along the floor until it spilled out through the cracks.

The prisoners pulled back against the wall.

"What the hell is going on?" Barraka whispered, looking back at Mastrada.

"They're afraid of us," Mastrada answered.

"We're friends," Barraka told the people. He lowered his carbine. "I'm Major Barraka."

"Partisans," a man in the shadows said.

"I'm an American officer," Barraka explained. "I command the partisans who've come here to . . . to rescue you."

None of the prisoners moved or spoke.

"They're frightened," Mastrada said. "Afraid we'll kill them."

Barraka was sweating. "We don't have time . . . if the Krauts discover—"

"Welcome," a soft voice said, coming from Barraka's left. "We've been praying and hoping that we'd be rescued." The man spoke slowly in English. He came forward and extended his hand. "I'm Mario Piatelli."

Barraka shook Piatelli's hand. "Major Barraka," he said again.

Mastrada stepped forward and introduced himself.

"Is there anyone here who can speak for all of you?" Barraka asked.

"Let him," a man said. "Let Mario do it!"

Barraka nodded, and speaking again in Italian he said, "Signor Piatelli then will speak for all of you, and I will consider him your leader. . . . Does anyone object to this?"

"Why should we object," a woman said, "he is already our rabbi."

Barraka wasn't sure what that meant, but he accepted it without comment.

"Come," Piatelli said, still speaking in English. "We have much to discuss, and your visit must be brief."

Barraka and Mastrada followed Piatelli. When they reached the light at the far end of the room, they stopped. "Here we will talk," Piatelli told them. He gestured to the table and makeshift chairs.

Barraka and Piatelli sat opposite each other.

Mastrada stood behind Barraka.

Barraka was surprised to find Piatelli somewhere near the age of Kip, his father. About fifty. He had kind eyes and hair that was beginning to turn white. He was very thin, almost fragile.

Barraka looked at the other men, who were some distance from him. They were emaciated and many were bent from malnutrition. All had wide and staring eyes. He turned back to Piatelli, who seemed to be waiting for him to say something.

"We've come to take all of your people out," Barraka told him. Even as he spoke, he realized he was looking at women as well as men. Since men and women alike were dressed in men's clothing, he couldn't easily differentiate one from another in the poor light.

"I want you to meet my nephew and niece," Piatelli said, beckoning to the two young people, who came out of the mass of men and women pressed back against one wall of the building. "This is Major Barraka and Signor Mastrada," he told them.

Manio, the young man, was not more than eighteen, of middling height, very thin, with coal black eyes and the beginnings of a moustache.

"And this," Piatelli said, "is Sarah. She was studying to be a doctor before the war."

Barraka shook her hand. She was a small woman, with wide, dark eyes, probably black, like her hair, which escaped from under a ragged kerchief. She wore pants and a man's jacket. She didn't look directly at him and mumbled something he couldn't hear before she moved back into the ranks of the people.

"My brother's children," Piatelli explained proudly.

"We're wasting time," Barraka said impatiently. "We must be out of here in a matter of minutes."

Barraka's eyes swept over the people pressed against the wall. For a moment, he found himself looking at Sarah. He hadn't realized she had moved away from the table.

Suddenly a woman cried out. "No . . . no . . . he's not dead. . . . My Nello isn't dead."

Another woman answered, "He is, Claudia. . . . You know he is. Please give him to me."

Barraka stiffened. He pointed the flashlight at the place where the voices came from. The beam fell on three women. He couldn't tell whether they were young or old. All of them were skeletal-looking. One cradled a child in her arms. The other two appeared to be trying to take the child from her. All of them looked toward him.

"He's not dead," the woman holding the baby sobbed. "Come look at my baby. He's just asleep."

Barraka wasn't prepared for what he saw. Despite the smell in the room, he was forced to take several deep breaths.

"To answer your question before you ask," Piatelli said, "the child is dead. Unless it is taken away from her, she will hold it in her arms until the soldiers tear it away and throw it on the garbage truck with the other bodies. There is no differentiation between the body of an adult or child, man or woman. Each is stripped naked and tossed into the garbage truck."

Barraka shook his head. He tried to speak. He wanted to say something that would ease their pain. But the words wouldn't form.

"Move your torch to the right," Piatelli told him. "There where the light is are two dead men. They too will be thrown on the garbage truck and taken away. Two or three die each night, especially among the very old and very young."

Barraka switched off his flashlight. Prickles raced down his back. An involuntary shudder shook him. He was in a cold sweat. He could feel his hands tremble and his stomach churn.

A woman's wordless scream slashed across Barraka's consciousness. The dead child had been wrested from its mother. To clear the knot in his throat, he swallowed several times. . . . The Germans really intended to kill these people for no other reason than that they were Jews. It was unimaginable, but it was true: The nightmare was real!

"Most of them will never make it across the mountains," Barraka answered, finding his voice. "Maybe none of them."

"But at least they will have tried to live," Piatelli said in a soft but passionate voice. "If they remain here, they will die; some here, and the rest in a camp in Germany."

Barraka hesitated. The silence in the room was so deep he could hear the roaring of his own blood. . . . If he succeeded, if he could lead these people to Switzerland, he'd have done something worth more than all the battles he had fought, worth as much as the bridges he someday hoped to build. Again, he looked at the people against the wall. Then to Piatelli, he said, "Crossing the mountains this time of the year is going to be the hardest thing any of them have ever done, and the Krauts will be after them all the way."

"There is no choice for them."

Barraka nodded. Despite Piatelli's lack of physical strength and his soft voice, the man was strong in a way that few men were.

"What can I do to help?" Piatelli asked.

"For now, answer my questions about the camp," Barraka said.

Crucci waited until he was certain Barraka was involved with Piatelli; then he made a dash for the guard building. In an instant, he was surrounded by soldiers.

The sergeant of the guard immediately summoned the duty officer.

"Tell the commandant," Crucci said, "I must speak to him. Tell him I have a message from Major Radish, the Eleventh Brigade's intelligence officer."

"Silence!" the duty officer shouted, slapping him hard across the face.

Crucci's head bounced back. Blood welled up in his mouth and gushed out of his nose.

"Lieutenant," Crucci said, spitting the blood from his mouth, "you'll have to answer to Captain Muller for this."

The lieutenant frowned at him.

"Don't be a fool. Take me to the commandant," Crucci demanded, knowing from the expression on the officer's face that he would acquiesce to him.

It took Crucci less than two minutes to tell Gissiking why he was in the prison camp. Within moments, Gissiking was explaining the situation to Kunstler.

"Don't do anything until reinforcements arrive," Kunstler said. "I am dispatching two full platoons. I repeat, don't take any action that would alarm the partisans."

"Should I stop them if they attempt to leave?"

"Do nothing. The camp is probably surrounded by partisans. Let Crucci rejoin Barraka. Once reinforcements arrive, we'll be in a better position to repulse an attack by the partisans."

Kunstler summoned Radish and Muller.

Both men arrived at his office bleary-eyed and somewhat disoriented from having been aroused in the middle of the night.

Kunstler had had time between Gissiking's call and the arrival of his two subordinates to wash, shave, and dress properly, so he was awake and brimming with vitality. "Gentlemen, Major Barraka, three other partisans, and Mastrada are in the prison camp at Servigliano," he said.

Muller frowned. "Captured?"

Kunstler shook his head.

"Please explain," Muller said.

"First," Kunstler responded, enjoying his coup, "I must tell you I've ordered two full platoons to head for Servigliano. Radish, you'll ride with me. So will you, Muller; once we're there, you'll direct two squads of your own men. I want them to cover the northwest slope outside the camp. The remainder will surround the camp. Then we'll move against Barraka."

"Yes, sir," Muller answered.

"To answer your question," Kunstler said, "Barraka and the others managed to breach the security of the camp. He's there, I'd imagine, to make a reconnaissance. I can't tell you precisely why, but we'll soon know."

"If Barraka is now in the camp," Muller asked, "why hasn't Gissiking taken him prisoner?"

Kunstler looked at Radish.

"Five men could easily be captured or killed by the prison guards," Radish said, choosing his words carefully to avoid offering support to Muller, or offense to Kunstler.

"Five men, yes," Kunstler agreed. "But do you really think there are only five men involved?"

"That is the number you just told us were there," Muller said.

"Do you think that five men would go inside a guarded facility without the rest of the partisans waiting for them outside? No, gentlemen, I can tell you that a good part of Volterra's entire strength is there. Should anything happen to the men inside, they most certainly will attack the prison in strength."

"But our soldiers are—" Muller began.

"Prison guards," Kunstler said contemptuously.

"They're not soldiers. If they were, they wouldn't have been posted at Servigliano. I've been under attack from partisan units on the Russian front. I know what damage they can do."

"I hope Gissiking is free to act if the partisans try to leave the prison," Muller said.

"I told him not to do anything to alarm the partisans," Kunstler replied. "If he stops Barraka from leaving Servigliano, do you think the partisans waiting outside won't attack? I don't want the prison camp left in ruins. It's my responsibility to protect it, not to destroy it. And to destroy it for one American major is not the kind of price I'm willing to pay." He looked at his watch. "The troops should be ready by now. If you get your coats, we'll be on our way. The weather's none too good. I suggest you come armed. Radish, meet me outside."

As soon as he was alone, Kunstler poured himself two fingers of brandy to fortify himself against the remainder of the night. He looked at his watch. It was 2430.

"Figure," he said aloud, looking down at Dmitri, "it will take us thirty to forty minutes to arrive there, and after that—well, as long as it takes to kill or capture as many of the partisans as possible."

He walked to the closet, took out his leather trench coat, and picked up his gunbelt.

Kunstler slipped the luger free of its holster, took off the safety, cocked the pistol and put it back in the holster. The last time he had used the gun was on the Russian front. It had saved his life. He had shot a Russian soldier who had wounded him and had decided to finish the job with a bayonet. Kunstler buckled the gunbelt around his waist and left the office. He and Radish reached the door of the castle at the same time.

"This will be my first action," Radish said tightly.

"I know," Kunstler said. "It'll also be Muller's."

The two men climbed into the staff car.

"It's a mean night," Radish said.

"A good night to put an end to the partisans," Kunstler answered.

Immediately after Barraka and the other partisans were out of the camp, Volterra had ordered the rest of his force to move toward the camp at Servigliano.

He had his men take up positions in a drainage ditch that ran parallel to both sides of the road just beyond the range of the searchlights on the tower nearest the main gate. He was taking the only course of action left open to give Barraka some measure of protection.

Silently, Volterra cursed Barraka. He did not enjoy lying in a ditch with freezing rain beating down on him. Since his encounter with the German patrol two nights before, he and his men had been living out of doors, building makeshift shelters wherever they could. None of them had had any hot food, dry clothes or real sleep.

Koss came up to him. "Nothing looks out of joint at the camp," he said.

"It's hard to tell in this rain," Volterra answered. "But I tell you this, next time Barraka wants to do something like this, I'm going to—" He turned toward his left, where the road went down the mountain. "Trucks," he said. "I heard them shift gears as they started the climb."

"I'll pass the word," Koss said, already moving into the blackness.

Volterra summoned two of his men and told them to go down the road and have a look. "Come back here at a run," he said, "if there are troops in them."

Yancy approached Volterra. "Koss says we have trucks comin' up," he said.

"That's right. Tell the men to be ready."

Yancy scrambled out of the ditch and ran across the road to where the group of partisans was positioned.

"Get ready. Trucks comin' up," he told them, as he settled down behind the BAR. He glanced at Rinata, who was close by.

She smiled at him.

"Take care," he told her in a whisper. "Wouldn't want any of those nice titties to get hurt."

"What about the rest of me?"

"What about it?"

She flung a clump of mud at him.

"Okay, okay, take care of that nice pussy too."

"That's better," she laughed softly. "That's much better. I like a man to appreciate all of me."

Yancy looked down the road. The sound of the trucks was pronounced.

"Troops," one of the two men said breathlessly, as he dropped beside Volterra.

"How many?"

"Five truckloads and two command cars."

"Where's Angelo?"

"Following the trucks."

Volterra began moving along the drainage ditch to tell the other men to wait for him to fire before they opened up.

The lead truck came into view. Its yellow blackout lights barely showed through the heavy downpour.

Volterra told the men to spread themselves out. He wanted to give them an ample field of fire. The first truck passed him. Its windshield wipers just about kept up with the torrent of freezing rain. He could see the driver hunched over the wheel, peering into the blackness.

He hoped the sound of the firing would alert Barraka to the danger and force him to leave.

Koss came up to him. "Do you think he'll get out okay?"

"Let's hope so."

Two of the trucks rolled by, followed by the command car.

Volterra could see two figures in the rear but he couldn't identify either one. Another truck passed. Its rear tarpaulin was rolled back around the arch-shaped frame. The benches were occupied by soldiers in full battle gear.

Another command car passed. Again there were two officers in the rear whom he could not make out. The last truck was in view.

"It begins now," Volterra said, raising his rifle.

"As good a time as any," Koss said.

Volterra aimed for the driver of the last vehicle and squeezed the trigger.

An instant later a barrage of small arms fire erupted from both sides of the road. The rear truck slewed sideways and came to a stop with its front angled into the drainage ditch. Two other trucks left the road. One of them turned over and exploded into flames.

"Keep firing," Volterra called to his men. "Keep firing." He had the advantage and meant to keep it.

Kunstler's driver stopped and rolled to the ground.

Kunstler and Radish dropped out of the car. Muller followed. Kunstler tried to see where the fire was coming from. He had his luger out, but couldn't find a target.

"The ditches," a soldier shouted. "They're firing from the ditches."

A grenade was lobbed toward the ditch on the right side of the road. The explosion threw mud in every direction.

"Use your grenades," Volterra shouted, tossing one toward the truck nearest him. It shattered the windshield and tore the metal top off.

The flames from three burning trucks cast a red glow over the nearby road and woods.

The crack of the rifle fire was constant.

The Germans were firing from a prone position, using the meager cover of burning trees.

Kunstler bellied over to two dead soldiers, took their rifles and ammo belts and brought them back to where Radish and Muller were. "Start firing," he said, "if you want to see the morning."

"This is your doing," Muller screeched.

"What?"

"You and the Jews," Muller shouted. "You betrayed the Fatherland."

"You're crazy!"

"Jew lover!" Muller screamed.

More and more fire was being directed at them.

"Shut up," Kunstler ordered. "Your screaming will get us all killed."

"I'll kill you myself," Muller yelled, pointing his pistol at him.

Kunstler didn't hesitate. The showdown between them had come at an unexpected time and place. He snapped the rifle he was holding over toward Muller and pulled the trigger twice. The first round struck Muller in the chest and knocked him over on his side; the second struck him in the face, turning it into a mass of bleeding flesh. Then he turned the rifle toward the partisans and began to fire at them.

After a few minutes Kunstler shouted to several of the officers to pull back toward Malveno.

Two trucks exploded.

Radish fired as rapidly as he could. A sharp pain slashed into his right arm. He glanced at it. Blood was pouring from it.

"Shit!" he exclaimed and continued to fire.

Gradually, the Germans were able to fall back.

"Keep at them," Kunstler shouted.

"Don't let them put their heads up."

For several minutes they poured heavy fire into the drainage ditches along the side of the road. Then they continued to pull back.

Volterra and his men harried them all the way down the mountain.

* * *

Barraka rested his elbows on the top of the table. He wanted desperately to light his pipe but realized the smell of burning tobacco would be unsettling to the people who had been denied it for as many weeks as they had. "Are there ever guards outside the fence?" he asked.

"Never," Piatelli answered. "The men in the towers are sufficient."

"Where are the arms stored?"

"Near the barracks."

"Are you sure?"

"They can't be anywhere else. The other side of the camp is a fuel storage area."

"Are the top wires of the fence electrified?"

"No."

"Has anyone attempted to escape?"

"No."

"How many guards?"

"Fifty."

"All German?"

"No. At least fifteen are Italian. The Italians are used for internal security. They check us several times a day. But only Germans man the towers."

"Could you give me a layout of the guardroom?"

"No," Piatelli answered. "I have never been anywhere near there."

Barraka looked over his shoulder at Mastrada. "Have you any questions?"

"How many old people do you have and how many children?"

"About fifty men and women over sixty and at least the same number of children below the age of ten."

Barraka shook his head. "You know they're not

going to have a snowball's chance in hell of ever making it."

"Major, at least there will be odds. Here there are none."

Barraka stood up and reaching across the table, he offered Piatelli his hand. "I want you to divide your people into groups of twenty-five. Mix the old with the young and strong. Each group will have its leader and assistant leader."

"Is there anything else?" Piatelli asked, getting to his feet.

Barraka actually pulled him up. The man was so light, almost weightless it seemed. "Don't do anything unusual," he warned. "We don't want to tip our hand to the Krauts. They could put a ring of steel around this place that could stop us cold."

"I'll wait for your message. . . . But how will we know when to be ready?" Piatelli asked.

"Be ready all the time," Barraka answered. "You'll know when we're here. You'll know, and so will the Krauts."

The two of them walked to the door.

"Did you know that the word *barrak* in the Hebrew language means lightning?" Piatelli asked, taking Barraka's hand. "It is a fitting name for you, major."

Barraka flushed. He was about to speak when two muffled explosions stopped him. "Those didn't come from lightning," he said. He was on his feet and at the door with Mastrada close behind him.

"I heard them," Fontana said.

"We better get the hell out of here. . . . That's rifle fire," Barraka told him, looking toward the road beyond the main gate. "Okay, get the others. . . . We damn well might have to fight our way out of here. . . . Stay inside," he called over his shoulder to Piatelli. "No matter what happens out here, you and your people stay inside."

Barraka ran toward the fence.

Conway joined him.

"There's firing—"

"Yes," Conway said, "I heard it. I was beginning to wonder whether you had."

Crucci came up to them.

"Where the hell were you?" Fontana asked Crucci. "I tried to get your attention before I heard the firing."

"I had to piss," Crucci answered.

The five of them made a dash for the hole in the fence. "Go through the powerhouse," Barraka shouted. "We won't have time to go out the way we came in."

Barraka rushed into the powerhouse. Lowering his carbine, he pushed the barrel through the steel bars and pulled off three rounds. The first caught the guard nearest him and flung him to the floor. The other two rounds hit the second man in the stomach and in the shoulder.

"Blow the fucking door," he ordered.

The four of them lobbed grenades at the wall. With a roar, the concrete dissolved into a cloud of dust and fragments.

They rushed against the steel door and pushed it open. They could hear the Germans shouting from the towers, while the searchlight beams were sliding over the ground outside the prison camp.

"Shoot the bastard out," Barraka said.

"I'll get it," Fontana answered. He stopped and raised his rifle.

A burst of machine gun fire stitched across his chest. He dropped without firing a shot.

Barraka, Mastrada, Conway, and Crucci scrambled down the side of the mountain with machine gun bullets ricocheting off the rocks around them.

XI

The morning sky was bright with sunshine. Kunstler was back in his office, looking drawn and rumpled. His boots and trousers were spattered with dried mud and there were large patches of dirt and spent powder on his face. He reeked of sweat and smoke.

After a forced march, the remnants of his force had reached Malveno. He had lost more than half his men. Only a few of the wounded had managed to survive. Radish was one of the lucky ones. And as for Muller—well, he had seen similar things happen on the Russian front many, many times. Now that the man was dead, Kunstler didn't waste any pity on him. He had hated the man and wasn't in the least bit sorry he had been forced to kill him. He had threatened him; he had had no choice but to pull the trigger first. Radish would back him in any court of inquiry. But to avoid that, he would list Muller with the other casualties of the action.

Kunstler looked down at the draft of the report he

had written to army headquarters and ground his teeth together. He had experienced similar actions in Russia, and because of them he had come to respect the partisans' ability to fight. But obviously, he realized, he had not respected it enough to have sent out point men. He had, in fact, moved up a twisting mountain road in utter blindness. He shook his head at his own mistake.

He was galled to have been so much on the mark about what Volterra would do with the main body of partisans and yet to have misjudged where they would be. He had expected them to be on the slopes just below the camp. That would have been their best position to mount an assault against the camp; that would have been where he would have placed his own men in a similar situation.

"But that is not where they were," he said aloud. "They were along the road, waiting for me!" He brought his clenched fist down on the desk.

Kunstler left his desk and went to the wall map. The more he studied it, the more confounded he became by what was so blatantly a useless mission. Freeing the Jews, especially at this time of year, would be an empty gesture. They couldn't go anywhere.

A knock at the door made him turn and call out, "Come in, Radish." He strode toward the door and when Radish entered, greeted him with a vigorous handshake. "Well, how does it feel to have—"

Radish flapped his bandaged arm. "It's nothing. Only a flesh wound. But the doctor says I'll carry a scar."

"And whenever you look at it, you'll remember where and how you came by it," Kunstler told him. "I know. I have my own." And he patted his right thigh. "I can even tell you what the man looked like who shot me. Did I ever mention to you that I shot him?" Kunstler walked back to his desk. "He was going to finish me with a bayonet. The Russian soldiers were told to conserve their ammunition and to use the bayonet whenever possible. I saw him coming at me and shot him in the face. His whole head dissolved, but his body kept moving. I tried to pull myself out of his path, but couldn't manage it. When the medics found me, my legs were wrapped around him."

Radish sat down in the chair next to the desk. From the display of friendship, he knew Kunstler was deeply troubled by what had happened and probably concerned about the repercussions from army headquarters.

Kunstler opened his cigarette box and offered one to Radish. "Well," he said, letting the smoke stream out of his nostrils, "what do you have to say?"

"For one thing, I've developed an intense hate for the partisans."

"Being wounded by one of them can do that."

"And as for the Jews," Radish said, "the faster we get them out of here, the better off we'll be."

Kunstler leaned back. "I won't argue with you on that point. But we must try to know what the partisans will do next. No matter how you look at the Jews of Servigliano, they can't go anywhere."

"Then you're assuming the Jews will be freed from the camp?"

"Not at all. I'm trying to find a rational explanation for what happened and what might happen."

"Are you going to ask headquarters for more troops?"

Kunstler's face darkened. "That kind of request would go straight to Kesselring and invite questions I'm not in the position to answer." He put his forefinger on the draft of the report. "This will raise enough comment. We'll make do with whatever manpower we have. I'd much prefer headquarters to offer reinforcements than to ask for them."

"I see your point," Radish said.

"By the way, Barraka and his men shot their way out. They killed two men and blew open a door made of steel bars. One of their men was killed by machine gun fire."

"Does Gissiking know how they got in?" Radish asked.

"They cut their way in. But why? What did they gain? No one went out with them. What was Barraka's purpose?"

Radish went to the wall map. "If we were closer to the sea," he said, "I could understand what the partisans would try to do. But we're too far away."

"I have called army intelligence and spoken to General Von Steiglitz. I asked for an estimate of what might happen. They have an overall view of things and perhaps can come up with a reasonable explanation. He said he'd be back to me before thirteen hundred hours. It's close to that now."

Radish sat down again. He didn't have too much faith in the ability of army intelligence to give a reasonable answer. So far they had not been able to predict one Allied landing from Sicily to Anzio, and they were usually wrong about the strength of the Allied forces.

"I also asked the general if his section had that additional background information you requested on Barraka and the other two Americans," Kunstler commented. "He said he would check into it."

For a few moments neither of the men spoke. Then Radish asked. "Have they brought back Muller's body yet?"

"None of them have been brought back," Kunstler answered. He purposely said nothing about the incident.

"Would you prefer me to write to his parents?"

"Yes, thank you."

Radish nodded.

The phone rang. Kunstler answered, put his hand over the mouthpiece, and told Radish that General Von Steiglitz was calling.

Kunstler managed to keep his voice noncommittal. "Yes, general, I am indeed anxious to know what the estimation of the situation is. What? Are you sure? Yes, general . . . and the tentative date is November seventeenth . . . yes, thank you. You expect to have information on the three Americans by tomorrow at the latest. Again, thank you, general."

Kunstler put the phone down. "They expect the camp to be assaulted by combined teams of Rangers and Commandos and that the Jews will be airlifted out. I've been ordered to prevent their escape at all costs."

"Airlifted out?"

"That's what I was told," Kunstler said in a tired voice. "That's precisely what I was told."

* * *

Immediately after Volterra broke off the action against the Germans, he ordered his men back to pick up the arms and the ammo from the dead Germans. Then they returned to their initial position and met Barraka, who suggested they leave the area around Servigliano and Monte San Martino for more secure positions.

Volterra led them north and west to a place where there was a forest of pine trees. They finally made camp at 0930 in the morning.

Though every one of them was exhausted, they were too flushed with their victory to sleep. Here and there, they started small fires and while warming their hands spoke in low tones about the ambush.

Barraka sat with his back against a tree and looked around. The fight had taken its toll. Though none of the partisans involved had been killed, five had been wounded, two of them seriously.

Barraka stood up. Taking hold of his staff, he made his way to where Volterra and Mastrada were resting. Hunkering down in front of them, he said, "The Krauts know what's going on, or they're soon going to make some damn good guesses about it. Because we don't have the element of surprise anymore, we're going to have to move quickly now."

"Mastrada thinks someone betrayed us," Volterra replied, looking down at the pine needle-covered ground.

"Anyone in particular?"

Mastrada looked questioningly at Volterra, who nodded.

"Wait a minute," Barraka told him, "since we're going to have a serious discussion, I want Koss, Yancy, Conway, and Rawlins in on it." And turning around he called to all of them. When they were assembled, he said, "I want you to sit down and make yourselves as comfortable as possible. This is going to be a long one."

"The only thing I could use now," Yancy laughed, "is a long sleep and a long drink of booze."

"Mastrada," Barraka said, "thinks we've got an informer in the unit. I wanted you men here when he names him."

Yancy's smile turned to a grim expression of anger.

"When we were in the prison," Mastrada started to explain.

"Excuse me," Conway said, "but before any names are given, I would like to preface whatever will be said by telling everyone that while I was a guest of the Jerrys at Servigliano several of the officers boasted to me that they knew every move you chaps would make before you made it—or at least most of your moves. Leftenant Rawlins, did you ever hear Jerry make any comments along those lines?"

"No, sir," Rawlins answered.

Conway looked at Mastrada and said, "I did not mean to interrupt but I thought you would want to know about it."

"Yes," Mastrada answered, "it is very interesting in light of what happened . . . Barraka positioned us inside the camp so that each man would be able to cover the other's field of fire, or most of it. I covered Crucci's, and Fontana, God rest his soul, covered mine. About ten minutes after we were in position, I tried to get Crucci's attention. But I couldn't. I tried several times. Then when the firing outside the camp started, I tried again. The third time, he answered by showing himself and waving. Later when I asked where he was, he told me he turned away to take a piss."

"Piss, my ass!" Yancy exclaimed.

"Koss," Barraka said, "you and Yance bring him here . . . he damn well better have good answers."

The two men started to their feet.

"Wait," Volterra said, holding up his hand. "If Crucci is an informer, I think it would be better if we used him for our own purposes rather than—"

"We're already doing that with Garjulio," Barraka said. "Crucci is with us. He can do a great deal of harm if he lets the Krauts know what we're going to do."

"Suppose we kill him," Volterra said, "and suppose he is scheduled to make contact with the Germans or someone who will carry the information for him to the Germans."

"What's all this supposin' goin' to get us?" Yancy asked.

"If Crucci doesn't show up," Mastrada said, "then the Germans will know we have found him out and probably killed him."

"Serve the fucker right!" Yancy exclaimed.

"Perhaps," Volterra said, shaking his head. "But I would like to know who his contact is, and if it comes to killing him, I assure you it can be done anytime. You have my word on it, I will do it myself, if it should need doing."

"Okay," Barraka responded. "He's your responsibility. I want him watched, and at the first sign that he's up to something—I'm holding you to your word, Chaim—you kill him."

"Absolutely, Mitch."

The two men looked at each other. It was the first time they had both addressed each other by their given names. Each nodded to the other and smiled.

Barraka filled his pipe and lit it before he said, "Now we have to find the way to get those people out of the camp, and I can tell you, it's not going to be easy. Any suggestions?"

"We might call for an airborne assault," Koss said.

"Then we'll have to get the jump boys and ourselves back through Kraut-held country after we bring the people up to the border. The more of us, the less chance any of us will have to make it back to our own lines."

"There is a large conduit," Conway offered. "We could use it as a tunnel. Perhaps dig at right angles to it?"

"It would take too long," Volterra said. "The Germans know we are going to try something. They too will remember the tunnel."

"Blow away part of the mountain," Yancy said. "I have enough plastic to do the job."

Barraka was about to reject that idea when Conway said, "Now there is something in that, major. But not exactly the way the sergeant suggested. Suppose instead, you arrange for an air strike . . . a low-level strike that would give Jerry a very difficult time."

"Possibility," Barraka answered, looking toward Volterra.

Volterra agreed.

"Is there a secondary target nearby that is of military value?" Barraka asked.

"A machine works," Volterra said, "that is used for repairing motor vehicles and some tanks."

"How far away?"

"Twenty kilometers to the southwest."

"That could be the secondary target," Barraka said. "Now I need some time to work out the overall plan, but by tomorrow night, I will ask for the air strike. I think if we're lucky, very lucky, we'll be able to pull it off. But it will require split-second timing, and once we have them out of the camp, the real work begins." He shook his head. "I still don't believe we can do it. A good many of those people won't make it to the border, and those that do will be in damn sad shape. But we're here to try," he said, getting to his feet, "and we will sure as hell try!"

"I don't think we should remain here too much longer," Mastrada said.

"An hour?" Barraka asked.

"No longer," Mastrada answered.

"Just some time to sleep."

"We could all use it," Volterra said, hiding a yawn behind his hand.

With his head pillowed by a blanket roll, Barraka looked up at the blue sky overlaid with a tracery of slender dark branches and green pine needles. Several times he closed his eyes and tried to sleep. But there was still too much adrenaline in his blood for him to relax, even though he was tired.

Because it gave him something to do, he mentally composed a letter to Kip, telling him things that the censors would never let pass. Explaining where he was, who he was with and why he was there. Had he actually written the letter he would also have said: *It is not the kind of mission I want or one that I think will be successful. All my previous experiences with partisans were in the nature of hit and run raids. Sometimes we'd go after an ammo dump, other times it would be something to do with communications or transportation. It was never concerned with the welfare of people other than the men on the mission. But this one is entirely different. This one has to do with people. To be more precise it has to do with three hundred or more Jews . . . I tell you Kip, I was inside the prison not more than twelve hours ago and the stench of the place is still in my nostrils. The men and women inside were more like phantoms than creatures of flesh and blood. These people are slated to be shipped to a death camp in Germany. . . . Kip, I still find it difficult to believe that there are death camps. But I have seen with my own eyes this camp at Servigliano, which is no more than a holding pen for the prisoners until transportation is available to move them into Germany, and I tell you that nothing you might imagine would come anywhere near the reality of the place.*

Barraka paused in his thoughts. He was somewhat surprised by his own reaction to what he had seen at Servigliano during his brief visit. He had not realized that the experience had had such a marked effect on him.

He sat up and looked around. Except for the men assigned to guard the others, everyone was either asleep or resting. He settled against a tree and returned to composing the letter to his father.

The leader of these people—of the Jews—is a man named Piatelli. Strange, I just realized that I've forgotten his first name. In time, I guess I will find out what it is. This man, in some strange way, reminds me of you. Not that you are in the least alike physically. He is very slender, but about your height. But he has blue eyes. Their color is the same as yours and they are set the same way in his skull. He is a rabbi. Have you ever met a rabbi? He is also about your age. Piatelli has no illusions about the battle that must be fought to free his people and the terrible ordeal that awaits them in their trek to the Swiss border. Many will not survive but those that do will have a chance for a new life. The risk is worth everything. They all know that once they reach the camp in Germany they will be killed. I guess it is better to die like a man than be slaughtered like a sheep. Piatelli has his nephew and niece with him. His brother's children.

Barraka stopped. Suddenly he remembered, or thought he remembered, what Sarah must have said to him. She had mumbled: "*We have been delivered into your hands.*" He was certain those were her words.

Barraka shook his head, stood up, picked up his staff and walked to where the trees gave way and the land sloped up to a small, rock-strewn ridge. Having remembered Sarah's words, he was disturbed by them. They had a meaning that did not rest easily with him. They put a burden on him that far surpassed the one he already had.

He went up to the ridge. From it he could see a splendid panorama of mountains, dazzling blue sky, and towering white clouds that truly looked like castles in the air. The letter he had mentally written to Kip faded from his thoughts and was replaced by the uneasiness engendered by what Sarah had said.

"They're not sure as hell delivered into my hands," he whispered. "If she thinks that, then she must be nuts." Again he shook his head. Turning, he was about to start down when he saw Volterra coming up toward him.

"I could not sleep either," Volterra explained. "One of the guards said he saw you go up the ridge."

Barraka was going to ask him what he thought about what Sarah had said but changed his mind. For some strange reason, he suddenly felt those words were meant for him and for no one else. And for him to have shared them with anyone else would have been wrong: the violation of something secret between him and her, though he did not fail to realize the absurdity of that, either.

"We are going to have to move in a few minutes," Volterra said.

"Where to now?"

"Toward the mountains," Volterra said, "and then back toward Servigliano . . . we must act soon, Mitch, or we will be too late."

Barraka nodded and said, "It must be perfect. We won't get a second chance."

"We might not be able to afford the luxury of a perfect plan," Volterra said, as they started down the slope. "Kunstler is going to try to move the date up for shipping the prisoners. . . . The sooner he gets them out of the way, the less trouble he will have with us. He knows that."

"The Krauts must be monitoring our radio—"

"I arranged certain code words with Keller before I left," Volterra said. "I'm sure Fennly has them."

"What do you call an air strike?"

"A home run," Volterra answered.

"A what?"

"A home run. Medical supplies is a base on

balls . . . an ammo drop is bases loaded . . . Keller was a baseball enthusiast. He played semiprofessional for a while. Didn't you know that?"

"No," Barraka said in a quiet voice. "He never mentioned it."

Barraka stood in front of a pine tree. Volterra, Mastrada, Koss, Yancy, Conway and Rawlins were gathered in a semicircle around him.

"I've worked out the details of our attack on Servigliano," Barraka said. "I'll lay it out, and if there are any questions, I'll answer them afterwards." He paused a moment. "Before I go into the operation, I want to know if any of you has any doubt about the physical layout of the camp and the topography about it? Okay, here's the plan.

"There'll be five coordinated attacks. The first will be the air strike. That will be directed against the main gate and the barracks on one end of the camp and the fuel storage and ammo dump at the other end. The strikes will be directed by me. They should take no more than three minutes. I'll let you know the precise time as soon as I know it.

"When the planes finish, we go into action. Yancy and six men will blow the east portion of the mountain . . . Yancy, I want it to sound like a mortar attack."

"Will do," Yancy answered. He was chewing on a dried blade of grass.

"Mastrada, you take a dozen men and hit the camp from the north. Keep the machine gunners busy in the northeast and northwest towers. If possible, knock them out."

"Okay," Mastrada said.

"A third group of fifteen men under the command of Major Conway will take up a position on either side of the road below Servigliano and stop anything attempting to come up. As soon as the air strike is over you come up top at a run and using the boulders in front of the camp, take up positions that will allow you to cover the main entrance.

"When the first prisoners come through, start moving them away from the camp. Go north. That means leaving the road. Understand?"

"Yes, sir," Conway responded.

"Two machine guns will be placed in the rocks, covering the gate. Koss and I will use them to stop the Krauts when they come after the prisoners."

"A fourth group under Volterra's command will go into the camp and bring the prisoners out. This will include most of the men not involved in the other units, with the exception of a dozen, who will be under the command of Lieutenant Rawlins. This group will hit the machine shops at San Viglio. They will attack immediately after the air strike. They'll join us on the march, north of here.

"Just to play it safe, I don't want any of this to get to the men until just before the attack. Each of you has your assigned sectors. The job is simple. Get Piatelli and his people out and kill as many Krauts as you can. Volterra will have the main responsibility of moving Piatelli and his people through the gate.

"Once that attack commences, most of the people are going to be scared out of their wits. Some might even be too frightened to move. It will be up to the men to move them.

"Wounded will not be taken. The people should be organized into groups of twenty-five; that should make them easier to control. Now, are there any questions?"

Barraka took out his pipe and sucked on the stem. Though he was used to telling men what to do, this somehow, he felt, was very different.

"About the wounded," Yancy asked, "what do we do with them?"

Barraka heaved a deep sigh and looked toward Volterra. "I don't see that we have much choice," he said, in a lower tone than he had been using. "Our men are supplied with cyanide capsules. They'll take them rather than be captured. But the others—what do you say, Chaim? What do we do with the wounded?"

"They can't be left for the Germans," Volterra answered.

Realizing the final decision was his responsibility, Barraka said, "They must be shot."

For a few moments none of the men moved or spoke.

Then Barraka asked, "Are there any other questions?"

"How long do we expect the entire action to last?" Rawlins asked.

"Fifteen, twenty minutes, at the most."

"Mitch," Volterra said. "I want you to make one change in your plans. I'll stay with Koss at the machine guns to cover you."

Barraka was about to object but changed his mind. "All right, you stay with Koss. Are there any other questions? Okay. You have the plan. It's not complicated. We should be able to carry it off. But once we have Piatelli and his people out, the hard part of the mission begins. We're going to have the mountains, the weather, and the Krauts against us. But maybe we'll be lucky. Maybe."

The meeting was over. With the exception of Volterra and Koss, the other men went off to get some sleep.

Later the same night Barraka, Koss, and Volterra huddled around the radio. A hard, cold wind had come up shortly after they had reached the ridge top on the north side of Monte Baldo. Their breath steamed in the night air.

"Is the radio on?" Koss asked.

"Yes," Volterra answered. "We should hear Captain Fennly any moment."

The radio began to static.

Volterra made some adjustments.

Fennly came on, using his own code name and calling for a response from Volterra.

Barraka took the mike. "This is operation Cross Over. I read you nine by nine."

"Roger, Cross Over."

"I need two sets of three home runs," Barraka said. "Do you read me?"

"Say again."

"I need two sets of three home runs."

"Negative."

"What the hell do you mean?"

"All home runs are being held."

"Listen, Fennly, this is Major Barraka, you damn well better get me those home runs with the right team or when I come back there, I'm going to blow your goddamn head off."

"Home runs can only be hit a certain distance."

"Captain, patch me into Colonel Dodd," Barraka said.

"The colonel is here."

"Your request is denied," Dodd said. "You do the best you can for your people without home runs."

"Listen, this ball game wasn't my idea. . . . But now that I'm here, I'm damn well going to play it my way or I'll play games with this fucking radio until General Clark comes down on you like a ton of bricks. . . . Get that message, Dodd?"

There were several moments of silence before Captain Fennly said, "Request approved. Need twenty-four hours notice for home runs to be hit. . . ."

"Roger."

"Take care of your people. . . . Over and out."

Barraka wiped the sweat from his brow. He turned to Koss and said, "I'm going to kick the shit out of that Fennly when I meet up with him. . . . I swear to God I will!"

"Mitch," Volterra said, "you have a bad temper."

"Only when I'm angry."

"Yes, I've noticed that. Have you noticed that, Bill?"

"Not too often," Koss answered, forcing himself to keep a straight face.

"I guess," Volterra said, "he doesn't like being told that three hundred Jews are his people."

Barraka shook his head. "They're your people, Chaim. I'm just here to—"

"They're our people," Koss said.

"I guess they are," Barraka responded. "I guess they're our people."

XII

At 1300 hours Radish entered Kunstler's office and handed him the envelope that had come over by courier from army headquarters a few minutes before.

Kunstler was at his desk putting the finishing touches on his report to army headquarters. He had redrafted it four times, but now it was finished and he handed it to Radish. "Sit down and read it. If you have any suggestions for changes, please note them in the right-hand margin."

"You read the information on the Americans," Radish said. "There are photographs of the officers but not of the sergeant."

Kunstler picked up the envelope, opened it, and pulled out three sheets of paper and two photographs. The first sheet of paper contained additional information on Barraka: "Barraka Mitchell, Maj. 0-2395674; born Nov. 30th, 1916 Duluth, Minnesota. Father's given name Kip. Pres. of Duluth Gen. Bank. Mother's given name Anita. Former Canadian Citizen. Sub. of this report graduate Univer. Minnesota, BS in Civil

Eng. 1937. No prior mil. ser. Fluent in Italian, French, and Spanish. Played football in HS and University. Long distance runner. Between 1937 and 1941 owned and operated sm. const. comp. Enlisted Dec. 8th, 1941. Comm 2nd Lt. Aug. 1942. Worked with Ital. partisans 6x in the last 9 mo. Interviewed by Ernest Pyle for Stars and Stripes. Promoted to Maj. Sept. 3, 1943." The photograph showed an ordinary face. Perhaps somewhat boyish.

Kunstler placed the first sheet down on the desk and read the second one: "Koss, William; 1st Lt. 0-8967592, born Berlin Feb. 22, 1918. Father's given name Otto. Father employed as a model maker by Sperry Corp. Mother's given name, Frida. Both parents left Germany in 1934. Sub. this report graduate City College of New York BA degree in Education 1938; enlisted Feb. 3, 1941. Com. 2nd Lt. Sept. 8, 1942. Former English and German teacher New York City school system. No prior mil. tran or ser. Has been with Maj. Barraka on three missions." Koss had a slightly more interesting face than Barraka. But he didn't appear to be very Germanic-looking.

He set the second sheet on top of the first and read the last one: "Yancy, Jack, Sgt RA 958634. Demo Expert. Enlisted Sept. 2, 1938. Court Martialed 2x. Served a total of eight months in stockade. Date and place of birth unknown. Age, not more than 30. No family. Has been with Barraka on all 6 missions."

Kunstler rapped the sheets with his fingers. "Not much to speak about," he said aloud. "The only professional is the sergeant. Barraka seems to have been lucky."

Radish finished reading Kunstler's report. "It's

fine," he said. "And objective. I don't think anyone in headquarters will find fault with it, or the way you handled the situation."

"I assumed we would encounter the partisans," Kunstler said. "But the weather made it impossible to see where they were."

"Absolutely," Radish answered. He knew Kunstler was covering his mistakes and wanted to be sure he would not at some future date take the cover off them.

"I've prepared a statement for your signature."

Kunstler stroked Dmitri's head. "The valley will be the place where the transports will land," he said. "There is no other area nearby that would give them the space they need to take off. Transports would have a difficult time getting in and out. Say there were fifty Jews per transport. That would mean they'd need a minimum of six. Say another three for the Rangers and Commandos. I don't think they'd attempt to make it back to their own lines on foot. The partisans, as usual, will melt away. But that means nine transport planes."

"Nine is right," Radish said. He went to the map and ran his forefinger along the Tenna Valley. "The nine transports would need at least twenty to thirty fighter planes to protect them."

Kunstler joined him at the map and said, "They could come from a carrier here in the Gulf of Genoa or from here in the northern area of the Adriatic. The Americans are adept at carrier operations."

Radish agreed.

"The way I think it will take place," Kunstler said, "is that the partisans will attack the camp at Servigliano, while the Rangers and Commandos will attempt to suppress our fire so that the transports will be able to land. We'll let them land, we'll even let them take the Jews from Servigliano—that is to say, we will not reinforce it. When the Jews reach a point within, say, five hundred meters of the transports we'll have our artillery open up and destroy the transports. Then the Jews will have no choice but to go quietly back to the camp at Servigliano and wait their eventual shipment to Germany."

"Then we'll emplace our artillery along the sides of the valley?"

"Yes. Four batteries of eighty-eights would do nicely. . . . Have them cover an area a thousand yards long and fifty yards wide. The transports will put down where the valley flattens out, here toward the east."

"What will we do about the Rangers and Commandos?"

"Take them prisoner whenever possible," Kunstler said. "I don't think we need concern ourselves with the partisans. Once they realize what's happening they'll make a run for it."

"Do you want me to write the orders for all of this?" Radish asked.

"I'd appreciate it," Kunstler answered. "I want to move three battalions of infantry into position along with the artillery. Once the planes are destroyed, I want them to be able to move against the Rangers and Commandos as swiftly as possible."

"Say, ten seconds after the barrage ends."

"Ten seconds would be excellent," Kunstler replied with a smile. "This time we'll put an end to partisan activity in this area once and for all. I also want you to offer a reward of five thousand American dollars for information that leads to the capture or death of each of the three Americans. Put out handbills. And, oh yes, try to get word to Crucci that if he tells us where we can find Volterra and Barraka, or when the attack on Servigliano will come, we would be willing to pay him ten thousand American dollars."

"He'd crawl through hell for that price," Radish laughed.

Kunstler poured himself a two-finger glass of brandy. "Join me?" he asked.

Radish nodded. Kunstler, once so distant, was now as amiable as a man could be.

"To our success," Kunstler said.

Radish touched his glass to Kunstler's.

General Kurt Wolfe, special assistant to General Kesselring, had flown into Malveno late in the afternoon. The single engine monoplane set down in a small field immediately outside of the town.

The first Kunstler had known of Wolfe's arrival had come from his own breathless aide-de-camp who had told him about it.

Kunstler had ordered his car to pick up the general and bring him to the castle. And now he, the general, and Radish were seated at a small table, covered with a white linen tablecloth and decorated with pine needle sprigs.

"A marvelous dinner," Wolfe said, "especially the wine." And he offered his glass to be refilled by the waiters who served him. "It's good to see that the amenities of civilized living have not been abandoned by you and your staff." He spoke in a peculiarly nasal tone that was out of keeping with his size. He was a stout man with a round face, several chins, and a completely bald pate. His eyes were small, brown, and very bright. His reputation as a gourmand was well known, as was his penchant for pubescent women. He was a friend of Hitler's from the old days and had always been a staff officer with varying degrees of authority and success.

Kunstler accepted the compliment with a modest nod. He had already spent part of the afternoon briefing Wolfe on the situation, but Wolfe had not made any remark that would give a clue to the real reason for his visit.

"I have some excellent cigars," Wolfe said. "We might enjoy smoking them in your office, colonel."

The three of them left the dining room. "You have a very comfortable headquarters," Wolfe commented, settling into the chair on the right side of Kunstler's desk. "It's almost as comfortable as home, though nothing is a substitute for what we have in the Fatherland."

Kunstler and Radish readily agreed to that.

"As you know, our position on the front here in Italy is not secure," Wolfe told them. "We're using it more to bleed the Allies than for anything else. The terrain is in our favor and they pay heavily for every meter they've taken. And because we are fighting so hard it will give them something to think about if they should bring the war to Germany proper."

"Is that a possibility?" Radish asked.

"Anything's possible," Wolfe answered. "But I don't think it will happen. Still, in Italy we must make the best of a bad situation, which is why I am here."

He paused significantly. "You see, we need some sort of a victory, something we can crow about to the people on the home front."

Kunstler knew exactly where Wolfe was going but he said nothing. The general was being swept along by his own words.

"We want you to foil the Allied attempt to rescue the Jews at Servigliano," Wolfe told him, looking straight at Kunstler. "We want you to become Germany's new hero. We are certain of their assault and we want them either destroyed or captured. Now you must tell me if you need more troops."

"Thank you, general, but we have enough," Kunstler said.

"From what you told me this afternoon," Wolfe said, "I can see that you've thought the action out . . . I agree completely with your defensive tactics."

"Thank you, sir."

"I cannot impress upon you the importance of this victory," Wolfe said. "We've not told the Führer about the Jews at Servigliano, but Himmler has dropped a few hints about an impending victory. You know the Führer—he has been scanning his maps looking for the place where that victory will happen. He's too proud to ask where, but rest assured, when it happens he'll be very pleased. I've been authorized to tell you that you'll become a general within twenty-four hours of the destruction of the Allies' assault team."

"We'll do our best," Kunstler answered.

"I must add that if the Jews are rescued—well, I don't think it necessary to go into that, because we both know the Jews will never be rescued, that they will be shipped to Germany on schedule. No, I'd much rather drink to your success and your forthcoming promotion."

"Wine or brandy?" Radish asked, getting up from his chair at the opposite side of the desk.

"Brandy, please," Wolfe said.

Each man held his glass, while Wolfe toasted Kunstler's success and the destruction of the Allies.

Pleased, Kunstler smiled. His heart was still pounding.

Barraka and his group of partisans circled back into the area around Servigliano and Monte San Martino. The large groups dissolved into smaller units of twos and threes with strict orders to avoid any contact with German patrols.

Barraka and Volterra surveyed the newly placed German 88s from a distance. Neither of them could figure out why the German infantry were so far east in the valley. They were encamped immediately behind the gun emplacements.

At night they returned to the village in San Martino and ate in Giorgio Pippi's house but dared not risk sleeping there.

Between Barraka and Volterra the final details of the attack were worked out. Not only would the secondary target be attacked by partisans, but some of the partisans involved on the assault on Servigliano would head west, leaving a broad trail for the Germans to follow. They would then break up into smaller units and rendezvous with the main body twenty kilometers to the north of Servigliano, at a place called Malcesine.

The two men also decided to call up more partisans from the other parts of Lombardy. Volterra assured Barraka that an additional thirty men could join their ranks within twenty-four hours.

Barraka set the date and the time for the attack on Servigliano. The air strike would take place just before sundown at 1645 hours on Friday, November 16th—three days away.

Word was sent out to the various units to group at 1500 in the woods on the southwest section of the Tenna Valley.

On the night before the assault, the group was at the table in Pippi's house. Very little was said. Barraka felt himself isolated from the others. He was anxious about the coming assault and tortured himself by thinking about the number of ways it could go wrong.

"Why don't all of you sleep here tonight," Giorgio offered. "It'll be a long time before you have a roof over your heads again."

"I'm for it," Yancy said. "What about it, Mitch?"

"What do you think?" Barraka asked, looking at Volterra.

Giorgio and his wife offered to remain awake all night. "If any one comes up the road," Giorgio said, "I'll hear them."

Much later, as Barraka lay awake in bed across from Volterra, he said, "Listen, no matter how it goes tomorrow, we'll give the Krauts a good fight."

"I don't think the Germans are prepared for us."

"I've been thinking the same thing," Barraka said. "Those eighty-eights should be trained directly on Servigliano, if they were expecting an assault on the camp. A few rounds and—"

Barraka sat up. "I know it's a long shot, but what if the Krauts were purposely led to believe that a strike is going to be made at Servigliano."

"I don't understand."

"Suppose army intelligence lets the word out that the people in Servigliano are going to be rescued?"

Volterra pulled himself up. "The Germans would try to stop it."

"Right. And that would explain why the eighty-eights and infantry are concentrated in the valley. It's the only place where transports and gliders can land. Chaim, I'm sure that's why they're there. The Krauts think some sort of air rescue effort is going to take place."

"Where does that leave us?" Volterra asked.

Barraka lay down again. "We should have the element of surprise completely on our side. Kunstler has prepared for something that won't happen, at least not the way he expects. But I still want to know what we're going to face when we attack. . . . If I were Kunstler I'd put some combat troops in Servigliano."

"I thought about that, too," Volterra answered.

"Then you know why I must go down to Malveno to see what's there."

"I'll go," Volterra offered.

"Chaim, I've got to do it myself," Barraka answered.

After a pause, Volterra said, "Go into the cafe. The owner, Calvino, is one of us. Ask him if he thinks the snow will come early this year. He will answer, 'Probably.' Then you will say, 'The snow means a hard winter.' After that, he will answer whatever questions you have, or help you in any way he can."

"I'll leave in the morning," Barraka responded.

Neither of them spoke any more. And Barraka watched the tip of Volterra's cigarette flare red each time he took a drag.

After having circled ten kilometers to the south of Malveno during the early morning hours, Barraka was lucky enough to meet up with a farmer taking a load of hay into Malveno by cart. He purposely kept his conversation with the man sparse, mentioning only that he was on his way to Milano, where he had relations. By the time they reached the town, a cold, mizzling rain was falling.

Barraka left the farmer at the piazza. He thanked the man for the ride and wished him good luck. Then he started to walk across the empty piazza. He glanced toward the arched doorway of the castle, where the XVIth Infantry Brigade was headquartered. Two German soldiers stood guard. They looked miserable, even though they wore warm clothing and ponchos to protect them from the rain.

Barraka continued toward the cafe on the opposite side of the piazza. Because of the castle, the town was more picturesque than some of the others he had seen. He particularly liked the church, which stood opposite the castle and was an excellent example of Romanesque architecture.

When Barraka entered the cafe, he was surprised to find three of the tables occupied. Two by German soldiers. One of them was a sergeant, a big burly man wearing an Iron Cross on his tunic. At the other table were three Italians conversing in low voices but gesticulating wildly.

Barraka went up to the zinc-topped bar and sat down on a high chair with a rattan back. When Calvino came up to him, he ordered a Grappa. Then he looked over his shoulder at the soldiers. They weren't the prison guard variety. They were field soldiers. Veterans of a good many battles. Probably pulled back from the lines at the Sangro River to protect Servigliano. He wondered how many more had been moved to Servigliano.

Calvino set the Grappa in front of Barraka and started to move away. "Do you think the snows will come early this year?" Barráka asked.

Calvino stopped and moved back to where his customer sat. He looked hard at him before he answered, "Probably."

"The snow means a hard winter," Barraka commented.

Calvino nodded and was about to speak when the sergeant called for two more bottles of wine. "We'll talk," he said in a low voice; then he went for the two bottles.

Barraka looked toward the window. A lone German officer walked hurriedly toward the cafe. A few moments later he opened the door and the sergeant immediately called the men to attention.

The officer nodded and said something to the men that made them laugh.

The officer moved directly to the bar and sat down, leaving an empty chair between himself and Barraka.

Calvino immediately came to serve the newcomer.

"A Grappa, if you please," he said, turning his attention to Barraka.

Calvino poured the Grappa and handed the glass to the officer.

Barraka picked up his own drink and offered a silent toast.

The officer immediately said something in German.

Barraka shook his head and in Italian he told the officer that he did not speak German.

"My Italian is none too good," the officer said in halting Italian.

"But manageable," Barraka responded politely.

"If you wish, colonel," Calvino said, "I will translate for you." As he spoke he kept his eyes on Barraka.

Kunstler waved the offer aside. "Thank you, but I will try it alone." He moved into the chair that was closer to Barraka. "Are you from this area?" he asked.

"Modena," Barraka answered. "I'm on my way to Milano to see my brother." He realized he was sweating and that Calvino was still looking at him.

"Colonel Von Kunstler," he said, offering his hand.

"Salvatore Caliendo," Barraka answered, hoping his moist palm wouldn't betray the sudden surge of fear that welled up inside of him.

"I passed through Milano on my way here," Kunstler said. "It reminds me of the industrial cities in Germany."

"I have never been in Germany," Barraka answered.

Suddenly the sergeant asked for the bill, and from the delight of the other men, he had obviously said he would pay all of it.

As the sergeant left, Kunstler turned and saluted him. "A matter of courtesy," he explained. "The man earned his Iron Cross on the Russian front, where I earned mine."

Barraka nodded and ordered another Grappa. His stomach was twisted into a hard knot. He had difficulty keeping his hand steady as he raised the second glass of Grappa to his mouth.

The three Italians paid their bill and left.

Barraka ran out of things to say to Kunstler. With each passing minute, he was becoming more and more anxious. He realized he could take this opportunity to kill Kunstler. But that wouldn't do anything more than bring more troops into the area and make his mission not only more difficult, but more than likely impossible to carry out. Suddenly Barraka realized Kunstler was staring at him.

"Excuse me," Kunstler said. "I didn't mean to make you uncomfortable. But I have the strangest feeling that I know you."

Barraka's throat tightened. His heart began to race. "Sometimes that happens to me," he said, after clearing his throat. "I think I know someone but it turns out I was wrong." He wanted to run. But if he did, he knew he would be dead, either before he reached the door, or as he ran across the piazza. He couldn't move until Kunstler left.

"You're probably right," Kunstler said, with a smile. "I have never been to Modena."

"And I have never been to Germany," Barraka repeated.

Kunstler finished his drink and said to Calvino, "Put Signor Caliendo's drinks on my bill."

"Thank you," Barraka said. "But that isn't necessary."

"Please. I consider it a pleasure. I don't often have or take the opportunity to relax with someone willing to talk to me as a man and not as a soldier."

Barraka extended his hand. "We are, after all, men," he said.

"If you come this way on your return trip," Kunstler told him, "stop by and ask for me—Colonel Von Kunstler at the headquarters across the piazza—and we will drink together again. Perhaps," he added, "we might discover that we have a few other things in common than just a mutual liking of Grappa."

"I am sure we have many things in common," Barraka said, standing when Kunstler stood.

"*Auf Wiedersehen!*" Kunstler said, touching the tip of his fingers to the peak of his cap.

"*Ciao,*" Barraka answered. He waited until Kunstler was halfway across the piazza before he uttered a deep sigh of relief. Then he turned to Calvino and said, "I better get my ass out of here."

"As fast as you can," Calvino answered. "Before he remembers where he saw you."

Barraka nodded and left.

Kunstler hurried to his office, closed the door and removed a file folder from the desk. He bit his lower lip, and, drumming the fingers of his right hand on the desk, he stared at the folder.

He could hear the thumping beat of his heart. He had known fear on the Russian front, especially after he had been wounded. But now he was close to panic. He stopped drumming on the desk and opened the folder.

Barraka's photograph was on top.

"I could have had him," Kunstler whispered. "I could have had him and put an end to whatever the partisans are planning to do." He picked up the photograph and studied it. The face of the man he had seen in the cafe was certainly older-looking than the one in the photograph. Most of the boyishness in the picture was gone from the face. But three years in combat would do that. The man in the cafe looked tired. There were dark rings under his eyes. He had at least a two days' growth of beard on his face. The lines radiating from the edge of his nostrils and around the corners of his eyes were deeply cut. Again, that's what combat could do. But there was essentially no difference between the photograph and the face of the man who called himself Salvatore Caliendo.

A knock at the door made him quickly replace the photograph into the folder and then slip the folder into the drawer before he answered, "Come."

Radish entered. "I've assigned two more squads of regulars to Servigliano," he said.

"Excellent," Kunstler answered. "Excellent!" He wanted to tell him that he had met and spoken to Barraka. But he dared not. That meeting must forever remain his secret. He could never risk sharing it with anyone, not even his wife, who might, in her heart of hearts, come to the conclusion that he was a fool for not arresting Barraka then and there in the cafe. He himself could not answer the question of why he had not acted.

"Is anything wrong?" Radish answered.

"No," Kunstler lied. "Nothing is wrong."

Radish smiled and Kunstler smiled back.

Though Barraka hadn't told the partisans what their objectives would be, all of them knew it would be Servigliano. Crucci was becoming more and more afraid he would be killed in the attack. Rather than take the risk of being anywhere near Servigliano, he planned to desert. But he knew that leaving prematurely would make the other men suspicious and might, if any of them survived, cost him his life. Men like Volterra and Mastrada had many friends who would be willing to kill him on orders from either one of them. Despite his fear, Crucci postponed his flight until just before the attack. He would be able to slip away while they were moving into position.

He had made his decision to wait in the morning. But now, in the middle of the afternoon, as he was walking along a trail on the way up from a stream, he spotted Koss and Rawlins. The two commanders were so involved with what they were discussing that neither of them saw him.

Crucci stepped off the trail and dropped down behind a bush.

"If Barraka thinks we can do it, then we might have a chance," Koss said.

"But Switzerland is not just a walk away from here," Rawlins answered.

"It's Barraka's ball game and we have to play it by his rules," Koss said.

They started up the trail. Crucci waited out of sight before continuing. He knew Kunstler would be willing to pay a greast deal for the information he now had. Fortune had finally favored him. He changed his mind and decided not to wait to desert.

A few minutes later he was on his way, and, at a run, he headed for Garjulio's farm, making sure to keep off the roads.

Several times he slowed, but he never risked stopping. "God," he whispered aloud, "God keep me safe from harm." His chest ached and his breath steamed in the late afternoon air. Cramps developed in both his legs, forcing him to stop running and eventually to stop altogether. He rubbed his legs until the pain eased and then he started off again. Half the afternoon was gone. He'd reach Garjulio's sometime after the nightfall. He began to run again; then suddenly his left foot twisted out from under him. A flash of pain went through him. He tumbled to the ground.

Barraka and Volterra moved as close as they dared to the prison camp. It was the last reconnaissance they would make before the attack at sundown.

Barraka hadn't mentioned his meeting with Kunstler earlier in the day. All he told Volterra was that new troops had been brought back in from the front and that they looked as if they could handle themselves in a fight. But now he said, "I met with Kunstler this morning."

"Met him!" Volterra responded with surprise. "How the hell did you meet him?"

Barraka explained what had happened. "Kunstler

said he thought he knew me, or more accurately, that he had seen me before."

"Good God!"

Barraka shook his head. "How could he recognize me? Besides, if he knew who I was, he'd have grabbed me."

"Maybe luck will be with us yet," Volterra commented.

"Maybe," Barraka explained, handing the field glasses to Volterra. "There's more wire on the fence and a lot of concertina wire around the outside," he said.

"It's the changes I can't see that worry me."

"Maybe the Krauts will concentrate all their effort in the valley," Barraka answered.

"Let's hope they do."

"I'll take the people out through the main gate," Barraka said. "I'll keep moving all night and most of tomorrow, if necessary. Where will you be?"

"See those boulders there about forty meters from the gate," Volterra said, pointing. "Koss and I with a couple of other men will cover your getaway from there. . . . The Germans will have one helluva time finding us and another helluva time trying to get us."

Barraka waved his staff in front of him. "Too bad it hasn't the magical power to part the mountains. Instead, we must make our own path and depend on our guns to keep it open." He shook his head. "We'll still need a miracle to make it to the border."

"I know," Volterra replied. "But we have part of one now."

Barraka looked at him questioningly.

Volterra smiled but did not explain. Instead, he pointed to the tops of the mountains. "Snow Giants," he said. "The people in the mountains believe that when the wind blows the snow off the tops of the mountains like that, someone will die. They say that the Snow Giants dance to tell the people that death is near."

"Many will die before the night is over," Barraka said, looking up toward the tops of the mountains.

XIII

Toward sundown Barraka moved his men out of the woods and into their positions. Yancy and his group approached Servigliano from the east. Mastrada and his band moved toward the camp from the north, while Volterra, with the largest number of men, approached from the west. Barraka and Koss, with two other partisans, stayed with Volterra's group.

Earlier the men under the command of Lieutenant Rawlins had started toward the secondary target, where the machine shops were located. They had to be in position to attack immediately after the air strike.

A radio link was established between the various assault units. But once the attack started, all of the partisans knew they would be on their own.

The shadows in the valley were lengthening. Within a matter of minutes the searchlights on the towers at Servigliano would be turned on.

Barraka looked at his watch. "Three more minutes," he said.

"I can't believe the Germans haven't seen us," Koss whispered.

"Maybe we're lucky," Volterra said.

"We're not going to be so damn lucky," Barraka said, "if those Snow Giants decide to start to do their dancing down in the valley within the next few minutes."

"They'll stay up on the tops of the mountains," Volterra responded with a wry smile, "and send their little brothers and sisters—some rain and perhaps some snow—to dance down here."

Yancy's voice came on the radio. "Everything checks out here. Rinata sends her love."

"We send ours."

Mastrada reported in. Then Conway said he was in position and waiting. Rawlins's transmission was weak. Barraka checked his watch. One minute to go before the flyboys made contact. He rubbed his sweaty palms together and found his breath coming in short gasps.

"Those damn Snow Giants are moving to the west," Koss said.

Barraka looked up at the mountains. The light above was a smoky yellow blended with a very pale green, and against that backdrop the Snow Giants danced.

A wind came off the mountains to the north. It was cold and had the feel of snow in it; even the air smelled of snow.

The radio began to crackle.

Barraka glanced at his watch and smiled.

"Cross Over, this is Home Run . . . Cross Over, this is Home Run . . . do you read me?"

"Loud and clear."

"I make it we're about twenty miles out . . . ETA about three minutes . . . second Home Run team departing now . . . any special instructions?"

"Come up at bat from any direction but the south end. Catchers in the sound end of the valley."

"Say again."

Barraka repeated his instructions.

"Read you."

"Home Run put down at the west end of the field."

"Roger . . . you other guys hear that . . . make them count on the west end of the field," the squadron leader told his pilots.

"What have you got?" Barraka asked.

"Six hitters with two five zero zero balls. And enough stuff for a two-minute round of ping pong."

"In sight," Barraka said, pointing to the planes moving in tight formation off to the east.

"Weather closing in. Have to move it."

"Ready for you," Barraka answered. "Good hitting. Over and out."

Barraka's eyes were on the planes. "P-thirty-eights," he said.

The planes circled around. One by one they peeled off to make their bombing run. They swooped low over the north end of the valley and came streaking down toward Servigliano. The roar of their twin engines seemed like the continuous thunder of surf smashing against a rock-strewn beach. The planes came one behind the other.

Barraka saw the first two bombs drop away from the lead ship.

The double explosion thundered over the valley. At

the same instant, the eastern portion of the slope on Servigliano rose up with a tremendous roar.

"Now," Barraka shouted. "Now!"

Leading his men, Barraka charged into the camp. A barrage of small arms fire came from the guardhouse. Two of the partisans bellied their way close enough to pitch grenades into the windows. The explosions silenced the firing.

The partisans ran for the barracks, where the prisoners were housed.

"Come on," Barraka shouted, "make a run for the gate!"

Even as he started, the planes came streaking back for a strafing run. The fifty-caliber slugs slammed into the fuel dump at the edge of the camp. A huge sheet of flame erupted.

Yancy and his men worked their way up the east section of the mountain, reached the camp, and immediately began to encounter machine gun fire from the tower in the southeast corner of the compound.

"I'm going to take that son-of-a-bitch out," he shouted, suddenly leaping forward.

The bullets followed him, chewing up the earth. But he bobbed and weaved, forcing the gunners to change their pattern of fire. Then he was below the tower. Raising his rifle, he emptied a clip into the underside of the wooden floor, splintering it and killing the men above him. Then he climbed the tower and lobbed a grenade into the observation post to destroy the machine gun.

Mastrada and his band of men made their way up the rock-strewn slope under continuous fire from the nearest tower. Several of the partisans were killed halfway up the slope and many more were wounded.

Barraka could see what was happening to Mastrada's force. "We've got to take out that machine gun, or none of those guys are going to make it."

Suddenly the planes roared down again.

The gun stopped firing at Mastrada and went after the planes. The third one was hit. Smoke and flames spewed out of its starboard engine. The plane turned slightly and within seconds slammed into the tower, taking the machine gun position with it in a flaming cartwheel that moved across the compound and dropped down into the valley.

Piatelli and Manio ran toward Barraka. "Sarah," Piatelli yelled. "They took her to the barracks."

"We've got to get the hell out of here!" Barraka answered.

"You don't understand," Piatelli shouted. "The Germans got her. I must get her. I can't leave her."

Barraka looked toward the barracks. There still had to be Krauts in there.

"You know what was done to her," Manio cried, "you know!"

"Stay with them," Barraka ordered four of the partisans. "If I'm not back in three minutes get them out of here, even if you have to carry them!"

"She's my sister. Let me go with you!" Manio cried.

"Hold him," Barraka ordered and turning, he ran toward the barracks. Part of the roof was on fire and tongues of flames were licking at the air from some of the smashed windows. A soldier started out of the door. Barraka fired from the hip.

The man screamed and staggered backward.

Barraka rushed into the smoke-filled corridors and kicked open the door of every room he came to.

He found Sarah in the fourth room. She was sitting naked on the bed, rocking slowly back and forth. There was blood on her thighs and legs. Her eyes were wide with fear. Her clothes lay in a pile on the floor.

"Get dressed," Barraka said. "Hurry, we don't have much time!"

Sarah started to moan.

He crossed the room and picked up her clothes. "Hurry," he said, handing the clothing to her.

"They raped me!" Sarah screamed hysterically. "They raped me!"

Suddenly Barraka heard sounds in the hallway behind him. He whirled around and fired two rounds.

One soldier was thrown against the wall and another fell headlong into the room.

Sarah began to scream.

Barraka spun around and slapped her across the face. "Get dressed or I'll take you out just as you are!"

Sobbing, Sarah dressed.

"Okay, let's get out of here," Barraka said, grabbing hold of an officer's tunic, which he threw around Sarah's trembling shoulders. She tried to push it off. "Leave it on," he commanded. "You'll be glad you have it." Taking hold of Sarah's hand, he pulled her into the hallway.

His first impulse was to run back toward the door, but that part of the hallway was filled with smoke. "To the far end," Barraka said, pulling her along with him. A few feet from the wall, he stopped. "When I say drop," he told her, "you fall to the floor." He took a grenade from his belt, pulled the pin, and said, "Now drop!" Then he hurled the grenade at the wall and dropped down alongside of Sarah.

The explosion thundered in the hallway and part of the wall came down.

Barraka grabbed hold of Sarah's hand, scrambled to his feet, and yanked her up. Within moments they were out of the building.

"Hurry," he said, "we have to move with the rest."

Piatelli and Manio saw Barraka and Sarah and came running toward them.

"Get the other people out of here," Barraka told them. "Help Volterra and Mastrada to move the people. . . . I'll take care of her."

"Is she—" Piatelli started to speak.

But Barraka cut him short. "Go, I said. . . . Go!" And still holding Sarah in tow he looked for and found Rinata. "Take care of her," he told Rinata. "She was raped." Then he let go of Sarah's hand and ran to where the prisoners were.

Moving from group to group, Barraka called to the people, "Keep moving . . . don't stop . . . as long as you move, you'll be safe." Then suddenly he was faced with a dozen old men. "Why aren't you with your groups?" he asked.

"We're not going! We're not going!" one of

them cried.

"You can't stay. . . . Once we're gone the Germans will kill you. Come, I'll lead you out myself."

"No . . . we're not going!"

"They are too frightened to go," one of the partisans shouted.

Barraka leveled his rifle at them and said, "Move, or I'll kill you myself."

The old men gathered themselves together, and with loud cries of dismay they hurried after the others.

"It's time for us to run," Barraka told Piatelli, catching up to him. And they ran after the column of prisoners hurrying through the smoke and rubble of what had been the main gate.

Yancy and his men crossed the compound from east to west and flanked the column to the south while Mastrada's group took up positions to the north.

Many of the newly assigned German troops had managed to find cover and began firing at the fleeing prisoners.

The partisans returned the fire.

There were screams from the women, and the children bawled in terror. Though darkness had long since fallen, the entire top of the mountain was illuminated by the red glow of flames that could be seen along the entire length of the valley.

"Hurry," the partisans called to the people. "Run . . . run."

Some of the partisans scooped up a frightened old man or woman, while others held children in their arms. All of them knew it would only be a matter of minutes before the German troops began chasing after them.

Barraka ran ahead to where Mastrada was. The first few people emerged from the smoke. They came out in a column of threes. Volterra and Piatelli were now up front.

"Move them," Barraka shouted. "Move them." He called to Mastrada and then to Yancy. "Hurry it up. . . . Hurry it up." He stood on top of the rock, holding onto his staff with one hand and his Carbine with the other. "This isn't a Saturday walk," he yelled in Italian. "You're running for your lives. Move faster . . . faster." Even as he was urging them on, several German soldiers managed to set up a machine gun on the other side of the smashed gate, and, firing it blindly through the smoke, sent a stream of slugs into the rear of the column.

The people panicked. Several went down. Screaming in terror, others tore off in every direction, only to be mowed down by the random fire from the machine gun.

"Get that machine gun!" Barraka shouted to the partisans. "Get that *gun*!"

Four of the men dropped back.

A thick pall of black smoke obstructed Barraka's view of what was happening. But he could hear the heavy chatter of the gun and see the glowing tails of the tracers.

A grenade went off!

An instand later the machine gun started up.

"They got them pinned down," Barraka shouted across to Koss, referring to the men who had gone after the gun.

"No way to get it," Mastrada answered. "They have the field of fire."

Barraka ran down to the roadway to move the people at a faster pace. About twenty of them had already been killed or wounded. "Hurry," he shouted at them. "Damn you, hurry." He was wet with sweat and the smell of smoke filled his nostrils.

"Krauts!" Koss yelled. "The Krauts are forming up."

Barraka looked toward the prison compound. Several squads were intermittently visible through the dense smoke. They moved grimly toward the gate.

Volterra ran to his machine gun and told the partisans with him to get ready. "We want to let them get down the road a bit before we open up," he said. "They won't know where the fire is coming from." Even as he spoke, a cold rain began to fall.

Gissiking was directing the counterattack. The first German troops came through the heavy smoke in a V-formation. They moved slowly, cautiously onto the road.

Volterra pulled back on the bolt and eased it forward, locking the belt into place.

Another V-formation stepped out of the dense smoke.

Volterra let two more formations move onto the road before he squeezed the trigger. The machine gun bucked, but not long enough to make Volterra stop firing. He gave one long burst followed by two short ones.

Koss did the same.

The screams from the road were almost inhuman.

Ten men dropped. Several more called for medical aid.

Gissiking and a dozen troops came running out of the camp.

Volterra said to the partisan with him. "Try your throwing arm."

The man picked up a grenade, pulled the pin and hurled it toward the freshly arrived troops. When it exploded, a shower of mud flew in all directions.

The blast picked Gissiking up and threw him down against a tree.

Volterra and Koss raked the road with short bursts.

There were more shouts for help.

The Germans were trying to locate the machine guns.

Several of them fired flare guns.

Volterra and Koss stopped firing.

More troops came rushing out of the camp. They began to throw grenades at the rocks along the road.

Volterra and Koss squinched down in the crevices between the rocks, while the ground trembled with explosion after explosion. When the grenading stopped, they went back to their machine guns and fired several long bursts into the troops who were moving along the road.

Through most of the night they harassed the Germans. When they finally ran out of ammunition they abandoned their hiding places and made their way to the rendezvous point on the north slope of Servigliano.

"We stopped them," Koss said. "Most of the people got out."

Volterra smiled. He turned to the men with them,

and with a nod told them to join up with Barraka.

"I thought we're all going together," Koss said.

"I want to see what's coming up from Malveno," Volterra answered. "We've got to know what the Krauts are going to send against us."

"Everything they can. You can bet on that."

"They're already doing it," Volterra said, looking up at the valley, where, despite the rain, the sudden flashes of bursting star shells were clearly visible.

"Let's join Barraka," Koss told him. "From the look of it, he's going to need all the help he can get."

"Okay," Volterra said after a moment's consideration. "Let's get out of here while we still can."

The four men moved quickly through the rain and swung north to link up with Barraka.

Volterra looked over his shoulder. Very little of the camp remained intact. Smoke still billowed out of various buildings and drifted with the wind down to the southern end of the valley, where Malveno was.

Early in the morning, General Wolfe had decided to postpone his departure from Malveno for at least twenty-four hours. He spent a portion of the day driving around the countryside buying wine, which he asked Kunstler to ship to him after he left. By 1500 hours he was quite exhausted and retired to his room to sleep for a while before joining Kunstler and Radish for cocktails before dinner. Though he had hinted broadly that he would appreciate the services of a young woman, neither Kunstler nor Radish seemed to understand him. Rather than push the matter, he thought it best to wait until he returned to army headquarters to satisfy his sexual needs.

While Wolfe was buying wine, Kunstler was busy making additional preparations to meet for the forthcoming Ranger and Commando attack. He moved a battalion of half tracks south of where he had previously positioned his infantry units. His plan, as he explained it to Radish, was deceptively simple.

"I am not really concerned if the Jews are freed from Servigliano," he said. "The measures I have taken there are designed to kill as many partisans, Rangers, and Commandos as possible before they move south to meet the transport planes . . . I will not even have the Luftwaffe send up fighters to intercept the attacking force. I want them down here where units of my command will destroy them. Resistance at Servigliano will crumble. The Rangers, Commandos, and Jews will make a dash for the planes. We'll let them board, and only when they attempt to fly out will we open up with the eighty-eights."

"Once they realize their position," Radish responded, "they will surrender."

"Precisely . . . they will surrender or be shot to pieces."

Radish nodded and congratulated Kunstler. "Not only for the plan," he said, "but also on your forthcoming promotion."

"And yours," Kunstler responded.

"What?"

"Surely you do not for one moment think that I would not take you with me to my new assignment? And I could not have you as my aide unless you were a colonel . . . so, my dear Radish, my good fortune will also be yours."

"I am immensely grateful," Radish said. And he was, though not exactly for the reasons that Kunstler would have thought. Radish knew that when the time came for him to surrender to the Allies, the higher his rank the better he would be treated. And afterwards, when he returned home, the higher his rank had been, the more chance he would have to become something more than the headmaster of a gymnasium. Perhaps chairman at a university, or even the director of such an institution?

"I have also recommended you for an Iron Cross, Second Class, for your actions against the partisans," Kunstler said.

"I'm deeply honored."

"In that case," Kunstler told him, "let's have a drink."

They toasted each other. Radish moved to the window and looked down at the plaza. It was divided into a large area of shade and a small one of sunshine. The old men of the town were sitting outside the cafe, enjoying the warmth of the sun. He was about to turn away when he noticed the windblown snow on the mountains to the north. Calling Kunstler's attention to it, he said, "The local people believe that it foretells the coming of death."

"Marvelous!" Kunstler exclaimed. "I'm always amazed by the explanations people have for various natural phenomena." He walked to where Radish stood and looked out of the window. "What was this morning's meteorological report?"

"I sent it forward to you—"

"I was too busy with making preparations to greet our visitors," Kunstler laughed.

"Clear today . . . rain tonight . . . snow in the higher elevations, and a steadily deteriorating condition with a seventy-five percent probability for snow at all elevations within the next forty-eight hours."

"Let's hope the weather will not keep the general here any longer than is absolutely necessary," Kunstler said.

Radish heartily agreed with Kunstler on that. He did not like Wolfe, or respect him.

The phone began to ring. Kunstler answered it and put his hand over the mouthpiece. "Gissiking is on the other end."

Radish nodded, came toward the desk and sat down alongside of it.

"Yes," Kunstler said. "I expected the partisans to begin their move against the camp . . . but they will not attack it until the Rangers and Commandos arrive. Don't worry, captain. The main thrust will not be at Servigliano. Do not, I repeat, do not prevent the Jews from leaving. Yes, you heard me correctly. Your primary mission is to kill as many partisans, Rangers, and Commandos as possible. We'll kill and capture the rest when they move to their transport planes. Thank you for letting me know what is happening." Kunstler set the phone down. "It looks as if the action is about to begin. Better alert our forces."

Radish stood up and asked about notifying General Wolfe.

"Not in this preliminary phase," Kunstler said, looking at his watch. "It is fifteen hundred fifty-five hours," he said. "Sundown should be down in another twenty minutes."

"More like fifteen in the valley areas."

"At Servigliano?"

"Twenty would be a good figure," Radish answered with a nod.

The phone rang again.

Kunstler picked it up. "Radar has picked up a dozen fighter planes heading this way," Kunstler told Radish, without bothering to cover the mouthpiece. "No, I don't want fighter interception," he told the officer on the other end and put the phone down. "Fighter planes? This is far north of their operational area."

"Auxiliary wing tanks would give the additional range," Radish commented.

Kunstler frowned. He did not think the transports would come in behind a screen of fighter planes. He thought the Americans would gamble on the element of surprise. He went to the window. Looking up, he said, "I did not consider having to deal with fighter planes." Then suddenly he heard them.

The roar of several tremendous explosions rolled down the valley. Kunstler's jaw went slack and the blood drained from his face. With his hand trembling, he picked up the phone and in a choked voice told the operator to put him through to Captain Gissiking.

He cleared his throat. "This is Kunstler . . . I am dispatching troops to your aid."

"They better come soon," Gissiking answered, "or nothing will be left standing."

"Stop the Jews from leaving."

"What? I thought you said—"

"Stop the Jews! Intelligence was wrong!" Kunstler

shouted and slammed the phone down on its cradle. "Radish, order all available troops to head for Servigliano. . . . Give me a battery of artillery to move up and lay down a barrage along the valley immediately around Servigliano."

Without knocking, Wolfe entered the office. "What the hell is going on?" he asked. "It sounds like the mountains are falling."

"Servigliano is under attack," Kunstler said quietly. "The partisans are doing what army intelligence said the Rangers and Commandos would do."

"What the hell are you talking about?"

"The partisans, general, under the command of an American major, are at this moment attacking Servigliano."

"You must be mistaken."

Kunstler shook his head. "It is no mistake," he answered. "Or to put it more correctly, yes, there has been a mistake made, and we were the ones to make it."

"But army intelligence—"

"Was wrong," Kunstler said sharply. "And now if you will excuse me, I'll try to help the garrison at Servigliano."

Garjulio saw the Snow Giants and stopped to watch them. They were larger than any he had remembered having seen in a long time. Suddenly a squadron of twelve fighters with American markings flew overhead. Within moments six of the planes headed west and the others continued north. He watched these six turn one hundred and eighty degrees and head directly toward Servigliano. His heart began to race. He sucked in his breath and waited for the first explosions to come. He saw a great plume of earth rise up above Servigliano before the thunderous roar of the explosion came rushing down the valley.

His wife and daughter came out of the house to see what was happening.

He shouted to them that the planes were bombing Servigliano.

He cursed the partisans and called upon God to strike them all dead. And then he saw Crucci come scrambling down the hill toward the house. From the way Crucci moved, he knew something was wrong with his right leg.

"For the love of God," Crucci shouted, "come and help me!"

Garjulio went toward him. "What happened?"

"Later," Crucci said. "Now get me into the house and help me bandage it. I think I broke my ankle."

Garjulio gave him support and together they went into the house. Maria fetched several old bed sheets cut into strips and helped her mother bandage the ankle.

Soup, bread, and wine were set down before Crucci, and he ate with gusto. "I must get to Malveno tonight," he said. "I must speak with Colonel Kunstler."

"I will go," Garjulio offered. "Tell me and I'll tell him."

Crucci shook his head.

"If I tell him you were hurt—" Garjulio began.

"No," Crucci insisted. "I must go . . . will you take me?"

"Yes. But on the condition that you tell me what information you have for the colonel. I saw what was happening at Servigliano. The partisans probably are on every road. I don't want to risk my life, unless I know what I'm risking it for and how much I'll be paid for the risk."

A short while later Garjulio helped Crucci up onto the wagon. Taking the reins, he guided the horses out of the yard and onto the road. "Are you going to tell me what is happening at Servigliano?" he asked.

Crucci told him about Barraka's assault. "Of course I don't know all of the details, but the partisans are going to free the Jews," he said.

"But what the hell will they do with them?"

"That's what I want to tell the colonel," Crucci answered. "I overheard a conversation between the American lieutenant and a British officer . . . they're going to take them to Switzerland," Crucci told him. "Don't be surprised. That's where they're going. They're going to walk them out of Italy and into Switzerland."

"Are you sure that's what you heard?"

"Absolutely certain."

Garjulio turned away from Crucci.

"Now you know why it's so important for me to see the colonel," Crucci said. "I think that piece of information is worth about two thousand American dollars and much more if they kill or capture any one of the leaders."

"A lot of money," Garjulio agreed, shifting the reins to his right hand and freeing a knife from his boot with the left hand. He swung around, thrusting his left hand into Crucci's stomach. The knife went in up to the hilt.

Crucci screamed, clutching his burning stomach. He tried to pull the knife out. He began to cough up blood, and after a few minutes he slumped forward.

Garjulio reached under Crucci, pulled the knife free, and, to make sure he was dead, plunged it into his back. Then he used his foot to kick Crucci's body off the wagon seat. It hardly made a sound as it rolled off the side of the road into the wet bushes.

XIV

Kunstler was angry. He spoke to no one, not even to Radish, who sat alongside of him in the rear of the command car through the long and dismal night while crews of men and machines worked to open the road between Malveno and Servigliano.

To Kunstler, the events of the previous few hours were all too reminiscent of his experiences in Russia, where the effectiveness of partisan units was always underestimated by intelligence. He uttered a weary sigh. There was no doubt in his mind that the same kind of bungling might have cost him his promotion.

A dull gray light was beginning to top the mountains in the east.

Kunstler got out of the car and stood by the side of the road to urinate. Star shells were still bursting in the upper reaches of the valley. He buttoned his fly, walked back to the command car, and, summoning his aide, ordered the artillery to stop firing.

"How much longer before the road is cleared?" he shouted to one of the officers directing the men.

"At least another hour, colonel. Perhaps more," the young man answered.

"Well, Radish," Kunstler said, "all my planning has been wasted. Here we sit, and somewhere out there are three hundred Jews and perhaps fifty or seventy-five partisans."

Radish nodded, aware of the strange, almost audible silence that filled the valley, now that the artillery had ceased firing. Sitting in the car all night had made his joints feel stiff and brought an aching pain to the muscles in the back of his neck. He swung himself out of the vehicle and wanted very much to shake his legs but dared not.

"Is food being brought up?" Kunstler asked, looking at the wet, tired men nearby.

"Yes," Radish answered. "I ordered it before we left Malveno. It should be here at oh-six-hundred."

"What about the attack on the machine shops at San Viglio?"

"Damage was negligible. The weather hampered the air strike and ground assault was successfully driven off. As of nineteen hundred hours last night, the partisans were falling back to the east. They lost about half their attacking force."

"Any prisoners?"

"None that I know about," Radish answered.

The light over the mountains brightened, but it was still a shade of gray. The dark smoke from Servigliano was clearly visible. Despite the rain it hung like huge black drapes between the top of the mountain and the lead-colored clouds.

Trucks carrying hot coffee, cold sausage, and bread made their way slowly toward the road block. In a few minutes the men working to clear the road and the soldiers waiting to advance on Servigliano were taking time to revive themselves with food and drink.

Kunstler and Radish ate and drank, too. They leaned against the side of the command car. Radish found no pleasure in the bitter coffee, the fatty sausage, or the hard bread.

"I've eaten worse than this," Kunstler said, waving a small piece of sausage. "Compared to maggot-ridden horsemeat, this is fare for a king."

Radish made no comment. He knew that within a very short time he would be suffering from heartburn.

"Well, Radish," Kunstler said, "we're going to have to bring those Jews back." He set his metal cup down and rubbed his hands together. "If you were leading them, where would you take them, Radish? I tell you," he went on, "it is insane to think that three hundred men, women, and children have any chance of surviving in these mountains. It is already the second week in November."

"There are two possibilities," Radish told him, speaking slowly. "They will head for one or the other coasts, where they will be taken off a beach by the American or British navy, or they will make a run for it to the south, in an effort to reach the Allied lines."

"We must find them," Kunstler said, "or we'll have to answer for what has happened, even though it wasn't our mistake."

"The weather will help us," Radish commented.

"I would like to think so," Kunstler answered. "But I cannot. In the end it will become—no, it is now—a duel between Major Barraka and myself. I will do everything to stop him, and he, in turn, will do everything to elude me. The weather will not help or hinder either of us. And each of us uses the weather to his own advantage."

Radish nodded and finished off his coffee. The men were going back to the arduous task of clearing the roadway. Kunstler climbed back into the command car to once again sit in absolute silence and silently rage.

As soon as he could, Barraka guided the prisoners off the road and had them move along the slope on the western side of the valley.

They walked and ran through the night. Many of the old people stumbled and fell, only to be picked up and urged on by their friends or by one or more of the partisans.

Yancy and several of the young men in the column dropped back to make sure that they were not being followed by the Germans. When it became apparent that the Germans were not behind them, they rejoined the column. "When do we rest?" Piatelli asked.

"In a while we will reach a place where there are caves," Barraka explained. "We will rest there and wait for Volterra, Koss, and the other men with them to join us." He pointed to the brightening light in the east. "We have to hurry. I want to be off the slope before the sun is fully up."

"But the clouds—"

"Regardless of the clouds," Barraka told him, "daylight is daylight. We could use three or four days of continuous darkness and heavy rain. But that's not going to happen."

"I'll see what I can do about quickening the pace," Piatelli said.

Barraka nodded and began to run.

Yancy came alongside of him. "Do you think Chaim and Koss got away?" he asked.

"I was just wondering the same thing," Barraka answered.

"Never knowin'," Yancy said. "That's the shit part of the war."

Barraka agreed.

Sarah ran alongside of Rinata. They were part of a long column of people struggling up a steep, rock-strewn slope. A strong, cold wind blew off the mountains. The night sky was patched with clouds.

Sarah's body ached. She could feel the caked blood on the inside of her thighs. She stumbled several times, but Rinata grabbed hold of her by the arm and stopped her from falling. And when she lagged, Rinata pulled her foward.

"I have to stop for a minute," Sarah said. "I have to stop."

More roughly than before, Rinata took her arm. "When Barraka says we stop, we stop. Until then we will keep going."

"I don't want to go," Sarah answered, coming to an abrupt halt.

"That's fine with me," Rinata said. "But first you tell Barraka. If he says you can stay, you stay."

Sarah stumbled forward, knowing if need be Barraka wouldn't hesitate to sling her over his shoulder, as if she were so much dunnage, and carry her. Because without her, he would lose her uncle and—

"Don't feel sorry for yourself," Rinata said. "What happened to you isn't anything unique."

Astonished, Sarah looked at the woman, almost as if she were newly introduced to her presence.

"I was raped," Sarah cried. "I was raped and abused. I feel dirty. Do you understand that? I feel dirty inside where I can never wash. . . . For God's sake, I don't want to be part of this . . . this second Exodus. . . . I want to die. . . . I want to die. Maybe then I'll feel clean again."

"I was fourteen when I was raped," Rinata said coldly. "I was fourteen when I was raped in the back room of a cafe and then sent out by the man who raped me to sell my cunt to anyone who'd pay me the few hundred lire he told me to ask for. . . . You're alive, aren't you? You have a chance to make it to freedom. . . . Don't be a fool and throw it away because some filthy German broke your cherry."

Sarah bit her lip. How could she respond to what Rinata had just told her? How could any woman who has ever been violated respond to the rape of another woman, except by experiencing in her mind the entire outrage all over again?

"A man risked his life to bring you out," Rinata said. "And a man raped you. You have to come to terms with that. One man was less than a beast. The other—well, you'll have to find out what he is yourself."

Sarah stopped again. "You don't understand," she sobbed. "I couldn't fight him. . . . I couldn't take the beating. . . . I just opened my thighs and—"

"So you opened your thighs. What did you think you would do? Fight back? Don't be stupid. He would have beaten you senseless and then raped you. Fighting him wouldn't have made any difference. You saved yourself more of a beating. Perhaps even a broken jaw or nose, or worse, perhaps an orgy of sadistic violence that might have left you physically maimed for life." Rinata took hold of Sarah's arm and eased her forward. "Come," she said in a gentle voice, "we must hurry and keep up with the others."

"I don't even know your name," Sarah said, stifling her sobs.

"Rinata . . . I'm Rinata."

"My name is Sarah."

Rinata smiled. "You're Piatelli's niece, aren't you?"

"Yes," Sarah answered, wiping the tears from her eyes with the sleeve of the jacket that Barraka had thrown over her shoulders.

Rinata reached Sarah's hand. "You think about what I said. You're young and strong. You've got a good chance of making it to Switzerland, and then a new life will start for you. But now you have to do everything you can to survive and to help as many of the other people as you can to survive."

"I'll try," Sarah answered. "I'll try. But I hurt, Rinata, I hurt in the very depth of my body, in the depths of my soul."

"In time it will pass," Rinata said softly. "Believe me, it will pass, and when you come to love a man, if God is kind, the hurt will vanish completely."

When he returned from Servigliano, Kunstler

found General Wolfe in his office. The general was calmly smoking one of his Cuban cigars and drinking coffee laced with brandy. He was dressed in a clean uniform, smelled of eu de cologne, and is face was freshly shaved.

As soon as Radish saw Wolfe, he grabbed hold of Kunstler's arm. "Whatever you are going to say, don't. This is not the time to let your anger show."

Kunstler wrenched himself away, and with a forced smile he bid Wolfe good morning.

"I've just been talking to Kesselring," Wolfe said. "He's disturbed by the turn of events here."

Kunstler removed his gloves and his heavy leather trench coat. He had seen what had happened at Servigliano and now had to face the idiocy of having to listen to Wolfe.

"Did you happen to mention that army intelligence—"

"I made note of that in my report," Wolfe said.

"Your report, general?"

"Yes, about the entire incident," Wolfe said. "Since I'm here I felt it my duty to report the situation from an unbiased point of view."

Kunstler nodded and looked balefully at Radish.

"The situation is very serious," Wolfe said. "The Jews must be recaptured as soon as possible."

"It's not my intention to allow them to be free."

"It's a matter of national honor," Wolfe said, standing. "We can't permit a racially inferior people to escape." He moved away from the desk.

Kunstler picked up the phone and asked his operations officer for a situation status report.

"There has been contact ten kilometers west of San

Viglio," the officer said. "Among the bodies of the dead partisans we found the body of a British officer. One of the two known to be with the partisans."

"Name?" Kunstler asked.

"Lieutenant Stephan Rawlins," the major answered.

Kunstler relayed the information to Radish and then asked about the main body of Jews.

"No sign of them," the major reported.

"Major, three hundred men, women, and children cannot disappear. . . . Find them, major. Find them!" And he slammed the phone down into its cradle. Kunstler walked to the window. The cloud cover had lifted. It was still raining. "Tell me, Radish," he asked, without turning, "where have the Jews gone?"

"We'll find them," Radish answered.

Suddenly Kunstler noticed the guards were forcing a man away from the building. He watched for a moment before he called Radish to the window.

"Is that man down there someone we know?" he asked.

"It is Garjulio," Radish said. "What is going on?"

"Send my orderly down," Kunstler said. "I want him up here."

Radish went to the door, told the orderly what to do, and then stepped back into the office.

"Who is this Garjulio?" Wolfe asked.

"A friend," Kunstler said.

A few minutes later Garjulio was in Kunstler's office, explaining the difficulty he had had with the guards. "But of course I understand they were only following their orders," he said. "I came to see you, colonel."

Kunstler nodded. "Go on."

"Crucci came to me last night." He looked suspiciously at Wolfe but was reassured by a nod from Kunstler. "He had escaped from the partisans."

"Where is he?"

"Dead," Garjulio said. "Badly wounded by the partisans. But before he died, God rest his soul, he told me to come to you with the information he obtained."

Kunstler leaned forward and Radish took a step closer to the desk.

"Of course, he also mentioned your business arrangement," Garjulio said. "And he was certain you would honor your end of the bargain."

"I will," Kunstler said.

"Crucci told me that the information would be worth at least ten thousand American dollars."

"You will be paid in deutsche marks," Wolfe said from where he was standing.

Garjulio glanced at him and said to Kunstler, "I must have the same terms as Crucci."

"Absolutely."

"I protest," Wolfe said.

Suddenly Kunstler was on his feet. "General, Servigliano cost the lives of seventy-five German soldiers, not to mention the complete destruction of the facility. How much do you think all that is worth? Surely much more than ten thousand American dollars. I want those Jews. Those were my men who were killed."

Wolfe did not answer. He went to the window.

"You will be paid what I would have paid Crucci," Kunstler told Garjulio. "Now the information, if you please."

"The Jews are going north," Garjulio said. "North to Switzerland."

"Impossible!" Wolfe exclaimed, turning to face him. "They could not possibly cross the mountains."

Kunstler went to the wall map. "There are at least a dozen ways to the border," he said.

Radish stood behind him. "The nearest pass is at Umbrail," Radish told him, stepping forward to point to it.

"It is insane," Kunstler said. "To reach that pass or any part of the border, they would have to traverse some of the most rugged terrain in Italy. There are sixty kilometers of—" He turned to Garjulio. "Where are the Jews now?"

"I don't know. I only know where they're going."

Kunstler went to the phone and ordered a small recon plane for himself. "And I want a pilot," he said, "who is not afraid of flying low."

Wolfe came over to the map. "The Jews would never be able to cross the mountains."

"You're probably right," Kunstler said, "but I want to make sure they remain on this side of the border." Then, turning to Garjulio, he told him he would be paid within twenty-four hours.

"I accept your word," Garjulio answered.

When Garjulio was gone, Kunstler told Radish to make out the usual voucher for the sum of ten thousand dollars.

"Surely you don't intend to honor that man's demands?" Wolfe asked.

"I do and will," Kunstler said. "What he just told us might help save the lives of other German soldiers, and if it does that and only that, then I must consider it a bargain. My plane is waiting . . . I must go . . . Radish, stay by the telephone. If there is anything interesting, I'll have my radio communications to ground patched into the telephone."

"Yes, sir . . . Good luck!"

The bells in the church tolled ten as Garjulio crossed the square to Calvino's cafe. He was feeling better than he had in a long time. In the not-too-distant future, the Germans would abandon Italy to the Allies and then the dollars he had accumulated would make him a rich man.

Garjulio entered the cafe and sat down at a table close to the fire.

Calvino came out of the rear room. "I saw you arguing with the German soldiers," he said.

"Nothing."

"That's good," Calvino answered. "It's better to have nothing with the Germans than something."

"This morning, I will buy you a drink. Drink what you want and put it on my score . . . For me, I will have Grappa."

Calvino left the table and disappeared into the rear of the store.

Garjulio stood up and went to the window.

The square was crowded with soldiers and vehicles. From the wide-eyed look of bewilderment on some of the soldiers' faces, he could tell they had been at Servigliano. Others just looked tired and miserable from having been up all night. Then he found himself looking at some of the women. One in particular held his interest. She was younger than the others. A full-breasted, wide-hipped woman. She was a widow. Her husband had been killed in Africa.

Garjulio felt a tightening in his groin. He nodded, and when Calvino returned, he went back to the table and sat down.

"Have you room for me to spend the night here?" Garjulio asked, picking up his glass.

"Yes," Calvino answered.

Garjulio picked up the glass and walked to the window.

Calvino watched his relative without any emotion.

"She is a beauty," Garjulio commented, gesturing toward the woman with his glass.

Calvino went to the window.

"That one near the fountain . . . the young one."

"Mellena Fracci," Calvino said.

"I would pay to spend a night with her," Garjulio said. "A night like tonight would be a good night." He looked at Calvino. "Do you think it could be arranged?"

"I don't know," Calvino answered. "But if she's approached, she'll want to know the price."

"Ten American dollars," Garjulio snapped off.

Calvino remained expressionless.

"Twenty American dollars," Garjulio offered. "That's as much as I'd pay for any woman."

"I'll make inquiries," Calvino said, lifting his glass.

Garjulio smiled, touched his glass to Calvino's, and drank most of his Grappa. A second draft finished it. He scratched his groin. "A woman like that makes a man's balls itch," he said.

Calvino nodded.

He shook his head, then suddenly his eyes went

wide. "Oh no!" he exclaimed. His knees buckled. He fell to the floor.

"Hurry!" Calvino called.

Two men rushed out of the rear and picked Garjulio up.

"He will soon be dead," Calvino said. "Take him into the mountains and drop him off a cliff. Make it look like an accident!"

The two men carried Garjulio out to the rear of the cafe. They placed him on the back of a wagon, threw several bales of hay over him, and covered all of it with a canvas tarp.

Calvino came out. "Tell Volterra when you see him that what he asked me to do has been done."

The man who held the reins nodded. Then he clicked his tongue and slapped the reins over the swayback of the old horse.

XV

They reached the caves shortly after the sky in the west turned the color of white ash. Exhausted and wet, they went into the many openings of the rock-faced wall. Like frightened animals worn down from the chase, they trembled and herded close to one another in an effort to hold a modicum of warmth.

None of the caves were deep and the ceilings of all of them were so low that even a man of middling height was forced to crouch, or go on his hands and knees in order to move.

Yancy and Rinata stretched out close to one another along the side of the cave. He cradled her in his arms. The arduousness of the last twelve hours had drained them of any desire.

Yancy called to Barraka. "How long you figure on holdin' up here?"

"A few hours," Barraka answered, hunkering down. "Not too long. I want to be at the north end of the valley by nightfall."

"Chaim and Bill are supposed to link up with us by

then, aren't they?"

Barraka nodded.

"These people don't look none too good," Yancy said.

"They're a lot stronger than you might think," Barraka responded.

"Maybe we don't look 'none too good' to them?"

"Don't think we do," Barraka told him with a grin. "Try to get some sleep."

"You too."

"As soon as I take care of a few things," Barraka said. He went from group to group, telling them to sleep. Finally he settled down next to Piatelli, Manio and Sarah.

"Thank you for—" Piatelli began.

With a wave of his hand, Barraka cut him short. "Get some sleep. It's going to get a lot harder." He glanced at Sarah. Her eyes were wide with fear. But otherwise she seemed to be all right. He found himself remembering what she looked like naked. Her breasts had jutted straight out and her nipples were pink—suddenly Barraka felt her eyes on him. Ashamed, he thrust the image from his mind, leaned back against a boulder, and pretended to sleep. The air outside the cave thrummed to the sound of a single engine plane. In an instant he was on his feet and scrambling for the opening of the cave. But before he could reach it, one of the partisans rushed out and fired several shots at the plane.

The plane was flying lower than the long ridges that formed the Tenna Valley. Kunstler had the pilot make several sweeps north, but he saw no sign of the Jews. From the air, Servigliano looked as burned out as it had from the ground. Smoke still rose up above the top of the mountain.

"Go closer to the slopes," Kunstler shouted to the pilot.

"Too close and we might be knocked against the side by a gust of wind," the pilot answered.

"Closer!" Kunstler shouted.

The pilot eased the stick over and brought his right wing within a few meters of the steep slope.

"There, along that cliff wall," Kunstler yelled, pointing to a secondary chasm that ran in a diagonal to the northwest off the east-west direction of the larger valley.

The small plane was tossed violently around by sudden upward drafts.

Kunstler's stomach rebelled, but he managed to keep himself from vomiting.

"Colonel," the pilot said, touching Kunstler on the shoulder, "we have more clouds coming in from the west."

Kunstler glanced in that direction. Large cumulus clouds were already covering the tops of the mountains.

Then suddenly two pings sounded off the strut under the starboard wing.

Kunstler looked down and saw a man pointing a rifle at the plane. "We've found them," he shouted, making a violent motion downward with the forefinger of his right hand.

Another shot tore through the thin doped material of the wing.

Kunstler saw another man run out of the side of the cliff and grab the rifle from the first. "Too late, you bastards," he shouted. "Too late." And picking up the mike, he radioed to the ground control station. "Patch me into Major Radish in my headquarters," he told the operator. "Radish," he said jubilantly, "I've found them . . . yes . . . I want a dive bombing attack . . . yes . . . twelve planes should do it. Yes . . . look at the map. According to the map I have with me the coordinates are oh-twenty-one and P-sixty-five . . . I want those planes in the air now. . . . There's weather coming in from the west."

"Heavy rains are predicted," Radish said.

Kunstler called the local Luftwaffe commander. "How long before your plane can get here?"

"Five minutes from takeoff time," the commander answered.

"How long to takeoff time?"

"Another five."

"Have we enough petrol to monitor the attack?" Kunstler asked his pilot.

The pilot nodded.

"I'll stay in the vicinity," Kunstler told the flight commander, "and radio you when I make signal contact with your planes." Kunstler signed off and put the mike back in its place. He felt satisfied with himself. If he put an end to this business of the Jews and the partisans, there still might be a chance for him to be promoted.

The sound of the plane roused Yancy, who had drifted into a light sleep. Even as he opened his eyes, the shots rang out. He pushed Rinata away and jumped to his feet. Within moments he was out of the cave.

Barraka grabbed the rifle away from the partisan and smashed its butt against the man's shoulder. "You stupid bastard!" he shouted. "You've told the Germans where we are." He raised the rifle again, and was about to bring it down on the man's head, when Yancy took hold of him from behind.

"It's done, Mitch," Yancy told him. "It's done!"

Barraka dropped the rifle and began to order the people out of the caves. "Hurry. Their planes will be here any minute."

"There's one now," Yancy said, pointing to the silver observation plane, moving back and forth overhead.

The people came out of the caves. They were confused and didn't seem to know or care what was happening.

"Move them, Mastrada," Barraka shouted. "Get them away from here. Move them up to the gorge. There's an overhang there that will give us some cover."

Yancy urged the people to hurry.

"How much time do we have?" Piatelli called.

"Minutes!" Barraka answered.

Suddenly the whole sky was filled with the heavy sound of the dive bombers. The prisoners heard the dull roar and began to run. Many of the older people fell and slipped down the side of the cliff. Though they cried out for help, no one was able to stop for them.

Sarah fell.

Barraka came up to her and pulled her up. "Run," he shouted. "Run."

The people ran, frightened they would never reach the overhang of the cliff before the bombs began to fall.

Then suddenly a terrible screaming sound rose above the roar of the engines. Within moments the face of the cliff where the caves had been dissolved with a thunderous explosion. The blast swept over them, carrying with it a cloud of dust that obscured the gray sky. More explosions followed.

Men, women, and children were crying hysterically. Splashes of blood stained the side of the cliff. Torn bodies lay scattered on the ground.

Barraka turned to Yancy. He tried to speak but couldn't. His tongue felt thick. He shook his head. He was helpless. Barraka had been in many battles and had seen men blown to pieces before. But for him this was totally different. These people, these Jews were his: He had freed them. They had followed him through hell. Barraka screamed at the dive bombers. "Bastards! You goddamn bastards! They can't take any more!" Then, grabbing the BAR from Yancy, he dashed out into the open and began firing at the planes. Suddenly one began to smoke; then it dissolved in a yellow burst of flames that smashed into the side of the mountain.

Barraka stopped firing. He lowered the BAR and breathed deeply, wiping the sweat from his face.

Yance pointed to the sky. "The clouds should stop them," he said.

"We've got to move the people," Barraka said. He ran over the debris of the blasted caves and passed the bloody bodies of some children and many elderly. Gasping, he shouted for Yancy and Mastrada to get the people out of there. "Move them," he yelled. "Get them moving." Then suddenly, he saw a middle-aged man holding the body of his aged father. "Come," Barraka said to him. "Leave him. . . . You can't do him any good now. We must get out of here."

The man looked up at him and sobbed, "Now, two minutes ago, I was his eldest son, and now, major, I am an orphan, a man without a living mother or father."

Barraka was brought up short.

"He was my father," the man said weeping. "My beloved father. . . . May God protect your father, major. . . . May God protect him."

Barraka nodded, bent down, and with his own fingers, closed the dead man's eyes. "Now come," he said gently. "Come. Your father would want you to live."

With a convulsive sigh, the man stood up. "I'm ready to go," he said.

Barraka put his hand on the man's shoulder and led him to the others.

The people moved out from under the overhang and into the narrowest part of the gorge. Barraka went to the head of the column.

Manio fell in alongside of him. "I want to help," he said.

"Some of the old people—"

"That's not what I meant, major."

Barraka glanced at him. He knew Manio wanted to become a partisan. "Did you tell your uncle what you want to do?"

"Yes."

"And he agreed?"

"He said if that is what you feel you must do, then do it."

Barraka was still about to send him back to his uncle; then he changed his mind. "All right. But once you pick up a rifle, you'll also have to accept all the other responsibilities. You'll be treated the same as any of the other partisans."

"I understand," Manio answered.

"That includes the discipline as well."

"I did not think it would be any other way."

"Drop back to Yance, and tell him I said to give you a piece and ammo; then come back here and stay close to me."

"Thanks, major, thanks," Manio said; then he turned and ran back to where Yancy was.

Barraka shifted the position of the rifle sling on his shoulder. He respected Manio for coming to him.

Before they reached the end of the gorge, the rain started. Torrents of water began to pour down the gullies that led into the gorge.

"We're not moving fast enough," Barraka shouted. "If we don't get out of the gorge, we're going to drown! There's more water coming."

"They can't move any faster," Yancy called out.

"Keep pushing them."

When they reached the end of the gorge, the rock face had been turned into a waterfall. Barraka began to climb it.

The people followed him. Barraka moved from ledge to ledge, grabbing on to rocks. His hands bled. Several times he was forced to stop and catch his breath. Near the top of the ledge, the water came down with force and almost tore his hands away from a rock he had hold of. With a sudden burst of energy he thrust himself through the torrent of water and up to the next ledge. A few feet above lay the end of the rock wall. He climbed again, clinging to the leafless branches of stunted trees. As soon as he was on the top, he reached down to help the man behind him. Over and over again, he pulled a man, a woman, or a child to the ledge. "Come," he said. "Come just a little bit higher." His arm ached and the faces he saw were blurred by sweat mixed with rain.

He found himself looking at Koss. "Chaim," he asked, "where's Chaim?"

"Behind me," Koss answered.

"And the other men?"

"All safe," Koss said, gaining the ledge.

Barraka reached down and grabbed hold of Volterra's hand.

"I'll bring the others up," Koss said.

"Thanks," Barraka replied. "I feel as if my arm is coming out of its socket." He stood up and with Volterra at his side he walked to where the people were waiting.

"We saw what happened," Volterra told Barraka. "We were at the far end of the gorge when the bombing began."

"I'm glad you and the others made it back to us," Barraka said. "Very glad."

After several hours of hard climbing all of them were out of the gorge and on top of a razor-backed ridge, where the wind was so strong they had to bend into it in order to stand up.

"That was the worst yet," Barraka told the people.

"Now we have to keep going. The Krauts will think we're still in the gorge. Let them think that, but we're going to be in the high mountain passes tomorrow morning."

"You mean we're going to keep going all night?" Piatelli asked.

"Most of the night, anyway," Barraka answered.

Many of the people started to complain.

Barraka ignored them. He took his place at the head of the column and raised his staff, shouting, "Let's move out. Let's move!"

Kunstler shouted to the pilots of the planes to bomb deeper into the gorge. He had seen the Jews flee and knew just where they were.

The planes dove down on the massive rock overhang and dropped their bombs.

The earth rose up, blooming huge chunks of rock that hurtled down close to where Kunstler thought the people were hiding. The air was filled with smoke and dust.

The planes came in low and strafed. Machine gun slugs slammed into the overhang, splintering the side of it.

Kunstler ordered his own pilot to fly low. "I can't see very much," he told Radish. "There are some bodies visible."

The flight commander cut in and told Kunstler he was returning to his base.

"I need another bombing run," Kunstler told him.

"Not today anymore," the officer answered. "That weather is just about to spill off the mountains."

Kunstler looked up and saw the black clouds like huge juggernauts advancing down on the valley. He thanked the flight officer for his cooperation and told his own pilot to head for home.

Kunstler had developed dark rings under his eyes from lack of sleep and Radish suffered continuously from heartburn.

Only General Wolfe remained untouched by the tense situation that swirled around him. Because of the sensitiveness of the situation, he had persuaded Field Marshal Kesselring that his presence at Malveno would serve to emphasize the importance with which the army viewed the operation against the partisans and the Jews. Kesselring was embarrassed by the entire situation and wanted to rectify it as soon as possible. He had enough trouble fighting the Allies. He did not want to have to be the object of the Führer's anger.

Wolfe made it a point not to intrude on the military operations conducted by Kunstler. He did not even ask for a desk. He spent most of the day in Kunstler's office, a silent, often grave-looking spectator to everything that went on. But at lunch and at dinner he was a convivial guest, amusing the other officers with a vast repertoire of jokes, even jokes about the Führer and Himmler. After only forty-eight hours, it seemed to everyone at headquarters that the general had always been part of the Eleventh Brigade.

Rendered impotent by the weather, Kunstler spent two days pacing the office. The rains made the movement of men or vehicles virtually impossible. His scouts had reported to him that the water in the gorge had become a rushing river.

He spent long periods of time standing at the window, looking up to where the dense clouds swirled around the top of the mountains. He was haunted by Barraka. He spent hours staring at his photograph, trying to figure out how an amateur could manage to do what Barraka had done and what he now was attempting to do. It defied logic. It was absurd. It was nothing short of being spectacular.

On the afternoon of the second day, Kunstler said to Radish, "I have always felt a certain neutrality toward the Jews. . . . My father told me that during World War One he had several superb Jewish officers on his staff. But now I have Jews served up to me for my enemy. I tell you, Radish, this war is—"

"Permit me, colonel," Wolfe interrupted, "to make an important observation."

Kunstler turned from the window.

"Had the Jews not caused the war, then you would not have to capture them now. The responsibility for what is happening to them was completely their own. And I tell you this: Many, many Americans and Englishmen know this to be true, just as we know it. I would not be surprised if this Barraka, who is with them now, feels about the Jews just as you had. But he will learn as you have learned, indeed as every German has learned, that the Jews were, and always will be, our enemy."

"Barraka," Kunstler told them, "is more my enemy than the Jews."

Wolfe frowned.

With a wave of his hand, Kunstler dismissed the

subject and returned to his window gazing. He had heard similar prattle from various other people for many years now. He took a quick glance at Wolfe and realized that such a man would never be silent about the Jews, who gave him and so many others something to hate. Yet, Kunstler had to admit that at this juncture he too hated the Jews, and he was certain Radish felt the same way.

The phone on Kunstler's desk rang. He did not bother to turn around.

Radish answered, "Colonel, Field Marshal Kesselring would like to speak with you," he said.

Kunstler turned from the window and took the phone.

"I have a letter," the field marshal said, "that was brought to me by General Stiefle. The letter was sent by SS Captain Muller to his mother."

Kunstler closed his eyes and took a deep breath. He could hear the blood roaring through his ears.

"I understand," the field marshal continued, "that Captain Muller was killed in action."

"Yes, sir, he was killed by partisans."

"This letter to his mother," Kesselring said, "is less than complimentary about you, colonel."

"We did not often see eye to eye, as the expression goes," Kunstler replied. "The differences in our respective military units and experience led to—"

"Yes, I can understand that," Kesselring said. "But I do not understand the allegation that you might be opposed to the way our leaders have decided to handle the Jewish problem."

"I can assure you, field marshal, that I know exactly what my duty is."

"That is what I told General Stiefle."

"Thank you, sir."

"These letters that sometimes come to us are in the main a nuisance. But because the unique situation in your area at the present time, the letter has much more impact, especially since Muller's mother sent a copy of it to Himmler."

Beads of perspiration popped out on Kunstler's forehead and upper lip. His heart began to beat rapidly. He forced himself to remain outwardly calm.

"Because of this situation, we must be very careful about what happens in the immediate future. We must make sure that the Jews are recaptured and the partisans destroyed."

"Those are my objectives," Kunstler answered, forcing himself to keep his voice steady.

"It pleases me to know that," Kesselring said. "I want you to capture the Jews. As for the partisans, you do what you must with them. But the Jews have now assumed a proportion that goes beyond our own command."

"I am afraid I do not understand," Kunstler admitted.

"The Jews must be captured and sent to Germany as planned. I do not want any more air attacks made on them. It should be easy to recapture them once you eliminate the partisans. But the Jews must not be allowed to tweak our nose."

Kunstler was silent.

"Himmler wants the Jews," Kesselring explained. "There is some nonsense about its becoming a matter of German honor." The general paused. "Kunstler, we are old friends. There is nowhere the Jews can go.

Keep after them. When they are exhausted, they will turn on their liberators, help you kill them, and go willingly back to the warmth and security of wherever you want them."

"Yes," Kunstler said, "I understand."

"Excellent. I've enjoyed our talk," Kesselring told him. "If there is something I can do for you, I would consider it an honor to do it."

"Thank you," Kunstler said and put the phone down. "Even dead," he told Radish in a low, angry voice, "Muller has managed to interfere." He removed a handkerchief from the inside breast pocket of his tunic and wiped his brow. "All the field marshal wants me to do," he explained, "is kill the partisans and capture the Jews."

"What the hell does he think we've been trying to do?" Radish asked.

Kunstler sat down at his desk. "Himmler is involved."

"Himmler?"

"A letter from Muller to his mother," Kunstler said, "and from her to Himmler."

"Then you must capture the Jews," Wolfe commented from the other side of the room.

Kunstler glared at him but refrained from calling him a horse's ass. Instead, he asked Radish to pour him a cognac.

"I think we could all use a drink," Radish said.

There was no way for Kunstler to exclude Wolfe and he accepted the general's conviviality with silent resignation.

The remainder of the day passed slowly, but by the following morning the rain abated. Immediately,

Kunstler ordered transportation, and with a full company of men he returned to the gorge where the bombing had taken place.

Water was still running down the gorge into the Tenna Valley, but it was not enough to prevent Kunstler from assessing the damage he had inflicted on the escaping Jews.

Several of the bodies were still caught in the rubble created by the bombing, a few others had been carried further downstream by the surge of the water.

"Well, Radish," Kunstler said, pulling up the broad collar of his leather trench coat, "now we have to find Barraka again." He looked up toward the end of the gorge and to the wall of rock beyond it. "He went that way," Kunstler told him, pointing to the north, "just as Garjulio said they would. By the way, did he come round for his payment?"

"I haven't seen him since the day he was in your office."

"Like the Jews, he has disappeared," Kunstler said sarcastically. "If we find him, he'll be dead. A man like him doesn't willingly stay away from money unless he is dead. The truth of the matter is that I can't feel too sorry for the Garjulios in this war. I have much more respect for the partisans than I have for men like him."

"He was a good source of information," Radish said.

"Which was probably why he was killed," Kunstler said. "But we can't worry about Garjulio when we have Barraka out there to occupy us. We have to find him and then go after him with our men. Kesselring, or Himmler, or both, want those Jews alive. I'm not to attack them with aircraft. That means, Radish, we will have to chase Barraka all the way to the Swiss border and either cut him off, or kill enough of the partisans to make it impossible for him to continue. And so far as we know, Barraka, Koss, and Yancy are still very much alive."

"That is true, so far as we know."

"I will tell you something," Kunstler said. "I would like to capture this Major Barraka alive and find out why he took three hundred Jews instead of just one, or even a half a dozen. He might have made it to the border with a few, but he'll never do it with three hundred."

"Perhaps, he's doing what he has been ordered to do, no more and no less."

"To take several hundred men, women, and children up that rock wall requires of a man that he do much more, very much more than just carry out his orders. I tell you this, Radish, this Major Barraka stands between me and the Jews. No one else and nothing else. To recapture the Jews, I must kill or capture him."

Radish did not understand Kunstler's attitude, or reasoning but he decided it would be wiser to remain silent than to ask for an additional explanation.

XVI

An icy wind-driven rain beat down on Barraka and his people as they struggled steadily northward toward the high passes of the pre-Alps. With little sleep and hardly anything to eat, they were exhausted, hungry, and very cold.

The first day Barraka had sent out parties of men to beg food from the farmhouses on the lower slopes, but the Germans had visited the farmers two weeks before and had, without exception, left only enough food for the particular farmer and his family to survive the winter. They had taken the rest of it to feed the local troops.

Though the two days of rain had shielded the column from the Germans, it had also slowed their progress toward the Umbrail Pass. Barraka had hoped they would travel at the rate of ten kilometers a day. But they were just barely doing seven. He was desperately afraid the weather would worsen before they reached the pass; it was the time of year when the first blizzard of winter would soon come roaring out of the Alps. He doubted if many of the people would be able to survive the rigors of such an experience.

At night Sarah stayed close to her uncle and brother. Barraka was never far away. He was the last to stretch out on the ground and the first one up. It seemed as if he needed no more than a few minutes' sleep.

Sometimes he looked at her, or rather glanced in her direction. But he didn't say anything to her. And when he did speak it was either to her uncle or brother. He always settled down to rest in the same way: on his back, with his hands behind his head. To shield his face from the rain, he covered it with the battered cap he wore.

There wasn't much talking when the column halted for the night. The people were just too exhausted. That was the way it was for the most part with her uncle and Manio. Sarah silently thanked God they had the good sense not to ask her how she was, or treat her with pity.

During the day, Sarah preferred the company of Rinata, who in so short a time she had come to admire and respect.

"That's my man," Rinata said proudly as she pointed to a thick-set, red-faced man. "He's a sergeant in the American army. His name is John Yancy. I tell you as one woman to another, I wanted him the first time I saw him."

The mention of sexual contact made Sarah cringe. But she kept her feelings to herself.

Later that morning, Rinata identified Lieutenant

Koss. "The three of them, Barraka, Koss, and Yancy, came here with Volterra and Mastrada, who are really the leaders of this group of partisans. . . . Did you know that Volterra and Mastrada are Jews?"

"No, I didn't know that," Sarah said.

The rigors of the march forced them into silence. But toward evening, Sarah touched Rinata on the arm. "What kind of man is Barraka?" she asked.

"Hard. A soldier," Rinata answered. "Yancy says that they don't come any better. But I can't tell you anything else about him. He doesn't talk much. Yancy said that when they started out Barraka was very angry at Volterra and Mastrada and there were even a couple of fights between them. But you wouldn't know that now, would you?"

"No," Sarah answered. "Now it seems as if they'd be willing to die for each other."

"No question about it," Rinata answered.

That night when Sarah rejoined her uncle and Manio, she said, "Thank you for saving me." And she kissed both of them on the cheek. "I love you more than I can ever say."

Piatelli wiped the tears from his eyes. "It was Barraka who saved you," he responded.

"He wouldn't let me go with him," Manio told her.

Sarah looked at Barraka. He was some distance from them, talking to Koss and Yancy. For a few moments she debated with herself whether or not to thank him. But she decided against it. Whatever she'd say would embarrass him. Intuitively she knew he wasn't the kind of man who needed or wanted to be thanked for the things he did.

Much later, when her uncle and brother had fallen

asleep, Sarah remained awake. The rain had turned into a thin drizzle and in the distance the clouds were beginning to break up, leaving patches of open sky.

Despite what had happened to her, despite the deep feeling that she had been irreparably damaged and would never again feel completely clean, she wanted to survive. She wanted to live. Maybe someday, as Rinata had said, she would come to love a man, and God will—

Barraka stirred.

Sarah narrowed her eyes and watched him. He pulled the cap from his head and sat up. He ran his hands over his face and through his hair. He put the cap back on his head and stood up. Then he turned and looked at her.

Sarah held her breath. He stood looking at her for almost longer than she could hold her breath. Then he walked away.

Sarah exhaled and opened her eyes, wondering what Barraka was thinking when he looked at her. Suddenly she was flooded with shame. She knew that when he looked at her, he saw her naked.

On the third day the rain stopped. But the clouds continued to cover the peak of the nearby mountains.

Barraka pressed on. Several times during the morning he moved back along the entire length of the column and shouted "Faster! You must move faster!"

Two of the elderly people suffered heart attacks and died. Their bodies were left practically where they had fallen.

Barraka and Volterra walked side by side. Neither

had the strength to waste words. Besides, during the short time they had been together, each one had learned somehow to divine the other's thoughts. Each of them was worried about the same thing.

Suddenly Barraka stopped. "Okay, we'll take ten."

"Good idea," Volterra answered and called out for the people to rest.

They dropped in their tracks.

Barraka stretched out on the wet, cold earth. "We're going to have more heart attacks, the higher we go."

"Can't be helped," Volterra answered. "Only the strong will survive this."

Barraka chewed on the stem of his pipe. He had lost the oilskin tobacco pouch during the attack at Servigliano.

"Did you think it would be this hard?" Volterra asked.

"I knew it would be hard," Barraka said, with a nod; then he added in a much lower voice, "There was no other choice for them. It was either this or the camps."

Volterra didn't answer.

They allowed themselves the luxury of closing their eyes for the remainder of the few minutes they had left to rest before continuing their march. When it was time to move again, Barraka stood up and called to the others to follow them.

During the afternoon it became progressively colder. Without any pretense of modesty, men and women stopped to urinate more frequently. The cold made their breath steam and cracked the skin of their hands.

Just before sunset, Barraka heard the drone of a single engine plane. "Company," he said to Manio, pointing in the direction of the sound.

Others in the column heard the plane and began to shout with fear. The column disintegrated. People ran in every direction.

"Yancy, Koss, Mastrada," Barraka shouted above the tumult, "get those people back here before they kill themselves."

Then Barraka saw Sarah move among the people, urging them to stay in the column and keep moving. "That's it," he yelled to her. "That's it, Sarah. Keep them moving." He went down the length of the column. "Stay with the column," he shouted, "if you want to reach Switzerland. It's your only chance of getting out of here alive."

Many of the people did not look at him when he spoke. Others listened intently to his every word and nodded. A few reached out and touched him with the tips of their fingers, as if he were some holy man.

"It's damn creepy," Barraka said to Volterra later when they were together. "Damn creepy."

"They need a hero," Volterra explained.

"Then they made a damn bad choice," Barraka said and looking up at the gray sky, he added, "It's too late for the Krauts to send up their bombers."

"Do you think they'll send them tomorrow?"

Barraka nodded.

"What will we do, Mitch?"

"Not much, I'm afraid. . . . Maybe if we get lucky, we can get a few good shots off and bring one or two of the bastards down."

"And how many of us will go down?"

Barraka didn't answer. He saw no point in stating what was so blatantly obvious. "Let's keep moving," he shouted. "Keep moving. . . . We still have hours to go before we stop for the night."

He turned, and, with the peculiar feeling he was harnessed to the people behind him, he plodded forward.

Captain Fennly looked up at Colonel Dodd and shook his head. "There's no response, sir," he said.

"What the hell happened to them?" Dodd asked.

The captain remained silent.

"We know they got out of Servigliano . . . I mean our recon photos show the place is a shambles. . . . Goddamn that Barraka!"

"Maybe atmospheric conditions aren't letting his transmissions through."

"Atmospheric conditions, my ass!" Dodd exclaimed. General Williams had asked for a status account of the mission and all he could tell him was that three hundred damn Jews had apparently gotten out of Servigliano, but he didn't know where they were or how many of them were alive. "Listen, if Barraka makes contact with you, I want you to have me patched in . . . I have something to say to that son-of-a-bitch."

"Yes, sir."

Frowning, Colonel Dodd left the radio communications center.

Kunstler was at the wall map, studying it. The Jews

had been spotted by an observation plane toward the end of the day at a point some twenty kilometers north of Servigliano.

"There's nothing there," Kunstler said to Radish and Wolfe, "except some scattered farmhouses. My guess is that Barraka will attempt to cross the Itillina River, which means he must come out of that high country to this area next." Kunstler moved the tip of his forefinger over the map. "That is where we'll be waiting for him."

"Just to play the devil," Radish said, "suppose Barraka decides to bypass that open area and move to the west?"

"You mean go into still higher country and cross into Switzerland at—"

"Anyplace along the border," Radish said. "Barraka probably has two, possibly four alternate crossover points. And once they're over the border, we won't be able to fire a shot."

"The two of you keep saying Barraka," Wolfe said. "You don't even know if he is alive."

"I'm sorry, general," Radish said. "I should use another word, or name. But I can only think of Barraka whenever I speak about their leader. My intuition tells me he is very much alive."

"What do you think?" Wolfe asked, looking at Kunstler.

"The same as Radish," Kunstler answered. "I am sure Major Barraka is alive."

When the column finally halted for the night, it was 0200 hours of the following day. There were huge open patches of star-filled sky in the cloud cover and it was bitterly cold. Barraka had gone as far as his own strength would sustain him, and then he stopped. The place he chose to rest for the rest of the night was a woods of stunted pine. "Pass the word," he told Manio, "that we'll camp here for the night."

"Any fires?" Manio asked.

"None. Can't take the risk," Barraka answered. He watched Manio move back along the column. Though they had never had the opportunity to get to know each other, Barraka wasn't the least bit sorry that he had accepted Manio's offer.

Barraka rubbed his badly bruised hands.

Yancy came over. "Do you think we lost 'em?"

"Maybe, if we were invisible," Barraka answered. "But at least we won't be where they last saw us. Now we could use another day or so of rain."

Yancy glanced up at the sky. "Not likely," he commented, getting up. "See you in the mornin'."

Barraka nodded.

Volterra and Piatelli came to where Barraka was. "Mitch, we need food and medical supplies," Volterra said.

"Why not mention warm clothing and blankets?"

"I think we should call for an air drop," Volterra told him.

"Believe me, major," Piatelli said, "the people have done all you asked them to. But they haven't had anything more than bread for three days. Some of them are so cold they are just sitting and weeping like children. We must have food and some medical supplies. Dr. Klaus doesn't even have any aspirin left."

Barraka took out his pipe and chewed on the stem.

"I agree with him," Volterra said.

"So do I," Barraka responded, removing the pipe from his mouth. "I'm as hungry and tired as anyone else."

"Excuse me, major," Piatelli said, "but you have been trained to take this kind of punishment. None of my people—"

"There's just a chance," Barraka said, pointing a pipe stem at them, "that we lost the Krauts . . . I'm not going to throw it away by calling for a food drop." He spoke in a low but determined voice.

"And that is your last word on the subject?" Piatelli asked.

Barraka stood up and said, "I want to save as many of your people as I can. But by calling for an air drop, I'll be giving the Krauts our address. Come on, Chaim, you know what will happen. We won't have a snowball's chance in hell. No air drop. That's it!" And he walked away, feeling very uncomfortable with himself.

Barraka moved through the pine grove without really looking where he was going. And suddenly he found himself face to face with Sarah.

Without speaking a word, Barraka took hold of her hand and led her to a large rock formation. He sat down on the flat side of the boulder and she seated herself next to him. Other than calling out to her the previous day, he hadn't said a word to Sarah since he had carried her out of the barracks in Servigliano, and then he had only spoken to her to assuage her fear. But the sight of her nude body had stayed with him, and now as he looked at her it came full-blown into his thoughts once again.

"You know," Sarah told him in almost a whisper, "I have watched you every day, and I have wondered what kind of man you were before the war."

"An ordinary man," he answered. "I owned a small construction company. And what about you?"

"A student in medical school at the University of Bologna," she explained. "But all of that is past, gone."

Barraka laid his finger against her lips. "We are alive," he told her gently. "Now, that is all that matters."

"You must think of the future sometimes."

"Sure I do."

"What do you think about?"

"The bridges I will build," he answered, feeling foolish for having spoken about his own dream for the future.

"So you are really an engineer?"

"Yes."

"And I thought you were a professional soldier."

He shook his head. "Yancy is the old professional," he told her.

"Major—"

"Mitch. My name is Mitchell. But everyone calls me Mitch."

"Why did you come after me back there in Servigliano?" she asked.

"Your uncle said he wouldn't go without you," Barraka answered. But after a moment he added, "I guess I just couldn't leave you to the Krauts."

"What if we don't survive? What if all this pain is for nothing?" she questioned in a rush.

"We'll have tried," he told her. "Trying. Only by trying will we know if we can do it." He stood up, took her in his arms, and kissed her.

She pushed against his chest. "You have no right to—"

Barraka kissed her again, this time with a growing passion. He had not been near a woman for months.

"I haven't the will to resist," she said in a choked voice. "I can't stop you."

He let go of her.

Sarah ran from him.

Barraka sat down on the rock and chewed on his pipe for several minutes. With a shrug he stood up and went back to where he had left Volterra and Piatelli. Only Volterra was there.

"What's the code name for a food drop?" Barraka asked.

"Seventh inning stretch," Volterra answered, looking up at him.

"Why that?"

"It was Keller's idea," Volterra answered.

"Okay," Barraka said. "Let's get us a seventh inning stretch . . . I've got to feed these people."

Volterra nodded and suppressed a smile.

With sleep still clouding his brain, Colonel Dodd held the phone close to his ear and listened to the conversation between Barraka and Fennly.

"We have to have a seventh inning stretch," Barraka said. "And a base on balls."

"Where the hell have you been?" Fennly asked.

"Listen, I've been walking."

"Your orders—"

"Fuck them and fuck you . . . just get me what I ask for."

Entering the conversation, Dodd said, "You better take it easy, Cross Over."

"That you, Dodd?"

"You crazy bastard, don't you know the Krauts are monitoring us?"

"Listen, colonel, I got more goddamn Krauts than I know what to do with. Let's cut the shit out . . . they probably know where we are and they also know how bad things are."

"That bad?" Dodd asked.

"Yeah, that bad."

"The general wants to know what the status is."

"Go."

"Are you sure? A helluva lot rides on it."

"Yeah, I guess the Krauts feel the same way."

"Okay, you'll get what you asked for. But when you get back here, I'll have a few things to settle out with you."

"I read you loud and clear, colonel."

"Give the info to Will-o'-the-Wisp," Dodd said.

Barraka began to laugh.

"What the hell is so funny?"

"Colonel, the Krauts know who we are. They probably know when we eat, piss, and shit, to say nothing of when we fuck, if we could fuck."

Dodd smiled and said, "You're probably right. But nonetheless keep to our code."

"Absolutely," Barraka answered. "Okay, Will-o'-the-Wisp, start writing . . ."

When Barraka finished with the transmission, he

and Volterra walked back to the fire. "Tell Piatelli we'll have food, with any luck, by tomorrow afternoon," Barraka said. "He'll sleep easier knowing about it. But also tell him not to mention it to anyone else. I don't want a few hundred disappointed and hungry people near me if the weather closes in and prevents the drop."

"What made you change your mind?" Volterra asked.

Barraka rubbed his hands. "I wish the hell I knew. Maybe, like the gambler said, it's the only game in town?"

Volterra nodded and went to find Piatelli.

Stretching out on the ground, Barraka put his hands behind his head. He did not want to tell Volterra that for some unknown reason his meeting with Sarah had changed his mind. He did not even want him, or for that matter anyone, to know he had met her, or that she had confused him, or that when he had held her in his arms and caressed her, he could hear her again say, "*We are delivered into your hands,*" though she had said something completely different.

Barraka pursed his lips and silently told himself that the encounter between them meant nothing. Just something that happened thousands of times during the war when a man who had not been near a woman for months suddenly held one in his arms.

"It means nothing," he said aloud and closed his eyes, drifting off into a light sleep, during which he dreamt about being in bed with Helen, who, by the time he awoke with a start, had become Sarah.

Barraka saw Volterra was asleep on the other side of the fire. He rubbed his eyes, stood up and moved away to urinate. Then he came back and shook Volterra, who bolted up and went for his .45.

"It's okay," Barraka said gently. "We have to move out . . . the sun will be up soon."

Volterra struggled to his feet. "It's cold!" he exclaimed, rubbing his hands.

Barraka agreed, "Maybe we'll get some sun today."

"It looks clear now."

Barraka didn't answer. He was already moving away and calling to Manio to get Yancy, Koss, and Mastrada.

Within minutes the column was assembled and the long day's trek begun.

"C'mon," Barraka shouted, "we've got to move faster. Let's move now!"

"We're going to have stragglers," Volterra gasped.

"You take the lead," Barraka answered. "I'll drop back and keep everyone moving. Remember that we must be on a fifteen-degree heading from where we are."

"Fifteen degrees," Volterra repeated.

Barraka dropped back to the rear of the column.

Radish was awakened by an orderly at 0300 hours and handed the transcript of the conversation between Major Barraka, Captain Fennly and Colonel Dodd. All voices had been authenticated. Radish read the report and then phoned Kunstler. The two of them arranged to meet in Kunstler's office within fifteen minutes.

Kunstler was already pacing the floor when Radish arrived. The colonel looked positively haggard. Radish handed him the transcript.

"They play games on the radio," Kunstler said with

disgust, "but we still don't know what they're up to. Seventh inning stretch. Base on balls. What the hell do those things mean?"

"A Home Run," Radish commented, "meant an air strike."

"That doesn't tell what these mean," Kunstler growled, going to the window and looking up at the clear night sky. "They talk about everything except the things that would tell us what we want to know."

"There must be someone in the brigade who knows something about baseball," Radish said. "Maybe we have such a man here in headquarters. As soon as we find him, or anyone—"

Suddenly Wolfe entered the office. As usual, he did not bother to knock. "I couldn't sleep," he said. "And when I went to my window, I saw the light go on in your office, Colonel, and realized that something of interest was probably happening. Is it?"

With a sigh, Kunstler handed Wolfe the transcript.

"I don't think we really know when they piss and shit. But maybe with a little digging we can find out when they fuck," Wolfe said, smiling broadly and waiting for them to laugh.

"General," Kunstler said, "from the transcript we know they are up to something. We know that it will be today, but we do not know what it is, or where it will take place. We do not know what a seventh inning stretch is, or a base on balls."

"A Seventh inning stretch is a pause in the game," Wolfe said matter-of-factly.

Kunstler glanced at Radish and asked the general if he was absolutely sure.

"Yes," Wolfe answered. "Before the war, whenever

I visited New York I managed to see a game if it was the season. A seventh inning stretch is a pause in the game."

"What happens?"

"People buy food and drink. Frankfurters, beer."

"Food," Kunstler shouted. "They're going to make an air drop of food."

"And what is a base on balls?" Radish questioned.

"It no longer matters," Kunstler said, moving to the map on the wall. "We know they're planning to make an air drop of food. My guess is that a base on balls would be some other type of supplies. Now all we have to figure out is where. We know where they were, but by now they've probably moved."

"Why think that?" Wolfe asked.

"Because, general," Major Barraka would not stay where he was spotted," Kunstler answered. "I would move, and I am sure he has, though he could not have moved very far. I would think that he and his people have spent the night in this area here, among the pine trees. Now we have to guess where that drop will be made."

"Excuse me, colonel," Radish said, going toward the map, "I don't think we have to guess at anything."

"Then you know where they're going to make the drop?" Wolfe asked.

"No, sir," Radish said. "But if we alert our antiaircraft units, they'll pick up the incoming planes and follow their course. We have the option of having them shot down by fighters or downed by antiaircraft fire, or both."

"Suppose a base on balls means fighter support," Wolfe suggested.

"Gentlemen," Kunstler said, "I have a plan that would negate their effort. I want those transports to come through, with or without fighter support. Radish was partially right when he said we would know where they'd be going. We'd also be able to follow them with transports of our own. Only ours would be carrying two companies of paratroopers. The American planes will come in, make their drop, and then leave as fast as possible. We'll follow them, make our drop, and finally put an end to this whole nasty business."

"Excellent!" Wolfe said. "Absolutely a first-rate idea."

Kunstler smiled broadly. He felt as if a great weight had been taken off his shoulders. He would soon have the Jews and Barraka. Secretly, he wanted Barraka more than he wanted the Jews.

"I think the trouble with the Jews," Wolfe said with a smile, "is that they never get over being circumcised. It makes them want more and more of something they can never have. I mean, gentlemen, what man wants to go through life with a shortened cock?"

This time Kunstler and Radish did laugh long and loud. They laughed until tears came to their eyes and spilled down their unshaved cheeks.

The drop zone was a bare, windswept knoll no more than three hundred meters long and less than thirty meters wide. Barraka left the main body of his people on the far side of a ridge to the east of the knoll, where they would be concealed by the lengthening shadows of late afternoon. He positioned himself, Koss, and ten other men on the west side of the knoll. To approach the drop zone the planes would have to fly north and then circle back, making the final run between two fairly high ridges. They would have a bumpy ride down to their drop altitude. Barraka had requested the drop to be made at no more than one hundred and fifty meters of altitude.

The sun was out and the sky clear, though there were some clouds off to the east. Barraka checked his watch. It was 1540 hours. The drop was scheduled for 1550. He expected to pick up the sound of the plane within a matter of minutes.

"How long do you figure before the Krauts show?" Koss asked.

"They'll be here soon enough," Barraka answered. "With luck, we'll have five, six minutes to grab what we can and run before they begin to strafe. The medical supplies will be marked with a red cross. Everything else will be food. As soon as you men have a bundle, run for those boulders to the south of the knoll. They'll offer good cover."

"I've already assigned two men to pick up the medical bags."

"Good," Barraka said. He was straining to hear the throb of the transports' engines. The sun had moved slightly lower in the west. Its light was intense. When the transports made their run, the pilot would not have any trouble spotting the knoll.

"They might be coming in from a different direction," Koss said, "before they make their final approach."

"Yeah," Barraka answered. He expected to see them fly in from the south, go north, and then swing back. "Fly boys all do things differently." The wind was cold but there was some warmth from the sun. He tried to enjoy it.

Suddenly he heard them.

Koss and the other men did too.

All of them strained to see the planes.

There was a flash to the north.

"Did you see that?" Barraka asked.

"Sure did. And there's another one. And another. Three of them. The sun must have hit the wings when they turned. Here they come!"

Barraka's breath made puffs of steam in the cold air. His heart raced. He licked his dry, raw lips.

The planes came swooping down on the knoll, growing larger and larger as they approached. And then they roared low overhead, as large bundles were jettisoned from their open cargo hatches.

Barraka and his men cheered.

The planes started to climb.

Barraka leaped up and ran for an open area of the knoll, where the first bundles were slowly drifting down. Before the first one touched the ground, another droning filled the air.

"Junkers!" Barraka shouted, pointing to the two tri-motor transports lumbering down at the knoll, "Grab what you can." He had gambled and lost!

The planes were overhead. One after another the German paratroopers came tumbling out of the transports.

"Keep them away from the column," Barraka shouted. He opened fire on the men coming down.

The others did the same.

Several Germans were killed before they reached the ground. But as soon as the others were down, they returned the fire.

"Let's get the hell out of here," Barraka yelled. He made a run for an area on the south slope of the knoll where the boulders were.

The paratroopers immediately began to advance.

"Fall back," Barraka said. "Fall back. We've got to draw them away from the others."

The Germans began to fire a light mortar, laying down a pattern that blew huge fragments of rock into the air.

"Hold your fire," Barraka ordered. "Make them come after us."

The mortar fire made a crisscross pattern on the southern slope and worked across the base. Then the firing stopped.

"Okay," Barraka ordered, "fall back. Come on now, move." He dashed down the slope and made it across to the base of several enormous glacial boulders. Breathing hard and soaked with sweat, he told the men with him, "I think we can hold out till tonight; then we can get the hell out of here. If they want us, they'll have to come and get us, and it's going to cost them."

The Germans set up two heavy machine guns on the knoll and began to pour fire down into the boulders.

"Just stay on your bellies," Barraka told them above the chatter of those guns and the pinging of ricocheting bullets. "Stay on your bellies."

Machine gun slugs chewed away at the boulders, filling the air with rock dust. Another mortar barrage started; then stopped. The machine guns also stopped.

Barraka eased himself up.

* * *

A light plane had just made a bumpy landing on the knoll. As soon as the aircraft came to a halt, Kunstler threw open the cabin door and eased himself out.

"Where are they?" he asked after a perfunctory salute.

"Among those rocks," the paratroop captain answered.

"I want as many of the Jews alive as possible," Kunstler said. "I do not care what happens to the partisans. But I want those Jews."

"Yes, colonel."

"How many casualties?"

"Five killed. Three wounded."

"Surround the entire area," Kunstler said. "And if they don't surrender, we will go in and get them."

The captain dispatched his men to encircle the entire area where the boulders were located. As soon as it was accomplished, Kunstler picked up a loudspeaker. "Major Barraka," he called, "we know you are there. We ask you to surrender."

Kunstler's words echoed off the slopes of the nearby ridges.

"Major, I urge you to think of the women and children with you," Kunstler said. "You are completely surrounded. There is no way out for anyone."

"I'll give you ten minutes, major," Kunstler said. "If I do not have an affirmative reply, I will have to use force."

Barraka motioned to Koss and the others to move deeper among the rocks. "We have at least a half hour before sunset," he whispered. "If we hold out, we can make it back to the column. But ten minutes is ten minutes. Listen, we can keep moving around these rocks for a while. He knows his casualties will be heavy."

"Why doesn't he just blast the hell out of us?" one of the men asked.

"Because he wants my people," Barraka replied angrily. "And I'll be goddamned if I'll give them up."

"But they're not here," Koss said.

"That bastard thinks they are. And we're going to fight as if they were here."

"The ten minutes are up," Kunstler announced. You leave me no alternative."

"Keep close and cover each other," Barraka told his men. "When you can use a knife instead of a bullet, use it. We're going to need all the ammo we've got. Okay, everyone follow me."

A burst from a machine pistol sent a shower of rock fragments behind the last man. He turned and fired.

Barraka moved quickly, his men following him. "In a few minutes everything will be in shadow," he whispered to Koss.

Another burst of fire! The slugs caught two of the men in the middle of the column. They screamed and dropped. More fire.

The German shouted he had made contact.

One of the partisans lobbed a grenade at the place where the sound came from. With a thunderous boom, the explosion sent a shower of pulverized rock into the air.

There were yells for medical aid from behind the boulder.

Barraka snaked his men around the rocks, stalking

the Germans and being stalked by them. He spotted a man to his right in between two large boulders and was about to reach for his knife, when the man turned toward him. Barraka dropped his carbine to his hip and squeezed off two rounds. A look of surprise passed over the German's face. One bullet struck the man in the left shoulder and the other hit him in the chest. A stream of blood gushed from his mouth.

Two Germans came running to the fallen man's aid, saw Barraka, dropped to their knees and began to fire.

The slugs pinged off the boulder behind Barraka. He bellied down and fired. Someone behind him screamed. He continued to fire.

Several more Germans joined the first two.

"Someone get to those fuckers!" Barraka shouted. He glanced over his shoulder to see one of his men leap up and try to throw a grenade. His head was suddenly mashed into a red blotch against the rock. Another partisan grabbed the grenade. There was no time left. The man pulled the grenade against his belly and threw himself to the ground. An instant later, the explosion lifted him up.

The Germans continued to fire.

"Take them out!" Barraka yelled. He fired as fast as he could, emptying his clip of ammo.

Koss fired from behind him.

Barraka inserted a new clip and resumed firing.

Then all at once there were three successive explosions in the midst of the Germans.

Barraka was on his feet and running past the place where the Germans had been and into another pathway between the rocks. The men followed him. He wiped the sweat and powdered rock from his face.

"How many got it?" he asked.

"Counting the two of us," Koss answered, "there's seven of us left."

"Shit!" Barraka exclaimed. "We've got to get the hell out of here."

There was a single shot from the knoll.

Barraka looked up. The white light of burning magnesium illuminated the sky, the knoll, and the boulders.

"That's not going to make it any easier," Koss commented.

"We're going to have to split up. One group of three and two of two. Each group goes off in a different direction. Koss, you go out with me."

The men dispersed quickly.

"It turned out to be a fuck up," Barraka said. "I figured on the Krauts sending planes, not men." He shook his head and once more started to pick his way through the maze of boulders.

Intermittently, there was a burst of bright white light above them that dimmed slowly over a period of two minutes as the flare descended.

Barraka could hear the Germans without difficulty. Often, they were on the other side of the same boulder, or in a place in front or in back of him.

The crack of rifle fire brought him and Koss to a halt.

The Germans were shouting.

"What the hell are they saying?" Barraka questioned in a whisper.

"They killed three men," Koss answered.

Barraka ran his hand over his beard but said nothing. Cautiously, he worked his way toward the southwest perimeter of the area covered by the boulders.

Another burst of fire. This time it came from the machine guns on the knoll. They weren't shooting into the boulders. From the tracers, Barraka could see they were going after targets on the east slope. A flare illuminated two men struggling to gain the ridge crest. The slugs from the machine gun whacked into the rocky slope and then caught each of the men in the back, knocking them down. The men rolled to where the steepness of the slope lessened and stopped their movement.

"The Krauts have to know by now," Barraka said in a whisper, "we're the only ones here."

"They know—"

A short burst from a machine pistol smashed into the back of Koss's head. He went down on his knees and then fell forward. He was dead.

Barraka whirled around and fired.

The German stumbled and fell. He was still alive.

With a growl of rage, Barraka drove his foot into the man's chest. Then, at point blank range, he fired into his face. Still quivering with fury and fighting back the sobs that wanted to wrench themselves free from his constricted throat, he ran.

Barraka looked up at a slowly descending flare. Beyond it the sky was heavily overcast. He hadn't noticed the change. Nor had he been aware until now that the wind had begun to blow harder. But he could hear it moan as it rushed through the mazelike pathway between the boulders.

More and more Germans, from the sound of them, were moving around the rocks. Several times Barraka fired his carbine in one direction and then in another to give the illusion of having more men. Once he tossed a grenade over a boulder because he had heard the Germans talking on the other side. From their screams he knew he had wounded several of them.

Barraka knew there was now very little chance of his getting out alive. But he was determined to kill as many Germans as he could before one of them killed him.

Then it began to rain. The combination of rain and wind shortened the life of the flares.

Barraka crept toward an opening that would lead him out of the boulders. In front of him a German leaned against a large rock in an effort to protect himself from the wind and the rain.

Barraka unsheathed his trench knife and moved in a crouch toward the man.

The soldier turned and faced him. Barraka dropped his carbine and leaped at him, slashing at his throat with a sideward motion. The blade sliced deep.

Barraka slashed again.

The man went down.

Barraka leaped back, grabbed his carbine, and ran for the slope. Behind him there was shouting, followed by rifle fire. But the Germans were shooting blindly.

Barraka ran up toward the crest of the rise, dropped over it, and began to move south. Sometime later he would turn east and north. During the night he would link up with the column.

He moved quickly, bending his body against the force of the wind. He had lost eleven men on the mission. Several times he swallowed the lump in his throat. Kunstler had outfoxed him. He had sent troops instead of planes. His gamble hadn't paid off; it had managed to kill his friend.

Barraka fought back the tears, but they came and mingled with the rain that beat against his cheeks. There was nothing he could do to stop himself from weeping, absolutely nothing.

Just before the rain started the paratroop captain reported to Kunstler that a total of eleven partisans had been killed. His men had not been able to find any Jews in the immediate vicinity.

"They're close by," Kunstler assured him and ordered that a thorough search be undertaken for several kilometers in each direction. He had all the dead partisans brought to one place, and from the identification tags on one body he discovered that Lieutenant William Koss had been among the casualties.

Because of the weather, Kunstler was forced to spend the night in a small tent on top of the rain-lashed knoll. When he returned to Malveno the following morning, he was cold, tired, and in a dark mood.

"I tell you," he said to Radish and Wolfe, "I had Major Barraka in my grasp and he managed to get out. And the damn Jews were not even there."

Wolfe and Radish were sympathetic.

"At least you managed to kill some of the partisans," Wolfe said.

"We lost twenty-five to their eleven," Kunstler responded dourly. "But I've ordered search patrols to go out and I will have the observation plane in the air as soon as the weather permits. We will locate them, and this time give them no rest until they are willing to surrender."

Radish went to the wall map. "To reach the border, Barraka must cross over this bridge here. It is the only one in the vicinity. We can hold him there. If we have the bridge, he'll have to remain on this side of the Itillina River."

Kunstler looked at the map. "That bridge is approximately twenty kilometers from where they are now, and about fifteen from the border. We have a twelve-man detachment at the bridge, and on the other side of it, about four kilometers away, we also have a lorry depot of eight lorries and twenty-five men. Radish, order half the men at the depot to the bridge. I want them to set up machine gun emplacements along the approaches. We'll block Barraka in front and come up on him from the rear. He'll be caught between our two units."

Radish went to Kunstler's desk, picked up the phone, and gave the necessary orders to deploy the men.

Kunstler stood looking at the map. "If I can harry Barraka, he might not have enough energy left to reach the bridge," he said. "I should think he's close to exhaustion now."

"Then, by all means, do it," Wolfe urged. "The sooner you have them, the better off you'll be."

Kunstler raised his eyebrows questioningly.

"Kesselring is being pushed from Berlin," Wolfe said. "The matter could not be hidden from the Führer."

Kunstler moved away from the map and poured himself a brandy.

"I explained to Kesselring the nature of last night's operation," Wolfe told him. "He was pleased."

"He's not going to be pleased when he gets the report of—"

"The field marshal has complete confidence in your ability," Wolfe said.

Kunstler downed his drink and poured another. He dared not say he wished he had the same confidence in himself he had had just a few days ago.

Barraka rejoined the column shortly after midnight. That he returned alone was sufficient evidence to everyone of the disaster that had befallen them.

"I'll rest for a while," Barraka told Volterra.

"We saw the Junker transports come in."

Barraka nodded and sat down on the wet earth.

"I'm sorry," Volterra said. "I should not have insisted that you ask for an air drop."

"Not your fault," Barraka replied, closing his eyes. "I knew it was a gamble and we had the short odds. Kunstler outfoxed me. I sure as hell didn't expect paratroopers."

Yancy came up to them. "Any chance of Bill making it?" he asked.

"He took a couple of slugs in the back of his head," Barraka explained, shaking his head.

Yancy reached out and squeezed Barraka's shoulder; then he walked slowly back to where Rinata was. He sat down, pulled up his knees and rested his head in his arms.

"We're going to have to make it on our own, Chaim," Barraka said. "By tomorrow we'll be too far into the mountains for any supply drop. Besides, the weather is too uncertain for them to risk it."

"Then we'll just have to make it," Volterra answered.

Without saying anything more, Barraka fell asleep.

Volterra removed his own jacket and covered him with it.

Piatelli came up to him. "How is he?" he asked.

"Exhausted and hurt."

"I wonder if he realizes what he is doing for us?" Piatelli asked.

Volterra shrugged. In the past few days he had often wondered about the same thing. "I don't know. But I do know that none of us will ever meet anyone like him again."

"What do we do now?" Piatelli asked.

"Whatever he wants us to do," Volterra answered.

Piatelli nodded and slowly walked away, leaving Volterra to watch over the man who would lead them all to the promised land. When he returned to his nephew and niece, they wanted to know what had happened and he told them. "Barraka was the only one to return. All of the others were killed."

"Is he all right?" Sarah asked anxiously.

Piatelli gave her a questioning look.

"Oh, please tell me," she cried. "Please?"

"He is hurt inside," Piatelli answered softly.

Sarah uttered a deep sigh of relief. "I'm going to him," she said. And without waiting for an answer, she went to Barraka and sat down alongside of him.

He opened his eyes and looked at her.

"Go back to sleep," she said, gently touching the top of his head.

"Why—"

"Because now you need someone to come back for you," Sarah answered.

He nodded, pursed his lips, and closed his eyes.

But Sarah could see the tears stream down his cheeks.

XVII

For two days and as many nights, Barraka moved his people north. He kept them going day and night, letting them rest when it was absolutely necessary. They were unmercifully flogged by the rain and the wind. They were exhausted and starving. There wasn't a child who did not whimper, or a man who did not falter. They were awake, but they were asleep, living through a protracted nightmare.

And following them were the German paratroopers, keeping close enough to watch their movements, waiting until they dropped in their tracks before they came in for the kill. Now and then they would move closer, fire a few rounds into the rear of the column, and then fall back, always leaving a few dead, or wounded.

Late in the afternoon of the second day, Manio was killed. Barraka had sent him to the rear of the column to help Conway keep the stragglers moving. Conway picked up the body and carried it forward, along the length of the column until he reached Barraka, who took the body from him.

Piatelli and Sarah had followed Conway.

"We can't stop to bury him," Barraka said. He swallowed hard. "The Krauts are behind us."

Sarah sobbed softly. Reaching out, she caressed her brother's hair.

"I'll carry him until we make camp," Barraka offered.

Piatelli wiped his eyes. "No need to, major. He would not have wanted you to give him any preferential treatment."

Barraka looked at Sarah.

"You can put him down," she told him.

Barraka gently laid Manio's body on the ground.

"I would like a few minutes to be with him," Piatelli said. "I think he would want a prayer said for him."

"May I stay?" Barraka asked.

Piatelli nodded, and then in Hebrew he began to recite the Kaddish, the prayer for the dead. Sarah added her melancholy voice to her uncle's, while Barraka stood silently nearby, aware that the strange language expressed his own feelings of grief. When the prayer was finished, Barraka stepped forward, and, picking up Manio's rifle, upended it in the rock-strewn earth.

"What's that for?" Sarah asked.

"To mark the place where a soldier lies."

"He will have no other marker," Piatelli said sadly.

The three of them turned and rejoined the column. Before they separated, Sarah said, "He was proud of belonging to you."

"He was a good man," Barraka replied.

"Yes, I know," she said, brushing the tears from her

cheeks. "He said the same about you."

Barraka nodded and went to his place at the head of the column.

On the morning of the fourth day, the sky, though not completely cloudless, was clear enough for Kunstler to send up a light plane to observe the Jews. The paratroopers stopped following them.

Kunstler was sure that the Jews were reaching the end of their endurance. He sent a plane over them to drop leaflets, asking them to give themselves up, promising them they would be given food and shelter. He had thought of this ploy, trying to think how he might foil a man like Barraka; he knew that if he stopped Barraka the Jews would be his. The leaflets said that if the Jews did not surrender he—Kunstler—would no longer be in a position to offer them the guarantees for noncombatants provided for in the Geneva Convention.

The leaflets created a stir among some of the men in the column. Arguments broke between those who wanted to continue the trek to the border and those who wanted to return to captivity.

"We're going to die out here," one of the men shouted. "Piatelli, you and Barraka are going to kill all of us."

And someone answered him, "I'd rather die a free man than go back to the Germans."

"To go back," Piatelli said, "is to throw away all we've gained." That any of the people would think of giving themselves up to the Germans horrified him. "Don't you realize Kunstler's promises mean nothing? When did the Germans adhere to the Geneva Convention. Don't be taken in by them." He turned to Sarah and in a low voice, he asked, "How can I make them understand?"

She moved her eyes toward Barraka. "He will do it," she answered. "He must do it."

Barraka ignored the leaflets. But the dissension became so violent, he was forced to halt the column.

Barraka listened to one group and then the other. He was on the upper slope of a ridge. The people were below him. He stood very still, holding on to the staff with his left hand and the carbine with his right.

The argument broke out again. Men from each group went at each other with their fists.

"Knock it off!" Barraka shouted. "Knock it off, or by the living God, I'll blow you bastards apart."

He had not spoken as many words to anyone other than Sarah and Piatelli since the debacle of the air drop. He was deep within himself, mourning for Koss, for Manio, and for all the men he had known who had been killed. The war had somehow shrunk to the dimension of his own purpose. Getting these people to the Swiss border had become the ultimate reason for everything that had happened to him in the army and perhaps throughout his whole life. He did not completely understand why that was so, but he intuitively knew it was. If there was some sort of a meaning to his life, he was living that meaning with these people, these Jews, whose leader he had so unwillingly become.

The men fell away from each other.

"Listen," he said, "too many good men have died to get you people where you are. You're going all the way. Listen, and make sure you understand me. I'll kill the first man who makes a move to go back. Is that clear? I'll kill him. No one is going back. No one. Now, form up into a column and let's move out."

There was a lot of grumbling, but the column reformed, and at Barraka's signal it began to move again.

Piatelli resumed his place in the line of march alongside Sarah. Ever since his first meeting with Barraka, he had been trying to reconcile the man with his mission. From Volterra and Mastrada, he had learned about Barraka's attitude at the beginning and how it had changed. Now the mission completely consumed Barraka with an inner fire so intense it had transformed him into another being. With the exception of Sarah, who was falling in love, or was already in love with him, Piatelli wondered how many people were aware of the fire in Barraka? He looked at the man's back and saw the staff in his left hand and the carbine slung over the right shoulder. "He will get us to the Promised Land," Piatelli said to himself. "He is the only one strong enough to do it." And for the first time in months, he silently cried, "Hear, oh Israel, the Lord is our God, the Lord our God is one." The tears ran down his cheeks, and he prayed, asking God to give Barraka the strength he needed to bring the people to safety. "Dear God, if it becomes a question of taking his life or mine, I humbly beseech you to take mine. I am nothing compared to him, nothing. In this place, at this time, the people need him more than they need me. And he needs you to walk at his side, to protect and guide him with your love. . . ."

By nightfall the people in the column caught sight of the Alps. The Swiss border was at the most another two to three days away.

Barraka kept going until 1900 hours, and when he called a halt he allowed the people to start small fires to warm themselves. Exhausted, he stretched out on the rocky ground and slipped into a light sleep.

He moaned softly and made wordless sounds. Suddenly his eyes were open. He was awake, looking at Sarah.

He sat up and said, "Go back to your uncle."

She did not move.

"Go back—"

"I didn't come here to be told to go back," she said resolutely.

Barraka stretched his hands toward the wavering flames. Aware of the flickering light on her face, he felt a surge of feeling toward her. He wanted to hold her in his arms.

"I came here," Sarah said, breaking the silence between them, "to ask you if you would have carried out your threat."

With a brisk movement of his hand, Barraka waved her question aside.

"I want to know how a civilized man could make

such a threat?"

"And I don't want to discuss it with you, or anyone else," he said.

"You don't understand. These people aren't soldiers. They don't understand a soldier's way or a soldier's reality. They only know that once they were free men; then they found themselves prisoners, and now they are neither free nor prisoners. They're in your charge. They must obey you."

"Yes," Barraka answered, "they must obey me, if they want to reach the border, if they want to live."

"Then tell them that," she said. "But don't threaten them with death. Tell them what you would tell any other man. Tell them what you would have told my brother, Manio."

Barraka did not answer. He knew she was right.

"For many of them," she said, "the future has no meaning, no meaning at all."

"And for you," he asked softly, "does it hold any meaning?"

"It is hard to believe there will be a tomorrow, when everything that happens today is a hair's breadth away from death."

Suddenly Barraka reached across the fire and took hold of her hands, standing up, bringing Sarah to her feet. He stepped over the fire and enclosed her in his embrace. His lips pressed down on hers.

"Sarah, I want you," he told her in a low, urgent voice.

She closed her eyes. The strength of his arms around her brought an unfamiliar surge of warmth through her body that quickened her heart and hardened her nipples. She rested against him.

He brushed his hand over her hair and again said, "I want you."

"But you know I have already been taken," she cried.

"I want you," Barraka repeated.

"It is not enough to be wanted for a moment," she whispered. "I want something more to believe in; something that would always hold us together."

"The war won't let us have more than a moment," Barraka said, still holding her in his arms. "If I promised you more, I'd be lying."

"It's not enough," Sarah repeated, shaking her head. "It's not enough. If I cannot have you for the rest of my life, I don't want you for the moment."

Barraka let go of her.

She reached up and touched his lips with the tips of her fingers. "For what it is worth," Sarah told him, "my heart and my body long for you, Mitch, as much as you want to have them."

Barraka pressed her fingers to his lips.

The guards on the east side of the encampment suddenly began to shout, "Men approaching . . . men approaching!"

"Quick, go to your uncle," he told her and called to Yancy, Volterra, and Mastrada. "Let's go," he told them, "hurry." He grabbed his carbine and the few grenades that were close by and ran toward the perimeter of the area.

"There," the guard told him, pointing to a place lower down on the slope where there were three men and two pack mules moving toward them.

"Yancy, cover me," Barraka snapped, as he started down the slope. He moved quickly, and coming up to the men, ordered them to halt. He pointed his carbine at the leader, a short man with a black moustache.

"My name is Sergio Petraroja, and the other two are Tito Scipo and Tanio Dela Rova."

"What do you want?"

"To help," Petraroja said. "We know who you are. We have brought you food."

Lowering his weapon, Barraka rushed toward Petraroja and embraced the man. "Food," he shouted to the others. "They come with food." Then to the three men, he said, "We can offer you nothing, only our gratitude."

Within minutes, everyone in the column had bread and cheese. And there was enough wine for anyone who wanted to drink.

Petraroja and his two companions said that they had heard about the escape from Servigliano from other people and they had decided to do something to help.

"We do what we think should be done," Dela Rova said. "We do it in the name of Christ, our Lord."

Barraka drank with the three men and Piatelli thanked them. "You have come at a time," he explained, "when we did not have the strength to continue."

"Others along the way," Petraroja said, "will try to help, if the Germans do not stop them."

"I understand," Piatelli answered.

After a while, the three men shook hands with Barraka and Piatelli and left the encampment the same way they had entered.

"Brave men," Barraka commented, as he watched them move down the side of the slope. "But what I don't understand is why they bothered. After all, they're Catholics."

"Yes, but they're also Italians."

"I still don't understand."

"The Jews are Italians first and Jews second. Italians have not surrendered Jews the way the French and Dutch did. The Italian way is to live and let live. It is a good way to live."

"A very good way," Barraka answered.

"Have you thought about the bridge?" Volterra asked.

"I know it's there," Barraka said.

"Kunstler will try to stop us there."

"Probably," Barraka responded with a nod. "Probably, but we won't get to the bridge until the day after tomorrow. We have to make it through tomorrow before we start to think about the bridge."

The two men parted and Barraka returned to his fire. Sarah was sitting on the ground next to the fire.

"I told my uncle," she said.

"Told him what?" Barraka asked.

"That I will spend tonight next to you."

"Next to me?"

"Yes, close to you," Sarah answered, looking up at him with her black eyes glistening with the light from the fire. "Nothing more than to be close to you. Would that be enough for you, Mitch?"

He nodded and stretched out alongside her, holding her to him.

XVIII

Despite the rain, Kunstler went to the bridge with Radish and Wolfe to personally supervise the placement of the machine guns. At Wolfe's suggestion, he added four mortar positions. Two of these guarded the southern approach to the bridge and two of them covered the northern end of the road that led away from the bridge. The last would be used only if Barraka managed to get some people across the river. He placed two battalions of armored infantry on the road eight kilometers south of the bridge. These units were on the road, leaving Barraka free to use the surrounding ridges to approach the bridge. And he assigned two companies of paratroopers to take up positions five hundred meters beyond the bridge to insure that his defenses would be absolutely unbreachable.

"By the time Barraka reaches the bridge," Kunstler explained to Wolfe as they entered the tent that served as Kunstler's command post, "he'll be unable to offer any kind of resistance."

"Do you mean the Jews or the partisans?" Wolfe asked.

"Barraka, of course," Kunstler said, taking off his gloves and warming his hands over a red glowing potbellied stove. He bent over a map of the area. "Come, have a look, general."

Wolfe stpped up to the makeshift table that served as the operations board.

"Major Radish predicted that Barraka would head up the Umbrail Pass. From where we are now, the road outside will take him there. You see, once the road leaves the bridge, it veers slightly to the west. He must stay on the road. That is why he must cross here, where the bridge is." To emphasize his point, he struck the map several times with the tip of his forefinger. "Now, all we have to do is wait and let Major Barraka lead the Jews to us."

"When do you expect the Jews here?" Wolfe asked.

"From our last report, Barraka was still a day's march away," Kunstler said. "And that was radioed by the pilot of the observation plane at dusk yesterday."

"And we have nothing more recent?"

"The bad weather has prevented any further observations," Radish offered.

"Permit me, general," Kunstler said, "to again emphasize that there is no other way for Barraka to cross the river. He must use the bridge. You see, it is all here on the map. The topography of the land dictates what they must do. He has chosen a route that must lead him here if he wants to reach the Umbrail Pass. The topographical characteristics of the region have already determined what will happen here."

Wolfe nodded appreciatively.

"And I used the same two paratroop units on the far side of the bridge that clashed with the partisans on the knoll. They have twenty-five dead comrades to avenge."

"Excellent," Wolfe said. "It's better when a personal motive is introduced into a combat situation."

"Absolutely," Kunstler agreed.

A dispatch rider from Malveno entered the CP. Radish signed for the pouch, opened it, and quickly riffled through the material. Only one was marked Top Secret, and it was addressed to Kunstler.

"For you, colonel," Radish said, handing him the envelope.

Kunstler read the message aloud. "You are hereby ordered to use every means at your command to completely destroy the Jews and the partisans. Take no prisoners." He paused a moment and then he said, "It is signed by Field Marshal Kesselring."

"Himmler must be involved in this," Radish commented.

Kunstler nodded and looked at Wolfe for confirmation, but the general remained expressionless.

"They will surrender," Radish said in support of Kunstler.

Kunstler went back to the map. "They will not have any choice. They must surrender. Barraka must give up his Jews."

"I do not see why it should make any difference whether the Jews surrender or not," Wolfe commented. "Your orders are clear. They must be destroyed. No doubt, Eichmann does not have the transportation available to ship them to Germany."

"I would have liked to meet Major Barraka," Kunstler said.

"That is not what this war is all about, colonel," Wolfe told him.

"Permit me, general, to say that though Major Barraka is my enemy, I am professional enough to respect his ability."

Wolfe turned very red. "As I just told you," he said, "your orders are very clear."

"Yes, sir," Kunstler responded. "They are very clear."

Barraka had originally planned to capture and hold the bridge for several hours, perhaps even as long as it was daylight. If the attack had been made at dawn, that would have given the column a good nine hours' travel time. And if they had continued through the night, they would have had a chance to reach the Swiss border by the following morning. Because of the mountains, there would have been little opportunity for the Germans to have bombed them.

The bridge would have been the last physical obstacle controlled by the Germans. Once they had passed it, the Germans would be forced to stay behind them. Barraka had intended to make that difficult by blowing the bridge. Then, for the last few kilometers to the Swiss border, they would have had to struggle only against the weather and their own exhaustion. Barraka realized, though the plan was militarily sound, it had failed to take into account the events of the past few days. He now had several hundred people to move across the bridge. He had to abandon it. He would leave the bridge to Kunstler and find another way to cross the river.

"How?" Volterra asked. "I agree with you; we can't use the bridge. But you still haven't told me how we are going to move these people across the river."

"I don't know yet," Barraka answered.

"If we had more time—"

"The *ifs* don't count," Barraka said. "We'll find a way."

Barraka dropped back along the line of the column to urge the people to move faster. The rain that had started during the night continued. It wasn't heavy, and often it was more fog than rain.

Within a matter of hours, the column would reach the river; then they would have to halt unless Barraka found a way for them to cross it. There was another bridge some sixteen kilometers to the east. But he was sure that Kunstler would reach it before he did, or failing that, force a battle that he and his men couldn't hope to win.

Suddenly Barraka realized he had another problem, and he ran forward to speak to Volterra about it.

"The Krauts are going to be expecting us at the bridge," he said. "And we're not going to show."

"That will give them something to think about," Volterra commented.

"That will make them suspicious," Barraka said. "We don't want them to think, and we sure as hell don't want them to be suspicious."

"How are we going to avoid—"

"We've got to send men to the bridge," Barraka said. "Enough men to make it look good, to make it look like we intend to take and hold it."

"And what will the rest of us do?"

"Cross the river," Barraka said. "Don't ask me how, because I can't answer that yet. But we're going to have to do it."

"Who goes to the bridge?" Volterra asked.

"Conway . . . four other partisans, and about two dozen of the elderly men and women. I want it to look like they intend to cross. In this weather, maybe we could get away with it. I mean the two dozen people. They might look like an advance group."

"Any chance of them making it?"

Barraka shook his head.

"What about Conway and the other partisans?"

"If they're very lucky and the fog becomes denser, or we have a blinding snowstorm."

"The fog has become worse," Volterra said. "Maybe they have a chance."

"We're close to the river now," Barraka said. "I'm going to halt the column and you and I are going to find a place where we'll cross. In the meantime, I'd rather not say anything about our plans."

"So far, Mitch, we really don't have any plan."

Barraka nodded and called a halt to the day's march. He went down the line to where Yancy was and told him, Mastrada, and Conway to take over. "Volterra and I are going to make a recon. We should be back in a few hours. No fires tonight."

"What about the bridge?" Yancy asked.

"We'll talk about it later," Barraka answered, and he walked back to Volterra.

Barraka and Volterra reached the river within two hours. They were closer to it than either of them had realized. The opposite bank was too far away to be seen through the fog and the river itself was hundreds of feet below them. They could hear the roar of its water, but they could not see it.

"We're going to follow it to the west," Barraka said. "Maybe we'll get lucky."

Volterra shrugged, but did not speak.

"I'm going down," Barraka said. "We've got to know what the hell it looks like down there. Give me an hour. If I'm not back, you and Yancy will have to find a way to get the people across. But I can't think of any."

"That means we'd have to surrender."

Barraka shook his head. "Not after all that's happened."

Volterra nodded.

"If you have to fight, make it a good one," Barraka said. "Make the Krauts bleed."

The two men shook hands.

Barraka picked his way down the side of the chasm. The rocks were very slippery and the fog thickened the lower he went. He lost his footing and slipped several meters before he could stop himself.

Somewhere near the bottom the vertical wall became a steep incline on which large pine trees grew with various types of bushes. This soon changed into another steep wall. But when he reached it, the fog was less dense than it had been, and he was able to see the river below, swirling white water, out of which rose enormous boulders.

Barraka worked his way down to the narrow bank. A fine mist came off the roiled waters. The trunks of large trees lay wedged between the boulders and along the narrow bank.

For several minutes, he stood looking at the desolate scene before he realized the river could be bridged. He would move additional trees into the river and wedge them against certain rocks until he reached the other side. It wouldn't be much of a bridge, not the suspension bridge he dreamed he'd build some day. There would be nothing beautiful about this bridge. Nothing graceful. But it would serve. Getting the trunks in place would be difficult but not impossible. The partisans had enough rope with them to pull the trunks to where he'd wanted them. By wedging them between boulders and lashing them together it could be done. It had to be done!

As soon as he formulated his idea, Barraka turned and started back up to Volterra. The climb was treacherous. When he reached the top, he threw himself down, and, breathing hard, he explained to Volterra what he intended to do.

"In this weather?"

"We don't have any other weather," Barraka answered. "That bridge has to be completed by tomorrow morning. I want us to be across and on the road by dawn."

"The odds are against us, Mitch," Volterra said in his calm voice. "You were right when you said I never thought the mission would be this hard. What will happen once we're across and on the road?"

"We'll make a race for the border," Barraka said, speaking the words before he thought about them.

"Mitch, we can hardly walk and you talk about racing."

Barraka pulled himself up on his staff. "Suppose we had trucks?" he said.

"And where are we going to get them from?"

"The German motor depot," Barraka answered. "That shouldn't be heavily guarded. We can manage it. A half dozen trucks and we should be on the way."

"Build a bridge, make a diversionary attack, and raid a motor depot. Is there anything else you expect us to do?" Volterra questioned.

"Reach Switzerland," Barraka answered, as he started back to the column. "You have to reach Switzerland."

Barraka gathered the people in front of him. To find some warmth and to escape the knife edge of the wind, they huddled close together. All were ragged and dirty. Like himself, the men had beards days old. The people looked up at him, and he felt the weight of their suffering and their hopes. He too wanted to survive. Now more than ever before. He sought Sarah out, and for a few moments let his eyes lock with hers.

Then he found his voice. "We must cross a river, and to do it we will have to build a bridge of logs." He paused until other words came to him. "There is a bridge a few kilometers from here. It is where the Germans will be waiting for us to cross. If we do not show up at the bridge they will know we have another way of crossing the river. We must make them think we intend to cross at the bridge they hold, even if it means a fight. To do that I must have a few men. Major Conway will lead the group. But I must have men—" again Barraka paused. The words were difficult to say. "I must have men who are willing to die so that the rest of the people might have a chance to live."

The people stirred uneasily.

"You're asking for some of us to commit suicide," one of the men said.

"I am asking for some of the men to sacrifice themselves for the others," Barraka said.

"Are you sure none will survive?" another man asked.

"If anyone did, he would be taken prisoner," Barraka answered. "The Germans would make him tell them where we are."

"Better he should die then," a woman commented.

"How does a man make such a decision?" another man called out.

"I don't know," Barraka answered. "But it must be made."

A silence fell over the people, leaving only the sound of the wind.

Barraka looked toward Sarah. She gave a slight nod and he knew he had spoken to these people in a way that pleased her, that did not lessen their dignity.

Suddenly one of the old men called out, "I'll go, major. I'll go!"

Another man volunteered. And then several more said they would go. Voice followed voice until twenty men agreed to die for the others.

"Major Conway will take your names," Barraka said. "Now everyone get some rest."

Sarah came up to him.

Barraka took hold of her hand and together they walked to where Piatelli was resting. They sat down next to him. Barraka leaned against a large rock and closed his eyes.

Sarah rested alongside him. "You never told me,"

she whispered, "if you have a wife or a girlfriend waiting for you at home."

"There is a girl," Barraka answered. "But when this is over, I'll write and tell her about us."

"What will you tell her?"

"That I found an Italian Jew with whom I have fallen in love and—"

"Do you realize how different we are? How different our backgrounds?"

He caressed her head. It was strange that Sarah had chosen this moment to ask him questions about his relationship to other women, when only a few minutes before he was asking men to die. But their situation demanded they shift their emotions to satisfy the moment. Their reality was the present moment. They could never be sure there would be another.

"You're not listening," Sarah chided.

"We'll worry about the differences later," Barraka said. "Now we have to worry about the next twelve or maybe fifteen hours."

"Are we really that close to Switzerland?"

"Yes," he answered. "Once we cross the river it will only be about sixteen kilometers to the border."

The entire column moved to where the river was. By letting them follow a rope, Barraka led the column slowly down to the narrow bank. Then began the backbreaking work of moving the trees into the swirling water and tying them together.

Every able-bodied man was involved in the effort. Those who could not swim hauled the trees to the water, while those who could swim went into the ice-cold water to work the trees into place. They labored throughout the afternoon, and when darkness came, they continued, calling to one another in the pitch blackness.

Barraka spent most of the night going in and out of the water until the opposite bank had almost been reached. Then he sat down next to Sarah, too exhausted to move and too cold to stop his teeth from chattering.

Volterra came and asked if they could build a few small fires.

"Back against the cliff," Barraka said. "And keep them small."

"You could do with some warmth yourself," Volterra commented.

"That's what I was thinking," Barraka answered, and forced himself to get up. He sat against the wall, where Sarah started a fire going. "I'm glad I didn't have to blow the stone bridge," he commented.

"Why? What's so special about it?"

"It's old," he answered. "Very old. Probably the base stones were put down by the Romans." Then he said, "Tomorrow is my birthday. I will be twenty-eight. But I feel like a hundred and twenty-eight. My birthday and Thanksgiving come out on the same day."

Sarah did not know anything about Thanksgiving.

Barraka explained the historical significance of the day and said, "I wish we could have some roast turkey and candied yams right now. I don't even have to close my eyes to see them." But he did close his eyes, and he was asleep.

Dawn came to the top of the chasm first and slowly

filtered down. It was gray and bitter cold, with the promise of more rain or the coming of snow. They were high enough in the mountains for the snow to come at any time now.

Barraka was awake. He lay very still. His eyes were still closed. He had awakened only moments before with a full-blown scheme for carrying out a raid on the German motor pool. He would use Mastrada, Yancy, and five other men. They would go up to the gate house, and, using their knives, kill the guards. Two of the men would throw grenades into the barracks area, two of the men would blow the fuel depot; then the seven of them, or as many as were alive, would take the trucks. If the attack was swift enough, they could get away with it. The trucks would roll north and pick up the rest of the column. After that, it would be a race between them and the Germans. The element of surprise would be in their favor. The Germans would not be expecting an attack, and if the weather held, the German observation planes would not be able to spot them.

He opened his eyes and suddenly realized that his right hand cupped Sarah's left breast. She was still asleep. Her face was turned into his chest. He kissed the side of her head.

She moved and whispered, "Happy birthday."

"Thanks." He was on his feet.

Within minutes, everyone was awake.

Barraka went down to the river's edge. The makeshift bridge had held. "Okay," he said, "soon we're going to start across it. If anyone goes over, no one will go after him. Go slowly. Be sure of your footing." And then he went to Conway and wished him luck.

"You'll know we arrived," Conway said, "when you hear the firing. Look, major, I am not at all good at this, but it has been a pleasure to know you and your men."

Barraka shook his hand and the hands of all of the men who were going to the bridge.

Several of the old men asked for guns. "If we have to die," one of them said, "let us die fighting for our lives, rather than just giving them up."

Barraka gave rifles to those who wanted them. And as he and Piatelli watched them climb into the fog above he said, "Pray to God to help them, to at least let their deaths have some meaning."

"I already have," Piatelli answered. "I also prayed for us and for you, major."

"I'm past praying for anyone or anything," Barraka said.

"Many people here pray for you, including Sarah."

Barraka nodded and quietly said, "I love her, professor." Then he turned and walked away, calling to Volterra to begin moving the people across the bridge.

Piatelli crossed the bridge, though not as quickly as he would have liked. More than once he felt as if he were on the verge of losing his balance. But he managed to stay on his feet and when he was on the other side, he sought Sarah out. He had to speak with her about Barraka, if for no other reason than to bring certain things into focus for her.

She was with Rinata, as she was every day since

Barraka had taken her out of the German barracks.

"Sarah," Piatelli asked, "may I have a word with you?"

"Yes, uncle," she answered and excused herself from Rinata.

Piatelli led Sarah a short distance up the bank, where there was a place for them to sit. For a while, he said nothing. He wasn't sure how to begin, and he was looking at the people as they came across Barraka's makeshift bridge. Like himself, they were exhausted and filthy. Many of their faces were raw and bleeding from the wind, and none of them had adequate clothing. If they had to spend another night in the open, he doubted they would be able to continue the next day. They had reached the end of their will to survive. They would have to reach the border within the next few hours, or the Germans would take them back, or kill them.

"What is it you want to say, uncle?" Sarah asked, breaking in on his thoughts.

"Soon," he said, "with any luck we will be in Switzerland and eventually we will go to the United States."

"Oh, Uncle, do you really think it will happen!" Sarah cried.

"Yes, I do. And that's why I have to speak to you now about Major Barraka."

Sarah started to say something, but Piatelli spoke first. "He loves you, Sarah. He told me so just before we started to cross the river."

"And I love him, Uncle," she said in a low, passionate voice.

"What will you do if he comes to claim you after the

war?" Piatelli asked.

"I will be his," she replied, looking directly at her uncle, then at Barraka, who was at the bridge.

Piatelli took hold of his niece's hands. "I love you," he said, "and I love Major Barraka. I don't want to see either of you hurt. These few days have compressed time and heightened emotions. The major is probably the most courageous man we'll ever meet and probably one of the most vulnerable. When he makes a commitment he makes it with his whole being, with what we loosely refer to as *honor*, with what he would give his life to keep."

"I understand that," she said.

"I hope you do, Sarah," he responded. "When we're in the United States he'll still be here fighting in the war. It might be years before he returns. He might return badly wounded, or not at all."

Sarah gasped and her hand flew to her mouth.

"There are tremendous differences between the two of you," Piatelli said. "Forgetting about the differences in your respective religions, since I know that many good marriages have come about between Christians and Jews. What I'm talking about has to do with culture, with everything that goes into making him what he is and you what you are."

"Uncle, I love you," Sarah answered. "I don't know what else to say to you. If he asks me, I will wait for him."

Piatelli nodded. "Please," he said, "do not be angry or annoyed with me for mentioning these things to you. I only wanted you to know how much I care for the both of you."

Sarah nodded.

"Are you sure you're not angry?" Piatelli asked, getting to his feet.

"Positive," Sarah answered, as she stood up.

Piatelli hugged her to him.

"What would happen if Mitch crossed over into Switzerland with us?" Sarah asked.

"He'd be interned," Piatelli answered, "and he would be delcared a deserter by the American army. His orders are to return to his unit when he finishes his assignment with us."

"But he'd be out of the war, wouldn't he?"

"Sarah, he'd never do it," Piatelli said. "And it would be wrong to ask him to. He knows that he must go back."

"Don't worry," Sarah responded. "I won't ask him. I know he must go back. He wouldn't do anything else."

Piatelli nodded. "Come," he said, "let's rejoin the others. We'll be moving again very soon."

Barraka stood on the other side of the river, watching the people slowly cross his bridge. The young made it over the makeshift pathway without any difficulty. But the elderly cautiously picked their way along the heaving tree trunks.

"Hurry," Barraka called. "You must move faster." He waved them on. "We don't have time. . . . Keep going . . . don't look down at the water."

"They're moving as fast as they can," Volterra said.

"Yes, I know," Barraka answered. "But I can't risk letting them slow down. We're almost to the border, Chaim. We're almost there." And then he said,

"Would you believe I love them?"

"I would believe it, and so do they."

Not one failed to look up at him when they passed. Some nodded and others wished him long life. None shouted as they had when they had fled from Servigliano. They were not caught up in the insanity of men killing men. They were more subdued. They were making a perilous crossing with the steady orderliness of men and women who had been tried and not been found wanting.

Yancy came up to him. "A few of the logs look like they are ready to break away."

"Have we any more rope?"

Yancy shook his head.

Barraka put down his carbine and staff and went into the river. Several of the logs had broken the lines that had held them. But it was easy enough for him to retie the severed ropes. He moved back to shore, numb from the icy grip of the water.

"It looks as if we have most of the people on this side," he said, flailing his arms and rubbing his legs to bring some warmth back into them.

Suddenly the sound of gunfire erupted. Barraka stopped moving and looked upstream.

"Machine guns," Volterra said.

Yancy came running over.

The people on the bridge stopped.

"Don't stop!" Barraka shouted. "You've got to keep going!"

The sound of three loud explosions thundered over the river. Another long burst of machine gun fire was immediately followed by the crack of rifles.

"Move it!" Barraka yelled.

There were two more large explosions. Then silence.

"It's over at the bridge," Yancy said. "Let's get the hell out of here before the Krauts get here. For sure as shit, they're goin' to come lookin' for us."

As soon as the last of the people came off the log bridge, Barraka formed up the column to begin its slow climb out of the river chasm. When they reached the top, he told Volterra how he intended to get trucks for them. "It's the only chance we have," he said, "even if it's a long shot."

"I'll go," Volterra said with a nod.

"No," Barraka responded. "I'll go with Yancy, Mastrada, and four others. You keep the column moving north, parallel to the road. We'll rendezvous about four kilometers from here. We could use snow, or rain."

"Maybe you'll get both before the day is out."

"Whatever keeps the Krauts off our backs for a while, I'll take," Barraka answered and summoned Yancy and Mastrada. He explained his plan to them.

They agreed it was worth trying, and Yancy said, "Rinata will want to come with us."

"Are you sure you want her?"

"That's the way she'll want it."

"I don't have any objections, if Mastrada doesn't."

"I have none," Mastrada said.

"Okay," Barraka told them. "Between you, pick four other men. Tell them what the score is. I want them to know we might not make it."

The two men nodded and went to choose the four partisans who would take part in the raid.

Barraka sought out Sarah and he led her off a short

distance from where her uncle was resting.

"I'm going away for a short while," he said.

"Where—"

"It doesn't matter where," he told her, placing his forefinger across her lips. "Chaim will lead the column . . . all the way to Switzerland if it comes out that way."

Tears welled up in her eyes and ran down her cheeks. "Hold me!" she whispered.

Barraka put his arms around her. "Take care of your uncle," he said. Then he let go of her and walked quickly to where the other members of the raiding party were waiting. "Okay, let's move." He left without looking back at Sarah.

Sarah continued to move up the steep incline that led away from the riverbank. There wasn't any path and the people were forced to make their own by pushing aside bushes, or breaking the low branches off trees that got in the way.

"Keep moving," Volterra shouted and a dozen voices picked up the words.

Sarah couldn't help thinking about her conversation with her uncle. The truth was that the kind of man she had thought about marrying had been as different from Barraka as the proverbial night from day. In that remote time, when she had still been a student and could still dream, she had dreamed of someday being the wife of a doctor. A man with professional standing. Perhaps a surgeon. A person like herself, who loved the theater. Read the latest books. Possibly could play a musical instrument. A man of a genteel nature, who wore expensive clothing and always had the faint odor of eau de cologne about him . . . someone like Barraka would have been impossible for her to imagine, let alone love. . . . Yet she did love him. Not because he had rescued her. But because he was substantial. His hands were strong and calloused. Bruised from climbing the rocks. He smelled of sweat and she hadn't the remotest idea if he read anything more serious than the daily newspaper. Yet from the first moment she had seen him, she had intuitively known he would save all of them.

"Keep moving," Volterra shouted. "Keep moving. Barraka will be waiting for us. . . . Barraka will be waiting for us."

Sarah smiled to herself. The love she had for Barraka was so intense it almost hurt. She wanted him so badly that often when they were close together she had to restrain herself from taking his hand and pressing it against her breasts.

In so few days, God had been good to her. As Rinata had said He might, He had made her feel as if the rape had never happened. She wanted to feel Barraka's body on hers. She wanted to give him the joy and pleasure that she knew she could give him.

Suddenly she realized her uncle was next to her.

"You look radiant," he said with a gentle smile.

"I was imagining how it someday might be between myself and Mitch," she answered.

Piatelli took her hand and kissed the back of it. "When the time comes, I will give you away," he said.

"I'd like that, Uncle."

"And in the giving I will gain—I was going to say a son, but—"

"Say it," Sarah said. "Say it. I know Mitch would want you to say it."

"And in the giving," Piatelli said, "I will gain a son."

"It will be," Sarah exclaimed. "With all my heart, I know it will be!"

"Keep moving!" Volterra shouted. "Keep moving. Barraka is waiting for us."

Sarah looked at her uncle and said, "Come, let's walk faster. I want to tell Mitch that you'll give me away."

"Where are the Jews?" Wolfe shouted, pounding the map board with his fist. "You told me it was impossible for the Jews to go any other way."

Kuntler gnashed his teeth, but he kept silent. Wolfe, though a fool, was still a general.

"I want you to tell me where the Jews are, colonel," Wolfe demanded. "Come to the map and point to them. Tell me what the topography of the area dictates."

"Barraka is in this sector," Kunstler answered.

"Major Radish," Wolfe fumed, "can you explain how a few hundred Jews and partisans were able to disappear?"

"General, the weather has made it impossible to send an observation plane—"

"Why were troops who were trailing them removed?"

Radish looked at Kunstler.

"General," Kunstler said, "there was no need to continue to chase the partisans. Once the weather clears, we will have no difficulty finding Barraka and finishing the Jews, I can assure you of that."

"You assured me we would have an end to this business of the Jews and the partisans," Wolfe said. "And what we have is more of it. It was a mistake to withdraw the paratroops, colonel. A serious mistake."

"I've sent out patrols to find Barraka," Kunstler responded.

With an abrupt movement of his hand, Wolfe dismissed Kunstler's statement. "If this is the way you and the rest of your brother professional officers handle themselves on the Russian front, it is no wonder why we are suffering such terrible reverses there."

Kunstler's complexion flared red. His breathing came in short bursts. "Sir," he managed to say, "if you would excuse me, I would—" He stopped. The words of subservience would not come. "I have seen too many of my comrades killed to allow you, or anyone else, to say that without demanding an apology, general."

Radish shook his head.

Wolfe's eyes bugged. He was livid; his lower lip quivered with rage.

The field phone on the desk rang.

Radish answered it. After a moment he said, "Colonel, this is for you." He tried to keep his voice steady but could not.

"Colonel Kunstler here," Kunstler announced, looking questioningly at him.

"Lieutenant Bosh," the voice on the other end said, "of the Twenty-first Transportation Battalion."

"What is happening there?" Kunstler asked, barely

able to hear the lieutenant above the background noise coming from the motor pool.

"Colonel, we're under attack."

"What?" Kunstler shouted. Before the lieutenant could explain, he told him he was dispatching reinforcements immediately. Then to Wolfe he said, "We have found Barraka. He has flanked us. He is attacking the truck depot."

"But how did he cross the river?" Wolfe asked.

"I wished to God I knew," Kunstler sighed. "I was certain Barraka couldn't get them across without using a bridge." He had hoped to put an end to Barraka and the Jews at the bridge. But now the bridge no longer mattered. Barraka had somehow built his own bridge. That a nonprofessional had completely outmaneuvered him was something his superiors would always hold against him. Unless he managed to stop Barraka his career was finished. He had to do it, if for no other reason than to salvage his honor as a German officer.

Barraka and one of the partisans went straight up to the gate.

A sentry challenged them.

The partisan lunged for the guard's rifle and grappled with him, while Barraka thrust a knife into the German's side. The man made a wheezing sound and slipped to the ground.

The instant the gate was cleared the other members of the team ran forward. Yancy and Rinata ran to the barracks and lobbed their grenades.

Mastrada and another partisan blew up the fuel

storage tanks. The explosion sent a huge sheet of fire up toward the gray clouds and along the ground toward the barracks.

"Get the trucks!" Barraka shouted.

Soldiers came running toward them.

A partisan dropped to his knee and squeezed off four rounds that sent two Germans crashing down. One against the side of the building, the other in the mud. The others scrambled for shelter.

The trucks were lined up behind the barracks. As soon as Barraka and his men went toward the vehicles, they were under fire from the upper windows of the burning building. The bullets pinged off the concrete and whacked into some of the nearby trees.

Barraka and Mastrada fired cover for the others.

Rinata screamed and went down.

Yancy whirled around and lifted her in his arms, running toward a truck.

A moment later an explosion inside the barracks sent flames out of the windows.

Barraka and Mastrada dashed for the trucks. "You drive one," Barraka said. "I'll take another. I want one man per truck . . . now let's go."

Yancy placed Rinata on the seat next to him and swung behind the wheel. A moment later he was rolling.

A few German soldiers were firing at them, but the raiders floored the accelerators and sped past them onto the road.

Yancy led the group. Now and then he glanced at Rinata. Her eyes were closed and her breathing was shallow. She had been hit below her right breast. Her jacket was stained with blood.

The trucks raced along the narrow road.

Barraka was surprised at how easy the raid had been. He had guessed right: Kunstler had pulled most of the men away from the motor pool to guard the bridge.

A snow began to fall.

Barraka switched on the windshield wipers and his lights. Driving became more difficult and Yancy in the lead truck was forced to slow down. Suddenly, except for the dark mass of the truck ahead of him, everything was gray. The whirling sound of the tires on the macadam road and the heavy grayness gave Barraka a strange, uneasy feeling.

"Some damn way to spend a birthday," he said aloud. And not being able to think of a follow-up, he whistled softly to himself and tried to remember the name of the song he was whistling.

The taillights on Yancy's truck flared red. The vehicle slowed and stopped. Barraka rolled to a halt and thrust his head out of the cab, yelling, "What the hell is wrong?"

"She's dead, Mitch . . . the fuckers killed my woman!" Yancy bawled.

"Yance, a lot more of us will be dead if you don't roll that truck!" Barraka yelled.

"Yeah . . . yeah," Yancy shouted. "I'll roll it." And he leaped back into the cab. A moment later the truck shot forward. Yancy looked at Rinata and said, "The trouble with you, cunt, is that—" His voice cracked and tears filled his eyes. "The trouble with you, cunt, is that I love you . . . yeah . . . yeah . . . I love you!" And he floored the accelerator.

Barraka raced after Yancy.

Finally, Yancy slowed and came to a halt where they were to rendezvous with the column.

Barraka pulled up right behind him, leaped down from the truck, and ran forward.

Yancy eased Rinata's body out of the cab and held it in his arms. "Best pussy I ever had," he said, looking up at Barraka. "I'm goin' to set her down there in the woods."

"You don't have much time," Barraka told him. "The Krauts are close behind us."

"I know that, Mitch," Yancy answered, walking off the road with Rinata's body in his arms.

Just as he turned from Yancy, Barraka saw Volterra and Piatelli emerge from the grayness. They were about a hundred meters from where he stood.

"This way," Barraka shouted. "This way!"

Volterra and Piatelli began to run. The others followed.

"Into the trucks," Barraka ordered. "Hurry, everyone into the trucks."

Sarah ran to him. Throwing her arms around his neck, she kissed him on the lips.

Barraka lifted her onto the rear of Yancy's truck. "I'll be right behind you," he said.

"Where's Rinata?" she asked.

"Dead."

"Oh my God!" Sarah cried.

Yancy came out of the woods.

"Are you fit to drive?" Barraka asked, putting his hand on Yancy's shoulder.

"Fit," Yancy answered in a choked voice.

"Okay, let's get rolling. We don't have far to go to reach the pass."

Moments later Yancy's truck pulled away.

Barraka followed and the other trucks came after his. For the first time since he had been given the assignment, he felt the odds had tipped in his favor. He'd be able to carry it off! Then what? He couldn't cross the border into Switzerland. He'd have to go back. Back to his unit; back to the war! He didn't have any other choice. Ahead, he saw Sarah sitting in the rear of the truck. He thrust his hand out of the window and waved at her. He loved her, but he still didn't know if he had the right to ask her to wait for him. The war wasn't anywhere near being over. He might yet be killed, or worse, come home maimed. . . .

She saw him and waved back.

Suddenly Barraka realized the people in the rear of his truck and Yancy's and those in all the other trucks were singing.

Kunstler led the armored column himself. He, Radish and Wolfe sat in the command car. Behind him were twelve armored cars, each mounting a 40mm cannon, and following them were an equal number of troop-carrying half tracks.

The heavy snow made it difficult for Kunstler to see any distance ahead, though the flames coming from the burning fuel tanks and the barracks in the transportation battalion area were visible for at least two kilometers.

The column roared past the fires, and in a short time it was again completely enveloped by the grayness of the snow.

Kunstler was in radio communication with the

commanders of each of the vehicles. "Keep close together," he urged. "Keep close together."

"How far to the border?" Wolfe asked.

"Approximately sixteen kilometers," Kunstler answered, now worried about the punishment he would receive if the Jews did manage to cross the border.

"And there is no way to head them off?"

"None. We must come up from behind them."

Radish leaned forward. "Go faster," he ordered the driver.

The sergeant nodded and pressed the gas pedal closer to the floorboards.

Kunstler realized his entire career, maybe even his life, was at stake. Should he fail to kill Barraka and all of the Jews, he would not only be removed from his present command, but he was certain that Wolfe and Himmler would make sure other disasters befell him.

"Colonel," Radish said, "there is something in front of us."

Wolfe peered into the grayness. "I don't see anything."

"Slow down," Kunstler told the driver. He turned on the two searchlights on either side of the car and brought their beams together.

"There, about two hundred meters in front of us!" Radish exclaimed.

"I see it," Wolfe said. "I see the truck."

"We've found the Jews," Kunstler said. "We found them! And now we'll stop them!" He switched on the radio and said, "Truck number one, adjust for a range of two hundred meters . . . fire two rounds."

The first round went short, blowing a small hole in the narrow road.

"Elevate slightly," Kunstler ordered calmly. He had the Jews now. He was saved!

The second round smashed into the rear of a truck, instantly turning it into a mass of flames that swung off the road and careened down the side of the mountain, falling into the canyon below.

The explosion from the first round brought an instant halt to the singing. And when the second round set fire to the last truck, the people began to scream.

Barraka gripped the steering wheel so tightly his fingers ached . . . he wasn't going to let Kunstler stop him now, not after bringing his people so far and so close to freedom. He had to do something to delay the Germans. . . .

Barraka had only one choice. He had made it days before when he had taken the people out of Servigliano. He hit his horn three times.

Yancy slowed down.

"You drive," Barraka told the partisan next to him. He slid out from behind the wheel, leaped down to the road, and ran forward to Yancy. "Take them through, Yancy. Take them to Switzerland."

"What the hell are you going to do?"

"Whatever I can to fuck them up!" Barraka answered. "You can make it to the border in ten minutes. I'll buy you that time."

"Mitch—"

Barraka dropped back to the rear of the truck. "You'll be safe with Yancy," he called up to Sarah. His eyes went to Piatelli. In the darkness he looked so much like Kip. "You know there's only one way to stop them?"

"Yes, I know," Piatelli answered in a quavering voice.

"Oh, God don't do it!" Sarah cried.

"I love you," Barraka answered.

"Mitch . . . Mitch, we can—"

"Your firstborn, Sarah," Barraka shouted, "name him after me!" Then he ran on to the side of the road, where the woods offered more cover.

Kunstler ordered two more rounds fired. . . . Now he could pick off the trucks one by one.

The first round smashed into the last truck, setting it on fire. But the vehicle continued to move.

The second round went short and blew another hole in the road.

Barraka darted in and out of the woods, racing to meet the column. Kip wouldn't understand what he was going to do. What he had to do? His mother wouldn't understand. But Yancy did. All of the people he had taken out of Servigliano understood . . . suddenly, a cricle of light surrounded him; then came the quick, flat-sounding burst from several machine pistols. He bellied into the snow.

Another burst of fire chewed up the branches of the trees above him and sent them tumbling into the snow.

The circle of light passed off to Barraka's left. He leaped to his feet and continued to run . . . he wasn't taking his own life; he was giving life. His life for theirs. It was the only way. If there was a God, He would understand, and if He didn't, He couldn't be much of a God. . . . Barraka was breathing hard and wet with sweat. The circle of light was searching for him again.

Then, through the trees, Barraka saw the command car. Holding a grenade in each hand, he pulled their pins with his teeth. He was sure the Germans wouldn't be able to see him until he was on top of them. He continued to run toward the command car, counting down from ten. . . .

When Barraka reached zero, he was almost alongside the command car.

"Kunstler," he shouted, and released the plunger on the grenades, leaping up into the slow-moving vehicle . . . Barraka's brain suddenly flooded with the image of himself and Kip watching the moose drink at the lake against the backdrop of a brilliant red and yellow sunset. . . .

The two explosions merged into one, fragmenting the image in Barraka's brain. The blast blew him and Kunstler out of the car. . . .

ZEBRA BRINGS YOU EXCITING BESTSELLERS
by Lewis Orde

MUNICH 10 (1300, $3.95)
They've killed her lover, and they've kidnapped her son. Now the world-famous actress is swept into a maelstrom of international intrigue and bone-chilling suspense—and the only man who can help her pursue her enemies is a complete stranger . . .

HERITAGE (1100, $3.75)
Beautiful innocent Leah and her two brothers were forced by the holocaust to flee their parents' home. A courageous immigrant family, each battled for love, power and their very lifeline—their HERITAGE.

THE LION'S WAY (900, $3.75)
An all-consuming saga that spans four generations in the life of troubled and talented David, who struggles to rise above his immigrant heritage and rise to a world of glamour, fame and success!

DEADFALL (1400, $3.95)
by Lewis Orde and Bill Michaels
The two men Linda cares about most, her father and her lover, entangle her in a plot to hold Manhattan Island hostage for a billion dollars ransom. When the bridges and tunnels to Manhattan are blown, Linda is suddenly a terrorist—except *she's* the one who's terrified!

Available wherever paperbacks are sold, or order direct from the Publisher. Send cover price plus 50¢ per copy for mailing and handling to Zebra Books, 475 Park Avenue South, New York, N. Y. 10016. DO NOT SEND CASH.